Shieldmaiden Sisters

*Three resourceful women,
not looking for but finding...love*

Loyalty is everything to half sisters Valda,
Brynhild and Helga. Their courageous
shieldmaiden mother had raised them to
be independent and, now that the family has
fallen on hard times, each sister must find a
way to help restore their fortunes. Being
resourceful, they have no need of men, but
the right ones come along just when
they're least expected.

Read Valda's story in
The Viking She Would Have Married

Brynhild's in
Tempted by Her Outcast Viking

And now Helga's story in
Beguiling Her Enemy Warrior

All available now!

Author Note

While researching herbal medicines of the early medieval period, it became clear that women had a great role to play in the health and well-being of their community. For example, Hildegard von Bingen was a medieval nun who wrote a book on medicine, actively encouraging women to have autonomy over their own bodies. If the past has taught us anything, it is that we should not persecute women for being different or wanting to control their own destiny.

This book is a thank-you to all women, past and present, but especially to the healers who help people with their knowledge, kindness and intuition. The world would be a darker place without you.

Also, a special mention goes out to fellow Historical author Lissa Morgan who helped me with my Welsh spellings and facts. Thank you!

LUCY MORRIS

Beguiling Her
Enemy Warrior

HARLEQUIN®
HISTORICAL™

ISBN-13: 978-1-335-72369-7

Beguiling Her Enemy Warrior

Copyright © 2023 by Lucy Morris

For questions and comments about the quality of this book, please contact us at CustomerService@Harlequin.com.

Harlequin Enterprises ULC
22 Adelaide St. West, 41st Floor
Toronto, Ontario M5H 4E3, Canada
www.Harlequin.com

Printed in U.S.A.

Lucy Morris lives in Essex, UK, with her husband, two young children and two cats. She has a massively sweet tooth and loves gin, bubbly and Irn-Bru. She's a member of the UK Romantic Novelists' Association. She was delighted to accept a two-book deal with Harlequin after submitting her story to the Warriors Wanted! submission blitz for Viking, Medieval and Highlander romances. Writing for Harlequin Historical is a dream come true for her and she hopes you enjoy her books!

Books by Lucy Morris

Harlequin Historical

The Viking Chief's Marriage Alliance
A Nun for the Viking Warrior

Shieldmaiden Sisters

The Viking She Would Have Married
Tempted by Her Outcast Viking
Beguiling Her Enemy Warrior

Visit the Author Profile page
at Harlequin.com.

For all the healers and wise women,
past and present.

Chapter One

Jorvik—AD 913

Brynhild and Erik would be lovers soon. Helga was certain of it.

A smug satisfaction warmed her heart as she watched them bicker, oblivious to her presence. Of course, they didn't realise their destiny, not yet, but it was clear their souls were bound together, like the entwined warp and weft of a tapestry.

Two fierce warriors, one dark and one golden. Strong, unyielding opposites, yet perfectly balanced reflections of one another.

Lesser men dived out of their way as they strode through the bustling crowds of Jorvik. Erik appeared calm, his voice low and sincere as they passed out of the market and into the alleys beyond. He had a lot to say—Erik, son of Ulf—which was odd in itself. Normally, Erik was as silent as a shadow with everyone, but it seemed Brynhild was the exception.

In contrast, Helga's eldest sister used her words like one of her weapons, with heavy and direct force. Her face was currently flushed with temper and her long strides would have forced others into a run. But not Erik—he matched her in all ways.

Helga began to lag behind, taking her time as she meandered through the market stalls at her own pace—she had given up trying to keep up with her sisters long ago.

Besides, she suspected Erik and Brynhild needed a moment alone together. Some of Helga's best remedies benefited from a little *maturing* time, without prodding or interference on her part. Feisty Brynhild would probably do well with similar treatment.

Soon it will be my turn.

A spark of excitement ignited the thrill in her veins as she thought about her own future. Valda had married Halfdan yesterday and if things progressed well with Erik and Brynhild, then both her older sisters would finally be married.

Then it would be *her* moment in the sun.

Unlike her sisters, she had always longed to find love. It would not be a cage—as they imagined it to be—for Helga, it would be a joy and she could not wait to fall in love.

Her sisters' marriages had always seemed inevitable to Helga. Like the cycle of the moon and the changing of the seasons, she had seen the fate of her sisters long before they had. She only hoped she would recognise her own as easily.

Stopping at a stall, she bought a loaf of fresh bread and a parcel of honey cakes. Before placing them inside her basket, she lifted them to her face and inhaled deeply. Her mouth watered at the delicious and sweet aroma that rose from them.

Valda's wedding feast had put her in a cheerful mood and, despite the lack of sleep from the all-night festivities aboard Halfdan's ship, she didn't feel tired. And it would do Brynhild good to have some time alone with a handsome man, especially one who so obviously wanted her.

Helga stopped in front of a craftsman selling turtle brooches and she took the opportunity to admire them. There was a bronze pair she rather liked—the swirling knotwork design each had a blue glass drop mounted in its centre.

'Try them on!' The owner smiled, unpinning them from the straw-filled cushion and holding them up to the morning light. The glass danced and shimmered before her eyes, like a sun-drenched summer sea. 'They would look ever so fine on a pretty maiden such as yourself,' he said with a genuine smile.

They *were* beautiful.

'Not today, thank you,' Helga said with a regrettable sigh. She leaned forward as if she were about to tell him a secret and he bent his head to hear her better. 'But, maybe next week? I am hoping our fortunes will improve considerably by then, but I wish to be sure my family is settled before I make a rash purchase... If I wait, I may even have enough to buy some beads, too. Brooches look so much better with a string or two of beads between them, do you not think?'

The craftsman's eyes lit up. 'Indeed, they do! I have plenty of beads that would match well with these brooches.' He gestured to a box filled with all colours and shapes of beads, mostly painted stones or glass, but all delightfully bright. He started to show her the variety of styles and she listened to him happily. Glad to give Erik and Brynhild some much-needed privacy, she flattered the craftsman with praise—maybe he would give her a good price when she returned so she could buy two penannular brooches, one each for her mother and Brynhild. They'd had to sell theirs last winter.

A strange prickle of awareness ran down Helga's spine, like a raindrop sliding down her skin. It was unexpected but not unpleasant, as if her ancestors were calling out to her, begging her to listen.

It didn't take her a long time to find out why. A very handsome and formidable man was staring at her from across the square.

Everything faded. The noise of the market, the voice of the craftsman, even the autumn light seemed suddenly dull compared to the vibrancy of the man watching her.

He stood apart from all around him, as if people were afraid to get too close. His eyes shifted to the side, distracted by a loud group of Norse youths who stumbled past him, their feet hobbled by too much ale. At his sharp glare they slurred an apology and left the square, using each other for balance.

She could understand why, he was an intimidating sight. Tall and slim, a dark cloak wrapped around his broad shoulders. Proud nobility stamped clearly on his face, with the confident up-tilt of his head and his finely sculpted jaw. His hair was as black as a raven's wing, curling slightly around his pale elegant face. He was not bearded, or ruddy like the Norse men she was used to. Instead, his skin shone like marble, his eyes bright, but deep set in his handsome face, and he looked around him with a hard sneer of disapproval, as if he were visiting from another world, a darker world, and he considered this land of mortal men both frivolous and weak.

Then his eyes met hers once more and they softened. Her own knees felt weak and she gripped the handle of her basket a little tighter, reassured by the creak of willow beneath her fingers.

Was this her dragon?

The thought was so strange and fierce that she gasped, shaken by the memory of her childhood visions.

A shadow of wings falling over her, stealing the warmth from her veins. Great talons wrapping around her body. Gently plucking her from the earth as if she were ripe fruit and carrying her up into the sky, her sisters looking up at her with crowns of flowers in their hair.

The dream had tormented her for many nights until casting the runes had explained her fate and that of her sisters—at least in Helga's young mind it had. They would all marry and if they cast runes together, it would foretell the *kind* of husband they would have.

A man of the sea, a warrior like Tyr and...a dragon. *Could he be the one?*

Never before had she felt such an instant connection with another person and it sent her heart racing with anticipation, although she could not move or think what to do.

How she'd longed for this and yet now she hesitated...

What if the runes were wrong and the dragon was actually a warning of something much worse to come?

Helga shivered, her thoughts interrupted by an insistent voice.

'Christian or pagan?' asked the craftsman and Helga blinked, her gaze forced back to focus on the stallholder.

'Sorry, what?'

'Crucifix or hammer? It makes a good pendant in the middle of the beads.'

'Oh, not today, thank you, though your jewellery is without compare. If I have enough silver next week, I will be certain to come to you first.'

Appeased by her compliment, the craftsman nodded. 'I can only give you a good price if you come back next week.'

'Thank you!' Helga beamed, feeling jubilant. Although

whether it was because of the handsome stranger, or because of the prospect of new jewellery, she couldn't be sure.

Helga looked back towards where the handsome man had stood, but the stranger had vanished and her heart sank with familiar disappointment.

Shrugging it off, she reminded herself that if it were fate, then they would see each other again. If not, then she had at least started her day pleasantly by admiring a handsome man.

After one last look at the brooches, she walked away with a renewed bounce in her step.

The finery of women was something she'd missed in the last couple of years. Her family's loss of fortune had been a hardship none of them had expected. All because one of Porunn's ex-lovers had stolen away with their hard-earned hoard. However, things were much better now, after Valda's voyage and marriage. Erik would help them find a suitable plot of land and, now that they had a connection to a powerful merchant, no Jarl could refuse them, even without a man at the head of their household. Still, she should be cautious about her spending until things were certain.

Was the handsome stranger a sign of good or bad fortune to come?

Helga was careful to watch for such things, messages from gods and spirits, which came in all manner of ways. In dreams, the weather, or even the fall of a feather in your path. Everything had symbolism and she read their meanings as if they were runes carved in stone. The world was always trying to speak to you, you only had to watch and listen.

One thing *was* for certain, change was in the air.

Her visions never failed her.

* * *

Lord Rhys continued to watch his beautiful prey from behind a cart filled with barrels. Three men stood with him, all loyal to the Draig ddu Gwynedd—the Black Dragon of Gwynedd.

Madyn spoke in a hushed tone beside him. 'See, a much easier quarry than that beast of a sister.'

Rhys had to agree that Brynhild would be a far more difficult capture. Not only was she built like a horse, she was also far better armed and had another warrior at her side. The inevitable fight could lead to serious bloodshed—of his men's, most likely.

Rhys nodded thoughtfully, trying to ignore the odd pleasure he felt regarding his decision. 'The youngest will be our target. Where is the mother, Heilyn?'

'I lost her in the crowd. She moves with surprising speed for someone who is lame,' Heilyn grumbled, a slight flush on his youthful cheek.

'It is probably for the best. The mother would also fight back. She was once a war leader under Rollo.'

Heilyn's eyes widened. 'A woman? They truly are unnatural.' He stared at the young maiden as she stopped at yet another stall and admired some woollen stockings. 'They say that one is a witch.'

Rhys shrugged, always pragmatic. 'She is a heathen, that is all. Do as I say and we will take her easily.'

It felt wrong to prey on the weakest of the three sisters, but it made sense.

Valda and Halfdan had left at dawn, sailing away from the mess they'd left behind. Brynhild Porundóttir was built for battle, as was the man she'd been walking with, who he'd recognised as the other son of Jarl Ulf, Rhys's enemy.

Ulf was the true villain here.

Could these poor women also be as tied up in Ulf's web of deceit? Either way he had to act.

After seeing Helga, his mind was firmly set on her. Slim and willowy, she was much smaller than the rest of her family. He could snatch her off the street and have her back in his fort within a week.

But that wasn't the only reason. Something else about her called to him.

He sifted through his first impressions of her carefully.

She was beautiful, although why he should care about such a thing was beyond him.

Was it the wilted flowers in her hair, or the dreamy way she walked and smiled at all around her…how she'd smiled at him? Softly, hesitantly, as if she'd been waiting for him to notice her.

She moved and he craned his neck around the barrels to see her better. Her messy blonde hair fell in a water-fall down her shoulders and back. Unrepentantly pagan, it proclaimed to the world her unmarried and ungodly nature.

It should disgust him.

But it didn't.

Instead, he found himself transfixed by the sway of her pale locks as she freely made her way towards an alley leading away from the square.

A part of him was angry that they would leave her out in the open like this. Alone and vulnerable. But he was also grateful for the opportunity. 'Madyn, Heilyn, circle round and head her off and be sure to check her kin are not waiting for her up ahead. Wyn and I will fol-low and grab her once we see you. Be quick, we do not have much time.'

Madyn and Heilyn hurried down the path adjacent to the one Helga meandered down, knowing that they would be able to stop her before the next crossroads. Wyn had family here and they had learned all that they could about the warren of streets before setting out on this mission of vengeance.

Rhys and Wyn began to follow behind her. There was no sign from her easy steps that she realised the danger awaiting her.

If only he'd arrived a couple of days earlier, he might have been able to protect his sister, Alswn, stop her from being abducted altogether. It would not have eased the burning need for vengeance, but it would have saved him from taking this woman as his hostage.

Anger curled his fingers into a fist when he thought of his missing sister and the havoc wreaked by Ulf's raiders on his land and people. He had sent Alswn into the lion's den as a sacrifice for the good of Gwynedd. A mistake he'd realised far too late, now that she and her guard— his best friend, Hywel—were lost to him.

Dead or taken, he wasn't sure and a part of him couldn't bear to know the truth…not yet.

Ulf denied all knowledge of their disappearance, yet his son had broken the marriage alliance on the same day they'd gone missing. All so that he could freely marry Valda Porunndóttir, this woman's sister.

Helga's pace remained slow and carefree, the basket of treats gently bumping against her hip as she hummed to herself. When she came to the entrance of the crossroads and saw his men blocking her path, she stopped and pulled her basket in front of her, as if to protect her paltry goods from being taken. For some reason the action made her seem even more vulnerable, and guilt weighed heavy in his stomach.

Madyn and Heilyn grinned at her in triumph and he

felt even more like a monster. It went against his nature
to frighten a woman like this, even if she were the enemy.

Remember Alswn! he reminded himself sharply. She
must also have been scared and could be hurt or dead
even now. At least Helga would come to no real harm—
he wouldn't allow it.

'If you fight us, it will not go well for you,' sneered
Madyn. Rhys was reminded that the man had lost both
his parents in one of Ulf's recent raids and therefore
would not behave kindly towards her. Still, he trusted
his men to never disobey an order and he'd told them to
take her without any unnecessary force.

She spun on her heel and hesitated when her eyes fell
upon him. A flicker of recognition ghosted across her
face and then…disappointment.

'We do not wish to hurt you. But you *will* come with
us. You are my hostage, until Jarl Ulf agrees to my demands,' Rhys said firmly and her eyes widened with
understanding. For a moment he thought she was about
to capitulate to him, her head dipped in defeat, her hair
sliding forward to mask half her face. Madyn stepped
forward and wrapped his fingers around her arm.

That's when Rhys realised he had misjudged her.

Her eyes narrowed with defiance and then there was
the flash of a blade as she pulled it out from the covered
basket and used it with impressive speed. She slashed at
Madyn's arm and he released her with a curse.

Heilyn jumped forward and she thrust her basket forward with all her might, charging at Heilyn as if she were
trying to run him down. He slipped in the mud and fell
backwards, clutching the basket with a slack jaw. She
pulled up her skirts and flew over his prone body with
an elegant jump that seemed effortless. Then she sprinted
away, baring beautiful slender legs as she did so.

Rhys charged forward, still shocked at the speed and ease she'd managed to thwart some of his best warriors. How had a woman with only a small dagger and a basket managed to elude four grown men?

While his own men stumbled in the mud, wondering how things had gone so badly in such a short amount of time, Rhys ran as fast as he could to catch up with his devious quarry. She was fast, but his legs were longer.

Wrapping one of his arms around her, he managed to pin the hand that carried her weapon to her side. His other hand he clamped around her mouth. She'd not screamed once, which was lucky—things could go even worse for them if she did and her family joined the struggle.

She strained against his body, writhing in a way that he quickly realised was deliberate and not solely due to panic. He knew her mother and sisters were fighting women, but he'd not expected this level of skill from Helga. The woman seemed so gentle...*so innocent*.

But she wrestled against him, her legs hooking around his ankles and trying to force him down with an expert strength that shocked him. If his men hadn't woken from their stupor and come to help him, he was certain he wouldn't have been able to hold her for long.

She began to grunt and scream against his hand, as he and his men worked together to disarm her. In the end, Madyn had to twist her wrist while Rhys held her elbow to force her to drop the weapon. If anything, the loss of the blade only increased her resistance, as she managed to free her other arm and punched out with it, causing Madyn to fall. Then she kicked out with her legs, sending first Heilyn, then Wyn into the mud. The force of her kicks threw Rhys back into the building behind him. The thin wattle and daub wall rattled, dropping dust on both their heads and winding the air from his lungs.

She clawed at the plaster as he dragged her down the alley, her fingernails dirty and bloody as she desperately tried to stop herself from being taken. Then she reached around and yanked at Rhys's hair and he hissed in pain as she tore out a few dark curls from his head.

'Stop it!' he snarled, hating that she was hurting herself.

She began to scream against his hand in earnest and he realised that so much had happened in only a few moments. He forced his mind to be logical, to think tactically and without emotion.

Gwynedd binds me.

The ancient oath of his family whispered in his ear, calming his mind and forcing away all doubt. The Vikings had taken so much from him, from his people and land. There was no room in his heart for sympathy.

She was his enemy and it was time for retribution.

Cold, hard resolve washed through him and, with a savage jerk, he pulled her close and lowered his head to her ear. 'There are four of us. If your screams bring Brynhild and Erik…there *will* be bloodshed. Is that understood?'

Her jerking eased as if she were considering his words.

'Leave the note,' he told Heilyn and the man pulled the parchment from his tunic, picked up the dropped dagger from the ground and stabbed the prepared note through the bread in the basket. He'd not bothered with a ransom note, being unsure if the women, or Erik, could read. Instead, he'd drawn his symbol in charcoal—the black dragon, wings unfurled in flight. Erik would recognise that at least, as it was marked on all his shields and banners.

Helga must have recognised it, too, because she sagged against his chest in sudden defeat. It appeared these women *were* aware of his sister's disappearance. He should have known.

Not so innocent after all.

'Good girl,' he whispered into her silken hair, his arm tightening possessively around her waist. 'Now *move!*'

Chapter Two

Helga stumbled, feeling as if she were trapped in a nightmare, her feet sliding in the mud as the handsome man she'd foolishly admired only a short time ago pushed her forward at a relentless pace. He must think he had subdued her by threatening her sister and Erik, but although his words had given her pause, it had been the note that had truly defeated her.

The black dragon.

A single thread in the tapestry of her life that linked her past, present and future. It was the same winged beast from her childhood visions. The image she'd become obsessed with, drawing it everywhere. Seeking the answer to a question she didn't fully understand in runes and symbolism.

Now, here it was, scratched on to cloth and stabbed into her lovely fresh bread.

To see it now could only mean one thing.

This was meant to happen...it was fate.

The past and future bleeding into one terrible moment. The last time she had seen it had been when she was a little girl of twelve winters and they'd cast their fortunes regarding their future husbands. Even though it had not been an official rune, she had placed a drawing of her dragon among them and had been unsurprised when she'd drawn it.

Valda had picked the Laguz rune symbolising growth, water and travel—it had foretold her fate well. Hadn't Valda had to do both? Grow and travel before she realised Halfdan was, and always would be, the man for her?

Brynhild had picked Tyr. The sacrificial warrior. Eventually Brynhild would wake up and realise that Erik was the man for her. The wounded warrior, who always put the greater good first.

And Helga had picked the dragon. Of course she had! *Why, then, did it feel so wrong?*

Squeezing her eyes shut and then opening them again to focus her mind, she looked around her at the men who had kidnapped her. They had dark hair and were all stocky and short, with the exception of their leader. She caught the attention of his piercing blue eyes and she shivered, her attraction to him mocking her, even now, and she looked away.

No! This blackhearted man was not her future husband!

He was a nightmare made flesh and bone. Her glimmer of foresight had been a warning of what was to come and it would not be a happy fate like her sisters. Fate was set, but how you behaved facing it was up to you. Helga's mind was certain. She would protect her family and make them proud of her.

A group of children were playing outside a workshop, toy swords in their hands and as the leader forced her through the doorway, he glanced at one of the older children, saying 'Remember what you need to do to keep those gifts.'

The boy gave a toothy grin. 'If anyone follows you, send them down the path to the market.'

'And?' asked the leader and she realised there was a strange lilt to his accent that she did not recognise. He was fluent in Norse, but he wasn't Norse or Saxon. Understanding dawned across her mind.

Was this the Welsh lord who was so angry with Halfdan for breaking the alliance? She'd always imagined him to be an older, more grizzled man...a man more like Ulf.

Helga realised none of the children seemed concerned about a woman being kidnapped. Then again, why should they? They were obviously poor and had been paid well for their silence.

A young girl cheerfully answered him from the back of the group. 'I am to deliver a message to Jarl Ulf.' She paused and stared up at the clouds as if in deep concentration. 'We have Helga Porunndóttir. She will be returned... safe and well to you if you return Lady Alswn to Lord Rhys Draig ddu Gwynedd's fortress before the end of the month. Shall I go now?' She stumbled a little over the strange name, but managed to say it well enough that the man nodded with approval. The little girl sprinted away on stick-thin legs.

So, he *was* Lord Rhys, the Welsh lord Halfdan had broken his alliance with.

The innocent girl had just explained everything, but Helga didn't have long to consider it.

The workshop was dim and dirty. Helga wondered if it had been abandoned, but then she saw the old man hunched in the corner, next to a young pale woman on the bed. The dark-haired leader placed a gold coin on the table. The woman coughed miserably from the bed, the sound like a rusty saw on wet wood, suggesting a chill that Helga would have fought with thick nourishing broths…something very much lacking in this home. The man paused and placed another gold coin on the table before leaving and the old man thanked him with watery eyes as they passed through the building and into the street beyond.

Helga had little time to contemplate the strange mercy of the leader. Maybe he knew the family well, or he only hoped to ensure their silence by adding more gold. Whatever his reasoning, her heart still sank as they stepped out into a new alley. It was an obvious break in their trail—no one would know to follow through here, especially if the children pointed them in another direction.

They continued to weave through several more alleys, further and further away from any hope of being tracked.

A cloth was tied around her mouth now and a heavy cloak had been draped over her shoulders and head. A man was in front and another behind her, with yet another beside her holding the end of the rope that tied her wrists in front of her. The leader was taller than she, his fingers wrapped around the back of her neck, almost fully encasing it in his punishing grip.

The leader turned to one of his men and gave an order in the language she didn't understand. She would guess it was an order to get closer and learn more information, by the way the man nodded and pulled up his hood as he left.

'Let us see what your new uncle makes of your disappearance,' Lord Rhys said, turning towards her, this time speaking in Norse. Then he pushed her into a decrepit old building filled with cobwebs, straw and a few old hens. It looked like a makeshift hen house, probably used by some of the grander halls nearby. They made their way to the back of the building and then the leader whispered, 'Sit.'

Helga obeyed, waves of ice-cold dread washing over her.

Why had they taken her here? What did they mean to do to her?

Through the gap-toothed timber of the wall, she realised they were facing the Jarl's square. Her attackers hunched in the shadows of the hut, their hands resting on the hilts of their swords, always ready, their eyes searching for threats.

All except *him*. Their leader, who sat so close to her she could feel the warmth of his body against her shoulder and side, his breath whispering through her hair.

'Your uncle is busy,' he said quietly. His blue eyes were focused on her—the ones she'd thought so beautiful.

What a fool!

She frowned and shrugged. It wasn't as if he could expect her to answer him, what with the gag in her mouth. But for some reason her confusion only seemed to anger him and he clenched his jaw so tightly she saw a pulse jump in his neck.

What uncle? Helga had no uncle. There was her mother and her two sisters and a father she barely knew. But he was far across the sea with a legitimate family of his own and he had no brother that she knew of.

Peering through the gap in the wall, she saw Ulf ordering his men. A surprising number of men—even for a jarl. It gave Helga an uneasy feeling in the pit of her stomach.

Ulf was gathering an army...and this man thought she had influence over him?

She shook her head fervently, dislodging the cloak from around her head.

He smiled with a wicked sort of satisfaction at her distress, but he had misinterpreted her reaction. 'Jarl Ulf has been busy since Halfdan married your sister. I *knew* your family couldn't be innocent in all of this. You have conspired against me. First, by capturing my sister and now by waging war against me.'

He's not my uncle! she wanted to scream.

Halfdan might now be her brother-in-law, but his father had disowned him for marrying Valda. Erik also hated him and had long since been treated as an outcast by him. In fact, Ulf was the last man in all of Midgard who would care what happened to her, or any member of her family for that matter. He probably didn't even know her name.

Desperate to explain she gripped his hands as tightly as she could with the rope binding them and shook her head fervently.

He frowned at her. 'Do not pretend you do not know him. I have asked around. For the past few months, you have had regular deliveries of food from Ulf's Hall. I heard of your sister's grand wedding aboard Halfdan's ship and how Erik is already trying to secure land for your family. Your uncle's devotion to you is clear and all know of the firm kinship that you *Vikings* feel for one another. It is the only decent thing you do honour!'

His lips had curved with disgust over the word *Viking* and she knew instinctively there was a bitter reason behind his hatred.

She shook her head again, imploring him with her eyes to understand, or at least, to remove her gag so that she could explain herself…

Ulf does not care for us! That was Halfdan! she wanted to scream.

Even the food hadn't been Ulf. She supposed it might have seemed like it came from Ulf's Hall, but as Halfdan had provided almost everything for his father up until recently that meant nothing. How could she make this man see that he'd made a terrible mistake? That his sister's disappearance was nothing to do with her family?

He growled in disgust at her silent denial and he turned back to look at the square. The girl from earlier ran up to Ulf and Helga held her breath, praying that the evil man wouldn't harm the child.

A large cart rolled across the path and they were unable to see Ulf's reaction, which was a pity as she was sure Ulf would have laughed at such an absurd demand. When the cart had gone, Ulf's back was to them and the small child was running home unharmed.

Two large figures walked past the hut and Rhys's eyes brightened with bitter triumph in the dim light.

Such beautiful sapphires, she thought, and wondered sourly when her anger at his stupidity would outmatch her foolish desire for him.

Belatedly she realised it was Brynhild and Erik who had passed by.

Helga lurched forward, intent on signalling to them where she was. With so many armed Norse men around, things would not go well for her captors if she broke free of them.

But Rhys had lightning-fast reflexes and he grabbed her before she could strike out against the wall. He rolled with her, taking the brunt of the force against his back, and held her tight to his chest, his breathing hot and laboured against her neck.

Fire and earth filled her nose. He smelled of warm spice, like the kind Halfdan had brought home in fine leather pouches. She'd breathed in their scent and marvelled at their taste—exotic flavours from a distant land. This man reminded her of them in a strange way, he was just as intoxicating.

His heavy scent did strange and confusing things to

her insides. She stared at the hard lines of his mouth and wondered if they would soften against her lips. Shocked by her body's aching response, she stared into his bright and unrelenting eyes as if they might offer her some answers. Only cold vengeance reflected back at her.

But then, why should she be surprised?

Nothing about today seemed to make any sense. She'd always imagined the dragon would steal her away to keep her safe, either from poverty or from some threat to her family—they'd had plenty of both over the last couple of years—but this man was the cause of her family's misfortune, not her saviour.

Typical. Not only had she failed to match her sisters in fighting, she would fail in this part of their fates as well.

Of course she would desire her enemy!

It would be comical if it weren't so painfully true.

Chest to chest she panted against him, her breathing hindered by the tight cloth between her teeth. Lord Rhys wasn't looking at her any more, he was looking towards one of his men who was staring between the gaps in the timber and held up one of his hands in warning.

A nearby hen and rooster had fluttered down from their perches, and Lord Rhys kicked a leg out towards them, deliberately spooking them. They flew out through one of the gaps in the wall, leaving in a flurry of feathers and squawking.

Afterwards the man dropped his hand slowly and smiled. A collective sigh of relief passed through all of them—except Helga. She cursed against the gag, then sank back against the floor in defeat. Her opportunity to alert Brynhild and Erik had evidently passed. Lord Rhys pulled her further into his arms and hauled her with him back to the wall, a bear grip around her body so tight she was helpless to do anything but breathe and watch.

'See how your vermin family run to Ulf for guidance!' he hissed in her ear and she had to admit that it must look like that, what with Brynhild and Erik speaking with Ulf immediately after her disappearance.

But then Erik might fear that it was Ulf who had taken her. Especially after Halfdan's unsanctioned marriage to Valda.

They were too far away to hear what was said and the square was growing heavier with more warriors and carts of supplies. But occasionally the crowd parted enough so that she could see them talking with Ulf.

Tostig, Halfdan's friend, joined them at one point, and then the next time the crowd parted all three of them were walking away from Ulf as he led his many warriors out of the square.

It seemed they would get no help from Ulf, but she had always known that.

The Lord's arms were beginning to pinch her rib cage and she guessed it was at the sight of so many warriors under Ulf's command.

The man who had left earlier to gather information returned. After a short conversation with their leader, two of the men left, leaving her alone with Lord Rhys and the last remaining guard.

Silently the three of them made their way back through the building, although this time Lord Rhys draped an arm around her shoulders and held her wrist tether tight. He marched her through the muddy streets, his arm pressing down just hard enough to keep her hooded head bent. He needn't have bothered, nobody paid any attention to them, and soon they were entering another building close to the river dock. Helga recognised some of the streets and she became hopeful of another opportunity to escape.

She had friends along the docks, friends who would

not let her leave without a fight. Except, just before the
dock, they entered another building. One belonging to a
wool merchant by the look and smell of the damp fleeces
filling the room. Lord Rhys spoke with the merchant in
a language she didn't understand, but guessed it was
Welsh by the lilt of it.

The man opened up a door at the back of the building, which led them directly on to a platform above the
river. Beneath it was a small boat. She could see they
were tucked behind a bend in the waterway, completely
out of sight from the docks.

There was no hope of rescue.

Chapter Three

Glancing up and down the river, Rhys could see no one that might hinder their escape. The ships coming in and out of Jorvik were few and far between at this time of day. It was a good thing his fleece merchant's platform was here. They could avoid walking among the many Vikings who infested Jorvik and in particular the riverside docks.

They were surrounded by the enemy—not unusual, considering they were in the heart of Danelaw, the old Saxon land now occupied by the Norse. These days it was a constant battle to keep his enemies at bay. Sometimes, when he was particularly exhausted like now, he wished he would lose—and quickly. Defeat would give him some peace at least. But he was too stubborn and proud to allow such a thing—his father had said he was more like his grandfather in that respect—and so he would fight on, until the bitter end.

Eager to leave the foul stench of Jorvik behind and not wanting to have his hostage out in the open for long, he slung her over his shoulder like bag of grain and stepped carefully down into the boat. It was little more than a bucket really, built for transporting small cargo back and forth between here and the docks. It had a wide, shallow bottom, a flimsy sail and a pair of dried-out old oars. A few supplies were already packed inside, with some fleeces to disguise them. Hopefully, they should be able to avoid any unwelcome attention.

They would sail and row down river, until they reached his army. His men had left the previous day as, with the alliance now broken, he'd rightly feared for the safety of his aunt and home. Seeing Ulf leave today with so many warriors had only confirmed his suspicions.

His men had been ordered to make up as much time as possible and only wait a short time for him at the arranged meeting point near Repton, before continuing home.

Even then, he feared it would be too late.

Helga glared and shrieked through her gag, jabbing him in the shin with a kick that sent shooting pain up his leg.

He took the tether rope around her wrists and tied it to the base of the rowlock. Not wanting to see the condemnation in her eyes, or risk her being seen, he quickly arranged the fleeces around her, laying one over her head to create a soft cage that would shield her from the view of any passing ships.

Then he turned to his last remaining warrior, still waiting on the platform's edge. 'God willing, Madyn and Heilyn will stop Ulf's messenger. If not, then I will meet with our men and do our best to reach Ulf's fort before the messenger arrives to order the deaths of our kinsmen. I will need you to continue searching for Lady Alswn, as we've have had no luck finding her here. So, try gathering information regarding any other possible locations and look in particular at Ulf's old holdings and alliances.'

Wyn swallowed nervously, but nodded. It was a huge task for one man, but hadn't Rhys been even younger when the mantle of leadership had passed to him? 'I will, my lord. But what if Ulf is right and she left with Hywel before the wedding could take place?'

'Then they will already be on their way home.' Rhys had little hope of that being true. Hywel would have left word for him—not let him worry like this. 'If before the end of the month you still cannot find her, then you should also return home. We will need every warrior available to man the walls if we are to avoid Cadair y Ddraig falling to the heathens. God be with you, Wyn.'

'And also with you, my lord.'

Rhys untied the boat from the platform and settled down to focus on raising the sail. The journey was easy here, the current doing most of the labour for him, and soon the water had carried them away from the muddy filth and smoke of Jorvik, the river meandering peacefully past lush trees and harvested fields. The tension eased in his neck and shoulders and, as the sun warmed his skin, he shrugged off his cloak, allowing himself a small sigh of relief that they had left Jorvik without incident.

It wasn't a long respite however—it never was—as soon his thoughts began churning through the mountain of duties and responsibility that plagued him daily.

Many battles were ahead of him. Potential plans and their possible consequences were spun like spider webs in his mind, each silvery thread intersecting with another. If one thread broke, he needed to have another ready to take its place.

So consumed was he by his worries, he almost forgot about the woman beneath the pile of fleeces. But then she kicked one of the wools away, punching a hole in his carefully made den, and abruptly reminded him of her presence.

Sitting up, she glared at him with pure fury and hatred and he remembered she was still tied at the wrists and mouth. He'd treated her poorly, but he quickly brushed any regret aside. Alswn could be suffering much worse under Ulf's hands even now. Helga should be grateful he was not so ruthless as her uncle.

Did pagans not care for their women's safety?

Was that why their women fought as warriors? Because their men offered them so little protection?

In truth, he knew so little about his enemy and it unsettled him. The Norse were a strange people, but he could not deny their prowess in battle, or how their alliances could prove beneficial for both parties. Rhys had wished for peace—if only to remove one adversary from his endless list of rivals. He had also truly hoped that Alswn would eventually be happy with Halfdan.

As he stared into the pretty eyes of his foe—a woman whose sister had ruined any prospect of such a future without bloodshed—part of him wished she'd remained hidden for the entire journey.

She shrieked against the cloth—although it appeared more in outrage than fear—and he realised she was berating him. He even recognised a few curse words in her garbled shouts. Her face was flushed and glistening with sweat. After a moment, she abruptly stopped in her tirade and sighed, as if her temper had burned away leaving only disappointment.

It made him almost feel…*guilty.*

Shame twisted in his gut. It was true, he did feel bad for kidnapping her—no matter how good his reasons.

Tying the steering oar into position, he allowed the wind and river's gentle current to carry them forward for a while.

'We are far enough away from Jorvik now. Your screams will not matter here,' he said, untying the gag.

She groaned and rolled her jaw tentatively, as if trying to ease the ache. Her lips were dry and cracked and she took a moment to wet them.

Her voice was dry and rough when she spoke, almost a whisper. 'Why the dragon symbol?' Her lack of anger surprised him, as did her odd question.

'Erik will recognise it as the symbol of my house. He will have confirmed to Ulf that I have you.'

She stared at him thoughtfully, raking her eyes up and down his face and body. 'You are the Welsh Lord, the one who had an alliance with Halfdan...before he broke it to be with my sister?'

He nodded, wondering how much she knew about the whole situation.

'And...*you* alone are the black dragon?' The question was emphasised as if she were checking a very pertinent detail and not merely asking him about the emblem of his family name.

'Some call me that,' he said, feeling uncomfortable under her pale blue gaze.

'I dreamt of you,' she said, frowning out across the rippling water as if it had insulted her.

As first conversations with a hostage went, *this* was most definitely not what he'd expected. 'You dreamt of me?' he asked stunned.

'Yes, as a child. I had a vision that one day I would be stolen by a black dragon with blue eyes...and here you are.' She waved her bound hands towards him and the big rope seemed almost ridiculous against her tiny wrists. 'Although I cannot understand its meaning...other than the obvious—that you would one day steal me from my family. Did you have any dreams about me?' she asked curiously and his stomach flipped.

She was trying to confuse and rattle him into bending to her will. Clenching his jaw, he snapped, 'Witchcraft does not frighten me. I do not believe in it!'

Shifting away from her, he grabbed the steering oar—though more for something to do than for any real need to check their course.

She laughed, the sound light and unbothered. 'I am glad to hear it. I would not wish to frighten anyone. But you did not answer the question. *Did* you dream of me?'

'No, thank God!' Again, there was that look of disappointment on her face. What dreams might he have had—if he *had* dreamt of her?

Lustful, wicked dreams, he thought with a shiver, and decided to row for a while, pulling on the oars with all his might.

He *shouldn't* desire her, but he did. Ever since he'd first seen her in the market that morning. The carefree way she'd walked among the stalls, the pretty smiles she'd given to the merchants and the way she'd stolen the air from his lungs when she'd met his gaze with heated interest.

After a few blissful moments of silence, she said, 'I cannot swim away… You may as well untie me.' She tugged on the rope again and he could see how it had rubbed her skin, causing thin red welts to bloom against the cream. It was no wonder the coarse rope had hurt her. She had pale, luminous skin that must bruise and mark easily, the kind that needed a tender, gentle touch. He swallowed down a lump in his throat.

'I thought all you Vikings were born from the sea?'

'We are born from ash and elm, not the sea. Odin and his brothers carved our bodies out of wood and breathed life in to us. But…many of us are master boatbuilders and skilled at sailing, so I can see why you might believe that.' She shrugged dismissively, before asking curiously, 'Where are you taking me?'

Dumbfounded by her calm reply to what he'd intended as an insult, he answered her honestly, seeing no reason to lie. 'To my fortress, Cadair y Ddraig.'

'And where is that?' she asked mildly as if they were discussing the weather and not her future prison.

'In the kingdom of Gwynedd, in Cymru…or Wales, as the Saxons call it. It is the land of the Britons and I have a fortress high in the mountains there.'

She stared at him as if he were mad. 'But…*why*?' Her eyes narrowed and she leaned forward, her voice as venomous as an adder, and he was promptly reminded of who and what she was. A shieldmaiden, a Viking woman with a pagan heart that thirsted for blood and treasure. 'Why did you abduct me, Lord Rhys? What made you think it was *ever* a good idea to steal me away?'

He matched her temper with his own, leaning forward to snarl, '*Because* Ulf stole my sister!'

Was he no better than Ulf?

The thought worried him, but in war you had to match the ruthlessness of your enemy, or risk defeat.

He continued more calmly, 'Your uncle is waging war against my people, stealing my land, slaughtering my livestock. Halfdan broke both his word and our peace treaty by marrying your sister. Now my kingdom is suffering because of it…' His simmering rage burst into flames when he saw her reaction and he roared, 'You *dare* roll your eyes at me!'

How dare she act as if the pain and suffering of his people were only a minor concern?

Halfdan and Valda had caused this, they were proof

that love—no matter how well intentioned—never ended well. It was a selfish emotion that always led to the suffering of others.

Her eyes focused on his with infuriating pity and she sighed. 'You have stolen the wrong woman. I mean nothing to Ulf.'

A strange dread crept through his mind like an unexpected frost.

Why did her answer sound so convincing?

No! He had seen with his own eyes how her family had run immediately to Ulf for help. She was lying to save herself. 'Well, that is a pity…' he said, sarcastically. 'Because if my sister is not brought back to me before the end of the month your family will never see you again.'

'Will you kill me?' she asked bluntly.

Staring at her in shock, he snapped, 'Maybe I will!'

It was only meant to frighten her. To put her back in her place as his hostage. But that appeared to be an impossible task because she didn't look scared by the prospect… just irritated.

'A pity. I would have hoped for a longer life. If it reassures you, I can confirm Brynhild and Erik will do as you ask. They will search for your sister and they *will* find her.'

'They need only ask Ulf!' he grumbled, regretting his earlier callous words, but being too proud and angry to apologise for them.

She smiled again. 'Ulf does not have your sister. Lady Alswn left of her own accord—Valda told me about it. Ulf would have forced her to marry him instead of his son otherwise and Halfdan would have felt terrible about it… He is a good man.'

'My sister and her guard would have come straight

home, if that were the case, and there was no sign of them on my journey here.'

'Maybe she didn't go home...' She said it softly, but her eyes were piercing and seemed to strip the flesh from his bones.

Alswn had always been against the alliance, but Hywel was honour-bound to fulfil his orders. Yes, he cared for her happiness, but he would not have ignored his duty, his responsibility to Gwynedd, and neither would Alswn. She knew Efa's life depended on it.

Rhys brushed the doubt aside. 'Alswn would not have done anything to jeopardise her aunt's safety.'

'Her aunt?' Helga's eyes widened with surprise. She was so expressive with her features that he found himself fascinated by them.

'She is being held hostage by Ulf.'

Helga muttered something rude and vulgar before she looked back up at him with a tight and bitter smile. 'If I am to be your hostage, please can you explain to me how this all came about? I am so confused. There seems to be a lot of women either missing or held hostage and I honestly cannot unravel any of it in my mind!'

For once Rhys was in agreement with her and wondered if maybe Helga *wasn't* privy to all of her uncle's wicked plans. 'It would probably be best if I explained everything from the beginning.'

'Well, I certainly have the time to listen.'

Rhys gave a huff of agreement at her mocking smile. She was incredibly likeable and he struggled to not smile at her wry humour. 'Ulf owns a small settlement near my border. We have never had trouble with the Norse farmers there before and have even traded with them from time to time. Last year Ulf ordered a fort to be built around his settlement and the farmers disappeared. More and more warriors arrived and then the raiding began.

'It was petty theft at first, but I fought back and managed to capture some of his men. I hoped that would be an end to it, that they were only testing our strength, but if anything, the attacks only grew in ferocity. Settlements were burned to the ground, families murdered in their beds, constant death and destruction across my land. They even managed to capture my aunt on the road and have held her prisoner ever since. Ulf said he had taken her to *"open negotiations"* between our people.'

'So, that is why you agreed to an alliance with Ulf?'

'I agreed that Alswn could marry his eldest son, Halfdan. I had heard good things about him, that he was a successful merchant with more wisdom than his father. I hoped that by sealing an alliance with Halfdan it would secure a better future for Alswn and end the raiding for good.'

'I am surprised you would trust a man like Ulf to keep his word.'

Chafing against the accusation, he glared at her with bitter fury. 'I was forced to accept either an alliance, or my aunt's brutal death. Which would you have chosen?'

Helga nodded. 'I see.'

For some reason he found himself explaining further, as if her approval mattered. 'When Halfdan delayed the wedding until the autumn, I had hoped to rescue my aunt before the end of the summer and save my sister from a marriage she did not want, but…I ran out of time.'

Had that been wrong of him?

To give Alswn hope, only to snatch it away from her at the last minute? She'd sobbed as she'd left, begged him to keep trying to rescue their Aunt Efa before she reached Jorvik. He'd said he would try…but he'd known even then that it wasn't enough time.

Helga interrupted his grim thoughts. 'Halfdan gave them horses, he told them to run. If he hadn't, Ulf would have married her instead because he needed the alliance just as much as you did. His power is failing in Jorvik and it would have helped him reclaim it.'

Exasperated at her lies, he replied coldly, 'It would not have made any difference.'

Helga gasped. 'You suspected Ulf might marry her anyway…even if Halfdan did not?'

Disgust coated his tongue with a metallic taste. 'My sister is beautiful and young. It was why I kept her from meeting him for so long. But…if he did choose to marry her instead, Hywel knew that I would have to agree.'

'You would do that? You know Ulf, you know what he is capable of!' Helga cried, horrified, and he clenched his jaw against her judgement.

Of course she thought him cruel!

He even agreed with her in his heart, but as a lord responsible for the lives of so many, he could not afford to listen to his heart. 'She is a high-born lady of Gwynedd, granddaughter of the great King Rhodri. We marry for duty and for the good of our kingdom. Not for love. As will I, if required. I asked nothing of her that I would not do myself.'

She laughed. 'You would let Ulf rut you, then?'

He choked on his own shock. 'You…' *You are right,* he thought miserably, but hardened his resolve to snap, 'You are a vulgar woman!'

'Hmmm,' she murmured, completely undisturbed by his insult, as if she didn't quite believe him and was even a little smug that she had proved her point so well.

Because she was right! When the time came, he would

not be in the same position as Alswn—because he was a man and would always have more power in a marriage than his bride. It was a worry that had robbed him of sleep more than once.

'So, you must admit that she *could* have run away by herself?'

'If that were the case, Hywel would have chased after her and left a message informing me of it,' he said firmly, remembering the last conversation he'd had with his friend.

'She will be distraught when she realises there is no hope of rescue.'

'You must stay strong for her, Hywel. Tell her that she is a daughter of Gwynedd and that her aunt's life depends on her. Remind her of that and she will do her duty.'

Hywel knew what was at stake and he was loyal. He had been Rhys's friend from child to man. If Alswn had been taken, Hywel would not rest until she was found and he would have sent word about her abduction immediately. Grimly, Rhys had to accept the most likely possibility was that Alswn had been taken and Hywel had died trying to protect her.

'Hmmm,' Helga murmured again, seemingly unconvinced.

'But…' He paused. 'In the very unlikely possibility that I am wrong—'

'Which you are.'

'*If* I am wrong,' he repeated with a scowl, 'your family will still do as I say, will they not? Search for Alswn and bring her home. Whether she is being held by Ulf, or she had somehow managed to run away of her own volition?'

Helga nodded, the immediacy of her agreement doing something to ease the knots of worry that strangled his stomach. 'They will. You see, no matter what you think of *my people*, family is everything to us. Brynhild, Erik and my mother Porunn will do everything they can to save me.'

'But not Ulf?' he asked mildly and smiled when he saw irritation spark in her narrowed eyes.

'Surely you cannot blame me for having *one* bad connection…especially when he is not related to me by blood and has now been disowned by both of his sons?'

Nothing seemed to faze her and he would give her credit for that. She was as brave and as fierce as her sisters, in her own way. Different, but just as impressive.

Sighing, she asked casually, 'So, what will you be doing while my family search for your sister? Sitting safe and pretty atop your mountain?'

Had she just called him pretty?

'I will be racing to try to save my aunt before Ulf's messenger arrives with orders to kill the hostages. After that I will be making plans to defend my land against Ulf's attack.'

Understanding dawned across her face. 'He has sent an order to kill her?'

'Yes. One of my men overheard him telling your family of his plans. I dispatched two of my men to intercept the messenger.'

'Oh, I had wondered why we were travelling alone. What of your other man?'

Rhys frowned wondering why he was telling her so much regarding his plans, but not finding any reason to lie. She would never be able to escape and tell Ulf. 'I have sent my remaining man to search for my sister, in case your family fails.'

'Just one man?' Helga asked, her eyes wide with disbelief.

Rhys inwardly winced, although he kept his face devoid of all expression. Helga had quickly cut to the heart of all his problems.

He didn't have enough men.

His land was sprawling, his warriors divided and pulled in far too many different directions. Sometimes he also felt as if he were being torn apart, with so many people relying on him.

The raiding had cost him the lives of many warriors and serfs, reducing his numbers significantly, and he'd received no aid from the King as yet. He'd barely been able to gather enough men to guard Alswn while she journeyed to Jorvik. Then Hywel and Alswn had disappeared, leaving their guards confused as to what had happened.

'If I could, I would order every man under my command to search for Hywel and Alswn. But I must consider the good of *all* my people and their needs must always come first above my own.'

Helga stared at him thoughtfully, a whisper of pity in her soft expression. 'I am glad I am not high-born.'

'To not be in my position, or Alswn's?'

She sighed. 'Both.'

He leaned forward. 'But you *are* in her position—you are my hostage, until my sister is returned to me!'

'If you say so, *my prince.*'

Rhys scowled at that. Intuitively she'd touched on a sore issue that still plagued him to this day, or at least it plagued the King, who still did not trust him. 'It is true that Alswn and I are the grandchildren of King Rhodri the Great, but we are not royalty. My father was one of his illegitimate sons, but he never wished to rule and gave up all claims to power. Even though in Cymru, land and title are equally divided between all sons regardless of legitimacy, he gave it up to ensure peace. The true King of Gwynedd is Anarawd ap Rhodri and I am glad of it.'

She yawned and leaned back against the fleeces, her eyes blinking slowly as if she were fighting sleep. 'You have the look of a prince.' Then, a moment later she murmured, 'Your father was brave.'

'Many called him weak.'

'It is never weak to choose peace.'

Rhys stared at the Viking woman in front of him with disbelief. *She valued peace?*

Helga was not like anything he would have expected in the daughter of a shieldmaiden. Not only was she beautiful and clever, but there was a strange magic about her, with her piercing gaze and wild locks. She had cut him down at the knees with only a few sleepy words and he had to remind himself that she was the one bound by a rope.

Why then did he feel as if he were the one trapped?

He had to be careful around her. There was something intoxicating about her that went past mere attraction.

The wind ruffled her hair and he realised she had fallen asleep, waves of pale hair spread out around her in a messy halo still scattered with flowers and thin braids. He wondered how it would feel tangled between his fingers.

He thought back to the market square when their eyes had met for the first time. How he'd felt a punch to his gut so hard that he'd been unable to breathe. Watching her like a fool, unable to think clearly, until her attention had finally been dragged away by the craftsman.

Maybe she was *a witch.*

Immediately he dismissed the thought as fanciful and stupid. He found her attractive, that was all.

In another life he might have gone to her, bought her one of the pieces of jewellery she'd been admiring and asked to walk her home. But he was Lord Rhys of Gwynedd and he could not ignore his responsibilities, or the fact that she was his enemy and could not be trusted.

Peace always came at a terrible price and soon he would have to pay it.

Chapter Four

Helga rubbed her eyes and stared up into the night sky. The waning moon and stars shone overhead, casting a strange dark blue light across the whispering river. The trees either side filled with dark shadows and the occasional hoot of an owl.

She shifted, tried to rise and failed. Her hands were still tied and tethered to the rowlock. Cursing, she had to wiggle for a while before she could sit upright. Tossing her loose hair over her shoulder with a huff, she asked, 'Are we not going to stop? Surely you will want to rest for the night?'

She must have fallen asleep against the fleeces because she hadn't seen the sun set. It looked as if they had crossed the mouth of the sea and entered into another inland river heading south. On this waterway they moved against the current and Rhys had been forced to row.

Had he been rowing for long? By the exhausted look on his face, and the sweat on his brow she would imagine he had.

'No. But now that you are awake, we can stop for a moment to eat.' He plunged the oars decisively into the water, guiding them to the shelter of some low-hanging willows.

She was a little surprised she'd been able to sleep at all. Granted, she had been exhausted from Valda's wedding feast the night before and then she'd been captured. But even so, to sleep so soundly in her captor's presence?

Except, she wasn't afraid of Rhys any more—not since she'd learned his motives. She actually felt sorry for him. He looked weary and not just from the rowing, but from the weight of responsibility on his young shoulders.

His sister was missing, his land and people in peril. She could not imagine adding the worry of an impending war to such a burden, or the responsibility of so many lives relying on him to make the right choice. She had been telling the truth—she *was* glad she was not highborn. It seemed too great a load for one person to bear.

After anchoring them, Rhys opened one of the sacks beside him and removed a loaf of bread, four hardboiled eggs, a chunk of cheese, four plums and several strips of dried fish. Using the blade of his oar as a table across his thighs, he began to spread out the food on a linen cloth.

'You're going to row through the night?' she asked, a little bewildered.

'Yes.'

'And then ride with your army back to your kingdom?'

'Yes.'

'And then you will attack Ulf's fortress and save your aunt?'

'I will try,' he said impatiently as he bit into a plum.

'With no sleep?'

'Eat!' he ordered, gesturing at the food.

Helga's own temper flared. 'How?' she snapped back, holding up her bound wrists and shaking them.

Using his dagger, he cut off a chunk of bread, loaded it with a slice of cheese and held it out to her. She began to eat, taking little bites so as not to fumble and drop the food. If this was all they had, it would be best if she did not waste it. 'Why did you take me over my mother or sisters?' she asked.

'I would have taken Valda, except she and Halfdan were eager to leave Jorvik and were already gone when I sought them out.'

'Valda?' Helga laughed, covering her mouth with her bound hands as she spoke through her food. 'You think Valda would have been easier? Both my sisters are fierce. They would have sliced open your guts before you had time to draw your sword.'

He smiled at her obvious pride in them, before hitting her with another barb. 'Then it appears I did take the right sister after all.'

Helga scowled. It had taken her years to accept herself. She wouldn't let some arrogant prince, or lord or whatever he was, make her feel bad for it.

'I have other talents,' she grumbled.

It was too dark to see his face clearly, but she saw the way he shifted in his seat, as if she had made him uncomfortable by her statement. Which was interesting and made her sit up a little in her seat.

Did she affect him as much as he affected her?

There would be some comfort in that at least. She was still unsure about how their fate entwined—it was death or love and both seemed unlikely at this moment in time. But if there was mutual attraction? Her hope fell when she heard his next words.

'As a witch? My men told me some people call you that.'

Tartly she replied, 'I prefer healer or wisewoman. I have a gift for growing things, telling fortunes and healing.'

'Who taught you? Your mother and sisters do not seem the type.'

'My Aunt Freydis. When they went to fight, she would look after me and I would help her prepare for the wounded. Being a healer is an important role and someone always has to stay behind to look after the supplies and children. I would guard them with my life, I am not afraid to fight.'

'How can I doubt that after seeing how bravely you fought earlier.' His voice was husky and it rubbed against her skin in the moonlight like a cat.

She grabbed one of the fleeces and wrapped it around her shoulders. 'Surely you have healers, too, in your own lands?'

'We do have healers. In fact, there is an old couple who grow remedies in my gardens. They are odd folk, but well meaning.'

Did he think her odd? Why should she care if he did?

Helga held out her hands for more food and he placed another chunk of bread and cheese in her hands. 'I know the Christian church disapproves of certain pagan beliefs and traditions. But a lot can be learned from them. Valda was telling me that in the east there are new herbs and spices, as well as techniques for healing. She promises to bring me some new ingredients on her next trip.'

Rhys began to peel the shell off a boiled egg and she found herself fascinated by the dexterity of his long fingers. He made no comment, and belatedly she realised he probably did not wish to speak of Valda and Halfdan. An awkward silence filled the night air between them and all she could hear was the rustling of willow branches, and the light crunch of egg shell being removed.

'I will have to speak with your healers…when we arrive at your fort,' said Helga, but Rhys said nothing in return, tossing the discarded shell over the side of the boat and biting into the soft flesh of the egg. Absently he passed her a flagon of mead and she drank from it before passing it back.

'They may know of cures that I do not. It will be good to meet others with my vocation,' she added.

He chuckled. 'They are nothing like you.'

Believing he was mocking her, she snapped, 'Why do you hate the Norse so? It cannot be only because of Ulf. Do not deny—'

'I do not deny it! I do hate them.' He glared at her and she felt icy fingers wrap around her heart at the viciousness of his reply. '*Vikings* are a pestilence on this land. Raping and pillaging. Stealing from good people. *Enslaving good people!*'

She did not bother to explain that *Viking* was a way of life and not the true name of her people. Who was she to correct someone who had so obviously suffered at Norse hands?

Quietly she replied, 'Not all of us follow that tradition. I do not.'

'Lies!' He leaned forward, his teeth flashing pearl white in the moonlight. 'Your people have plagued our shores for years and you never want peace! It was not that long ago that we repelled your brethren horde at Anglesey. We have not forgotten the people who were killed that day, or how you meant to take our land by force!'

'Not all of my people want to kill and enslave. Many of us wish to farm, build settlements, make crafts and live in peace—'

'It is not your land to farm! Or even the Saxons!' They came to the land of the Britons like you did, many years ago. A flood of settlers that pushed mine further west into the mountains. Well, we will never make the same mistake again. Your people are not welcome!'

Helga's fists were clenched so hard she could feel her nails cutting into her flesh.

If this man was destined to be her future husband, then she would rather be torn apart by wolves!

There was no blissful future here. The rune had been a warning, nothing more. Maybe she would never marry and, after meeting this loathsome lord, she was beginning to think a life without men was definitely preferable.

The ropes were chafing her skin and she tugged on them in irritation. She would do anything to be rid of them. If her fate was set and she was to be his captive, she would rather be a comfortable one.

'Think what you like! But surely you see how ridiculous it is to keep me tied up like this? What if I give you my word that I will not run?'

He laughed. 'Your people have no honour—why should I believe you?'

The last thread of her patience snapped and she lost all grip on her temper, letting it flow out of her like a raging storm.

'You are so ignorant! Honour means everything to us. *Everything!* Are you so stupid as to ignore the first rule of war? Let me remind you of it: know your enemy better than you know yourself. If not, then you will only ever learn defeat. Your prejudice has made you blind.'

She expected him to rage back at her, but to her surprise, he leaned back as if she'd struck him.

Unable to stop her tirade now that it was loose, she continued. 'Do you think I *want* to remain alone with you? So out in the open? There may be war bands in this area and they would see your fine clothes, and think to themselves...' She spoke with a comically deep voice. 'That poor farmer's boat is a trick! Look at him! He is wearing a handsome tunic. He must have lots of silver with him.' Losing the mocking voice, she hissed, 'They would sooner slit our throats than wait to see how heavy your purse *really* is… And…' She paused, a little embarrassed by her next words. 'I…I will need to relieve myself soon. I cannot do that bound to a boat! I may be your hostage, but I am still human and I have basic needs!'

Sucking in a calming breath, she leaned forward and place her bound hands against her heart. 'I give you my word, on the lives of my sisters and mother, that if you untie me, I will not try to escape. Unless…' she thought of Loki, the God who never made a deal without a way out '…unless I see one of them stood directly in front of me. I will not leave you. I will even help you row. We can take it in turns to rest and navigate the river.'

His eyes had widened in surprise and she wasn't sure if it was the vow, or the fact that she'd pointed out how vulnerable they were, but he seemed to consider her words properly for the first time.

Calmly he replied, 'I will protect you. As my hostage, I am duty bound to ensure your health and well-being… until your family pay the ransom.'

'I am sure you will try to protect me, but after so long rowing, would you be able to offer much resistance if we were outnumbered?'

He looked out into the darkness with a frown and then, after a long pause, he reached forward, gripped the bonds around her wrists and tugged her forward. Their faces were so close she could feel his breath against the tip of her nose. Then there was a flash of a blade in the waning moonlight and the ropes fell to the deck.

'Let us see if you can keep your word.'

Chapter Five

Dawn broke on a fresh, clear sky. The autumn light was warm against Rhys's skin and sparkling white upon the river's surface, while a brisk wind whipped his hair forward, forcing him to keep pushing it back out of his eyes.

He didn't risk falling asleep, but he did rest while Helga rowed.

There was much for him to consider. Was he mad to trust her?

In the market square she'd spoken so softly to the merchant, her movements gentle and light, her beauty delicate and otherworldly, reminding him of the Tylwyth Teg, the fairy-folk he'd heard tales of as a child. Strange, mythical creatures who could transform into mist or birds at will.

Well, Helga could certainly transform when provoked. She'd fought hard with a strength and will that had shocked and impressed him. He could not fault her courage, or her wisdom.

Was she right? Had he allowed his own ignorance and hatred to cloud his judgement?

Usually, he considered himself a firm but fair leader, judging a person on their own merit and actions alone. Hadn't he cursed his own King's petty mistrust of him, yet had he behaved any better in his treatment of Helga?

No, he had behaved much worse.

She was not his enemy, but a casualty in a war that was not of her own making.

What else had she said? *Know your enemy better than you know yourself.*

Wise words.

In fact, much of what Helga had said was full of insight and common sense. Although he would rather pluck out his own tongue than admit it to her.

They'd not argued since their talk beneath the willow. Keeping their words brief and pragmatic instead, which seemed to suit both of them. With her hands unbound their progress was swift and their necessary stops short and infrequent.

Time was slipping through his fingers like water and it was imperative that he re-join his men before it was too late. After already failing his aunt once, he refused to do it a second time.

Thoughts of Efa soured his mood. He should have protected his aunt better. Banned her from going out into the villages, even if it was to help those who were sick and wounded. If he'd been stricter, she would now be safe at home and he would never have had to make any alliance with Ulf in the first place.

Her life, and that of those captured with her, depended on a wild rescue plan. An idea that he wasn't even sure could work, which relied on the extraordinary efforts of a few good men and barrels of luck.

One wrong step could end in disaster.

They passed a few fishing boats, followed by a settlement close to the water's edge. Heeding Helga's earlier warning, Rhys had already taken off his elaborate tunic, leaving only the linen undershirt beneath.

'The wind will help us for a time.' He reached for

the oars and took them from her, their fingers brushing against one another, and a shiver of heat ran up his arm as he placed the oars on the deck. He bristled at the unwelcome reaction, feeling as if he had broken some code of honour by touching her, if only by accident.

He focused his attention on steering the boat as they passed the clamour of a large settlement. The banks were bustling with trade, fishermen and people washing their clothes and he breathed a sigh of relief as they passed by unscathed. The landmark was a good sign. It wouldn't be long until he reached his army. Before noon, God willing.

'So, how do you plan on saving your aunt?' Helga asked pleasantly. He could almost believe she was looking forward to the rescue.

'It will depend.'

'On what?'

He frowned. 'That is not your concern.'

'Oh, but I think it is,' she said with false sweetness. 'I presume there will not be enough time to take me to your fortress first. Therefore, I will most likely join you on the raid, or at least be close by.' At his scowl she smiled in triumph. 'Exactly! I should like to know your plans—'

'Do you think me stupid?'

'At least then,' she continued, deliberately ignoring his outrage, 'I will know if it is a good plan, or not, and I can then prepare accordingly.'

'And how would you prepare?' he asked, a ghost of a smile fighting to be free and he had to deliberately repress it.

'Well, if your plan is a bad one and things turn sour, I will hide and await rescue. If it is a good plan, I will help.'

Her honesty was refreshing and he chuckled. 'Help? Why would you wish to help me?'

'Why not? Your aunt has been kidnapped and held

against her will. I understand her situation far better than you ever could and, yes, I would try to free her. Ulf is not a man I would ever choose to side with.'

Astounded by her answer he asked in disbelief, 'You would fight against your own people?'

She rolled her eyes with a heavy sigh. 'Have you heard nothing I have said? Ulf's men are not my people. Ulf does not care for me at all. Why should I care if he is defeated by you? In fact, I am sure he deserves it.'

'He does. He has raided my lands and caused countless deaths.'

'See! So, I am happy to help you in any way that I can. I am not good with a sword, but I am accurate with a bow, or if you plan on trickery or negotiation, my Norse could be very useful to you.'

'I speak Norse. I am speaking it right now!'

He looks so angry, thought Helga and she deliberately forced down the giggle rising in her throat. *Why was she enjoying teasing him so much?*

'Your accent would give you away within a heartbeat, if not your looks.'

'My looks?'

'You are tall and strong, but lack the bulk of a Norseman, and your features are too...' She paused, suddenly aware that she was about to say *fine.*

'Too?' he prodded.

'Pale. You look as if you have never seen the sun.'

He chuckled. 'As do you.'

'I wear a cap or hood to avoid burning in the summer, but there has not been much sun in Jorvik to warrant either. It rains much of the time.'

'I am afraid you will have much of the same in my kingdom.'

'I do not mind the rain. As long as I have food and a warm bed.' Helga had spoken without thinking and a rush of heat flooded her face when she realised what she'd admitted.

It was disturbing how easy she found conversing with her captor. Had she really just told the man who held her hostage that she liked a warm bed?

Rhys cleared his throat and busied himself checking the sail, as if to distract them both. 'You and your family. Whereabouts did you live in Jorvik?'

'Do you not already know?' she asked, feigning surprise. 'It is truly miraculous that you were ever able to find me—what with so little planning!'

He scowled at her mockery. 'I only learned of Valda's marriage to Halfdan two days ago, when I arrived and learned my sister was missing. I asked for someone to point out Halfdan's ship and they pointed you out as you were leaving, said to speak with one of you if I needed Halfdan. They were most helpful in telling me all about you.'

Helga chuckled dryly. 'To think I might never have been captured if someone had been a little less forthcoming.' Rhys looked at her as if she were mad and she threw up her hands with a laugh. 'Fate is a funny thing. Nothing is ever chance, yet it all appears to be. Do you not think that strange?'

'I *would* have found you eventually.' Something in the way he said it felt almost possessive and a shiver ran down her spine, twisting and curling into something hotter.

'Perhaps… Although, by then you would have realised how little we actually meant to Ulf. Especially if you had seen where we live. We are not rich. We do not live in a grand hall. We live in a hut, close to the stench of the tanning yards and the raw meat of bone alley. Our home barely fits four of us eating together and I sleep next to Brynhild under the one blanket we share. Our fortunes only changed for the better when Valda returned from her voyage with Halfdan.'

'Because she seduced him into marrying her?' he asked with a raised brow of condemnation.

'If anything, Halfdan seduced her!' she cried. 'My sister made her own silver on that voyage, then had the good sense not to let the love of her life go for a second time. I am sure they did not realise how their rekindled love would affect others. Well, perhaps Halfdan did, but he probably thought he had solved most problems arising from his broken engagement.'

'He did not.'

'And you think your problems would have been resolved by making an alliance with Ulf?' she asked gently, not wishing to prod his anger further, but needing him to realise the truth. 'You think a man like Ulf would happily form a trade agreement with you and allow you to live in peace?'

Something hard and venomous flashed behind Rhys's eyes. A darkness she had not fully seen until now. 'Oh,' she said softly, as understanding dawned slowly in her mind. 'You did not plan to live in peace with him...did you?'

'If Halfdan proved worthy of my sister, then I might have let him live. But Ulf? I cannot make deals with men I do not trust. I planned to overthrow him eventually. I only needed more time.'

The cold intelligence and ruthlessness of his statement shocked her.

'And what of Ulf's people? The men and families in his fortress?'

'They would die defending it or be forced to leave when I burned it to the ground.'

'So, that is your plan. To arrive before Ulf's army and destroy his fortress. But what of your aunt?'

A muscle jumped in his jaw and his voice was raw with barely concealed pain. 'I will try to free her. But if I fail, then I must still destroy his fort. Otherwise, he will continue to use it as a base to launch his attacks from. It will make the defence of my own land and settlements impossible.'

'That makes sense,' she said sadly. She had never approved of killing and war, but she understood it; she had followed her mother and sisters long enough to know that strategy and not compassion meant the difference between victory or death. Still, to be so cold when talking of his aunt's death? Did the man have no feelings?

'It looks as if the wind is easing. I shall have to row again,' Rhys said with a frown, settling back on the bench and beginning to pull on the oars.

It was strange, everything Rhys said sounded so cold and unforgiving. He'd insulted her family and countrymen repeatedly, captured her without a care for her own freedom and disregarded her when she'd sworn no fealty to Ulf.

He was a villain in every way.

Yet she found she could not hate him. There was a backbone of honour and loyalty in everything he did that she could not ignore. Behind his angry bluster and hard decisions there was a burning need to protect and care for his people. Everything he did was for them and not his own ambitions—or at least, not as far as she could tell.

He'd also not hurt her, as other men might have done. She shivered, imagining what horrors his aunt might have suffered as a hostage under Ulf's 'care'.

No, she would not pity him, or accept him as her fate. He had disregarded his sister's thoughts and feelings in the same way he had ignored hers.

He did not deserve her and she *definitely* did not want him.

Leaning back into the fleeces, she watched him row. She might have admired his resolute strength and courage if he was not, with each beat of the oars, taking her further away from her family.

Chapter Six

Rhys saw his dragon banners flapping in the breeze and felt the knot in his shoulders loosen.

They had made it.

There were many steps ahead of him and so much had gone wrong, but the relief that something was finally going his way was overwhelming.

There was still hope for Efa.

Not only that, they were also far safer travelling in a group—Helga had been right about that.

He looked towards her. She sat with a dignified grace, her eyes fearless as she coolly assessed the camp from the boat. There had been no tears or wailing from her as anyone might expect from a hostage, not even once. Resilient, pragmatic and wise were not the character traits he would have presumed when he'd first seen her.

She caught him staring and he quickly looked away, busying himself with the steering of their boat towards the riverbank.

His body ached from the long hours of rowing. He'd thought himself to have a strong stamina, especially in battle. But the monotony of the rowing for endless hours had burned through his muscles, leaving him weak. The lack of sleep hadn't helped. But at least it was all worth it.

The camp was pitched between the water's edge and the forest. He whistled, high and sharp, to announce his arrival. Madoc, his current next in command, came to the riverbed with a serf boy.

The sun was high and he could hear the sounds of the camp being dismantled. Would he have made it in time without Helga's help? Probably not.

It was strange to think she deserved his gratitude, but she did, and he wondered how to show it without appearing weak in front of his enemy.

If she was indeed his enemy. Speaking to her had scrambled his thoughts on all manner of things. At least there was hope for Alswn's return now. If he had to use Helga's family to find out the truth, then he would do so gladly, whether they were innocent in Ulf's plans, or not.

Although, after listening to Helga speak, he suspected that she knew very little of Ulf's plans. Maybe her warrior siblings and mother didn't bother to tell her about such things? Part of him hoped that was the case.

Rhys threw the boat's rope to Madoc, who swiftly pulled them in. Hywel was officially his second, but after his friend's disappearance, Rhys had been forced to choose another. Madoc was young and enthusiastic, with a cheerful disposition and a ruddy complexion. What he lacked in experience, he made up for with diligent obedience.

Madoc was a good man and an excellent warrior. But Rhys missed Hywel's easy companionship. He always gave his opinion without formality, restraint, or flattery. But, more than that, they had laughed together.

A friend and a brother. Gone. Alswn, Efa and Hywel. Washed away like footprints in the sand.

Pushing the gloomy thought aside, he called out before

the boat had even hit the riverbank, 'Madoc, prepare the camp, we leave immediately, there is no time to waste!'

'Yes, my lord,' said Madoc, and then with more hesitation, 'What of the others?'

'They will join us later. Instead, we have a hostage. This is Helga Porunndóttir.'

Madoc looked a little horrified by Helga's presence, but gave a polite nod and then returned to the camp, shouting orders as he did so.

'Thank you for the introduction,' Helga murmured dryly with a roll of her pretty eyes and he chuckled.

The young serf steadied the boat and Rhys leapt from it, splashing into the muddy shallows up to the tops of his boots. He was about to offer Helga his hand when he noticed how wobbly she was on her feet. Her arms and feet were spread wide, as she stood and tried to maintain her balance, the boat rocking from side to side as if in a storm.

'I will help you,' he said and, before she had time to refuse, he scooped her up from the boat. Her body soft and warm in his arms and, as he waded through the boggy water, he realised how empty his life had become.

Helga swallowed a yelp of surprise when Rhys lifted her up from the boat. He held her as if she weighed no more than a bag of feathers and placed her gently at the bottom of the steep riverbank. As she gripped his forearms to steady herself, his fingers cupped her elbows, and had she imagined it, or did his thumb brush the crook of her arm?

Their eyes met and heat flooded her face and neck.

Hunger and torment were cut into the hard lines of his face, as if holding her hurt him in some strange way. Her fingers pinched into his forearms. She wanted to reach up and stroke the dark stubble of his jaw, but knew instinctively that she risked far more by doing such a reckless thing.

The boy began emptying the boat of all useful items and, as a fleece dropped beside their feet, Rhys let go of her and took a step back.

Picking up her skirts in haste, she tried to climb the riverbank, but her shoe slipped in the mud, and she would have tumbled back down into the water if it wasn't for strong hands reaching to grip her waist.

Humiliated by her clumsiness, she immediately bunched the cloth of her skirts in one hand and grasped the long grass above her with the other.

Rhys cleared his throat, his voice deep and gruff behind her. 'Shall I carry you again?'

'No!' she snapped and pulled herself up with a mighty heave, scrambling up with both hands and feet.

However, as she crested the riverbank and triumphantly stood upright, she felt her balance shift. One foot had slipped back down the slope and her upper body had dipped back with it. She was moments from tumbling down the hill when a firm palm slapped against her rump and propelled her forward with a hearty push.

Mortified, she stumbled forward, but at least she was safely on flat ground.

Rhys followed behind her, deliberately avoiding her eyes. 'Forgive me, I thought you were about to fall.'

Hot embarrassment threatened to engulf her in flames and she would gladly have been swallowed by the bog for all of eternity.

'I was,' she gasped and then cleared her burning throat with a humbled, 'Thank you.'

The little lad clambered up shortly after, a pack twice

his size strapped to his back, and she felt even more of a fool.

Dropping her skirts, she shook the mud from them with angry slaps. After being captured, dragged through alleyways and hen houses—not to mention sleeping against dusty fleeces—she realised how pitiful she must look. Hardly a temptation for any man, she must have imagined the desire in his eyes.

Usually, she took pride in her appearance. Even when they'd had no silver, she'd cared for her apron dress carefully, washed and combed her hair every day. It made her miserable to know that she must look and smell no better than cattle.

It wasn't my fault! she reminded herself, allowing some of her pride to return. Straightening her back, she looked out at the camp with a critical eye. It looked as if they'd been dismantling the camp when they'd arrived, as most of the tents were down and rolled up. There were no carts with them, only horses. Men were packing the final supplies and saddling them.

'Is this your army?' she asked with growing unease.

There were at least a hundred men, all heavily armed with spears, shields and bows. They were clad in protective mail shirts and helmets, with dark woollen clothing and matching cloaks, presumably made from the black mountain sheep their homeland was known for.

They would have been impressive—if she had not seen Ulf's army beforehand.

Sombre countenances were on all of their faces, as they sat in their saddles with straight disciplined backs. Helga recognised them immediately as seasoned warriors. But no matter how skilled the warrior, numbers always meant more in open battle, and that was something Ulf had plenty of.

'They are my *teulu*—it means family—and they are my personal guard.'

'Then you have a larger force back home?' she asked hopefully.

He frowned and she had the distinct feeling that he had fewer men than he would like. 'Yes, the rest of my men are back in Gwynedd. These are my elite warriors who travel with me.'

'I see—and that is why we must get back to your fortress quickly? Because otherwise your force is divided?'

A muscle in his jaw flexed and he gave a sharp nod. He took her gently by the elbow and led her towards a huge grey stallion. 'I would be outnumbered on the open field. But within my fortress, we have a good chance against Ulf's army.'

Helga swallowed nervously. From what she'd experienced so far with Rhys, she would rather be under his control then Ulf's. 'A good chance?'

He mounted his horse swiftly and reached down to offer her his hand. Gold rings and a sapphire winked down at her from his fingers. 'I do not believe in fate. Nothing is ever certain.'

'Except death,' she answered grimly.

He gave her a cold smile and nodded. 'Except death. But no one knows when death will come for them. Not even you.'

She shivered.

Was the dragon of her dream taking her to the Halls of the gods? Was that the meaning behind it? War would be one of the easiest and most straightforward paths to the afterlife.

Still, he was right. No one truly knew their fate until they walked it and she would walk it with her head held high.

She took hold of Rhys's warm hand and set her foot

firmly in the empty stirrup. As he pulled her up, he turned her, so that she sat in front of him. Due to her long skirts she had to perch sideways in front of his saddle, but after shifting a little she felt secure enough.

Rhys wrapped his arms around her and murmured in her ear, 'Hold me if you need to, or lie back against me. We will ride hard to keep ahead of Ulf.'

She nodded and showed her acceptance by resting her side against his chest. Wrapping his cloak around them, he tugged firmly on the reins and ordered his men to ride.

As they moved forward, she asked, 'Will you sleep now, while we ride? You must be exhausted.'

'You worry about my welfare, Helga?'

She bristled at the humour in his tone. 'If you fall off your horse, you might take me with you!'

He chuckled, the sound rich and smooth like Frankish wine. 'Have no fear, I can last a long time without sleep.'

Her spine stiffened and he cleared his throat awkwardly, having belatedly realised the double meaning of such a statement.

'I mean…I…sleep only for a short time most nights.'

'I see,' Helga replied pleasantly. She was glad he couldn't see her flushed face, or the smirk upon her lips.

They swept down and across the land, entering the kingdom of Mercia, the land bordering his own. Its ruler, Aethelflaed, the Lady of Mercia, was sister to Edward, the King of Wessex, in the south. Those two kingdoms were a threat to his people's independence, even more so now that they were so closely linked, but Rhys could not deny that they were currently more of a threat to the Danes than to his people, having already taken back land in Anglia, and successfully defeating encroachments from the Norse of Northumbria. Still, he hoped it would be a long time before the powers of Mercia and Wessex combined and looked west once more.

The Benedictine monastery they approached was called St Peter's. The lands surrounding the abbey were well cultivated with fields of grain, orchards and gardens, but the main buildings and livestock were encased within a stone wall. It was a humble monastery, following strictly to the Benedictine vows of stability, fidelity and obedience.

How the kindly Abbot Cuthbert would feel about Rhys's hostage, he wasn't sure.

Cuthbert was already hurrying towards them, his bald head gleaming in the light of his torch. 'My lord, what a pleasant surprise to see you again so soon.'

'Can we beg your hospitality for another night? My men will make camp just outside as they did before.'

'Of course! And you and your...' He paused, obviously trying to see Helga better, but being unable to, what with her wrapped so heavily in his cloak. She peeked out from the shelter of the cloth and smiled brightly down at the Abbot, who blinked back his surprise and cleared his throat. 'You and your guest are welcome to stay within our walls. I will have two lodges prepared for you, with some refreshment.' He nodded to another monk beside him who hurried away. 'We have already eaten our evening meal so you will have to eat alone tonight, but you and your men will be well cared for.' He gulped a little and Rhys knew the poor man must be worried.

'Thank you, that is very kind. You will, of course, be compensated for your hospitality, so that you may help other less fortunate travellers in the future,' Rhys said diplomatically, hoping to ease the Abbot's concern.

Helga chose that moment to dismount with a loud exhale of relief as she stretched her arms over her head. 'I am glad to be down from that horse,' she said cheerfully and the Abbot visibly paled when he heard her speak the Norse tongue.

'A heathen?' he whispered, horrified.

Rhys considered lying to Abbot Cuthbert, but decided his soul had enough things to pay penitence for as it was. 'She is my hostage and will be until my sister is safely returned to me—Lady Alswn is missing.'

'As well as your poor aunt?' Cuthbert frowned, but nodded. 'I cannot say that I agree with the taking of young women as hostages—usually it is men and for good reason,' he grumbled, looking pointedly at Rhys reproachfully. 'But I suppose you had no choice?'

Rhys nodded at the kindly man. 'I had no choice, Abbot Cuthbert.'

'And you will treat her well?' He looked at Helga then and the few wilted flowers still clinging to her hair like weeds. The muddy apron dress and lack of a cloak made her seem more vulnerable, although her eyes flitted back and forth between them with sharp intelligence as they spoke. Wild and innocent all at the same time.

'Of course.' Although something stopped him from claiming anything more than that and the Abbot frowned as the silence stretched between them.

'Well…' Cuthbert said eventually, breaking the tension. 'Let me show you to your accommodations, then.'

'We will only need one guest house,' Rhys clarified. 'My hostage must remain with me at all times.'

The Abbot spluttered in horror. 'But…that…that… cannot…'

Rhys smiled. 'It is for you and your brothers' protection. Unless you have another room. One I can lock her in?'

The Abbot shook his head. 'No Is she truly so dangerous? She seems harmless enough…' He paused as

Helga's eyes narrowed on him. She must have learned some Saxon living in Jorvik.

Rhys reassured him. 'On my honour, she will be treated as if she were a high-born lady of my house. No harm will come to her.'

'Very well, come with me.' Abbot Cuthbert sighed with obvious displeasure.

They passed the church and then a tall timber building, which must have housed the refectory, and the monks' dormitory, as the Abbot led them to a small but handsome timber and thatch building not far from the kitchens.

'This is where we lodge our most noble and venerated guests. Even so, it is still humble compared to what you are used to—we are not a large abbey.'

'It will suit us perfectly well, Abbot Cuthbert. We will leave shortly after dawn anyway. Tonight, we rest our horses.'

'Then I shall see you after lauds in the refectory to break our fast together before your departure.'

'Yes, Abbot.'

The Abbot opened the door to the guest house and used his torch to light the fire in the centre of the room. The fire was placed at about waist height on a large stone plinth and had a carved-out hole in its base for storing logs.

The monk from earlier arrived with a large basket of supplies, which he placed on a table near the door. Two benches were placed either side of the fire, with two beds at the end of the room.

'The chest has extra blankets,' said Cuthbert, with another pointed look at Rhys.

Did the man think him incapable of controlling himself?

It was almost laughable. Except he'd touched her far more than was acceptable already. Holding her in his arms for hours while they rode, not to mention those awkward moments at the riverbank. The press of his palm against her bottom to stop her from falling, and the embrace before that. When his loneliness had got the better of him and he'd desperately wanted to kiss her.

Not that he would ever behave so dishonourably.

'If a man uses his strength as a weapon, he only proves how weak he truly is,' his mother had told him once and it had always stayed with him.

Weak men did not deserve power and it was his duty to protect Gwynedd from men such as Ulf.

As the fire began to burn more steadily the Abbot took his leave with a hesitant smile at Helga. 'I hope you will be…comfortable. Is there anything else you need?' he asked, his worry clear. He might have been nervous of her Norse heritage, but he was still concerned about a young woman spending a night alone with a man, no matter the oath he'd sworn.

Her smile was almost blindingly bright in the gloom of the little room. 'No, thank you,' she answered in Saxon, before adding with a mischievous expression, 'Do not worry, Lord Rhys will be safe with me.'

The Abbot looked a little horrified by her teasing at first, but then he chuckled and shook his head, seeing the humour of it.

'Goodnight to you both,' he said and left.

Leaving them alone, with only the crackle of the fire filling the silence.

Chapter Seven

'I am *ravenous*!' Helga declared as she walked over to the table and began unpacking the basket cheerfully. 'I wonder what they have for us.'

He wasn't sure why her positive manner bothered him. Shouldn't he be happy that she did not fear him? Except, it made their time together somehow more…intimate. As if she were not his hostage, but a companion. The absence of which, he'd come to realise, he felt keenly.

Which was ridiculous!

He was a leader, with no time for such frivolities.

Should he order her to sit down, to not move or speak without his permission? Regain some form of boundary between them and remind them both of the conflict that stood between them?

But such petulant behaviour seemed even more ludicrous.

Oblivious to his inner turmoil, Helga exclaimed gleefully, 'They eat well, these priests. Look! Half a roasted hen, bread, cheese and a salad of autumn vegetables… and, what's this?' She picked up a clay jug and uncorked it to sniff the contents. 'Wine! Oh, it has been a long time since I tasted wine. Not since our days in Francia. I am surprised they can grow vines here—I thought it only grew in the south?'

'Most things grow well in this region. The soil is good and the Abbot manages the land well.'

'Then I look forward to trying it.' Helga piled up the food on to one large platter, then carried it and the jug towards the fire. 'I will need to share your knife again,' she said, before sitting down on one of the benches.

So, the single platter was for them to share? It was the kind of gesture a courting couple might make and it sent a shiver of anticipation down his spine, even though he was certain she did not intend it in that way. There was no formality with Helga in how she behaved with anyone, whether they be lord, abbot or serf.

He sat beside her and took out his eating knife. Leaning back, she gave him room to cut up the food into sizeable pieces. He tried his best to avoid accidentally brushing against her as he worked, realising belatedly that it would have been simpler if he'd just moved the platter from her lap to his.

She uncorked the jug once more and took a sip above his head. 'Mmm…' Helga moaned with pleasure and his knife paused. 'The wine is delicious.'

Uncomfortable with the turn in his thoughts, he moved back, sheathing his blade. 'That should be enough for now.'

'Here, try some.' Helga offered the jug with an innocent smile, as if they were old friends. It only made the emptiness inside him echo louder.

He shook his head and stared into the flames. He did not want to eat or drink. Instead another hunger gnawed at him, filling him with shame.

'Fine!' she replied tartly, nibbling on a chicken leg. 'I will not let your bad humour spoil this meal for me. I am famished from sailing and riding all day with barely any respite! I am sure you are just tired and ill-tempered after not sleeping for so long.' She pointed the greasy leg at him. 'But let me be clear—even if I am bound to you by fate, I have no inclination to fall into your bed this night!' Then, with less conviction she muttered, 'You would have to prove yourself worthy of me before I even *considered* it!'

Shocked by her outburst, he laughed. 'Worthy of *you*?'

'Yes,' she replied firmly, adding a glare for good measure. 'So, do not try anything!'

He smiled softly, amused by her, in spite of himself. 'Have no fear, Helga. I would never do anything to harm you.'

With a nod of acceptance, she began to dig into the food with gusto and he found himself relaxed enough to eat as well, as if she had chased the shadows from his mind.

After an easy silence in which they ate most of the food, he asked her curiously, 'You talk often of fate and dreams—as if the future were already known to you. What do *you* think will happen?'

Her shoulders slumped and it surprised him to see her suddenly so downcast. 'I do not know… It is frustrating.'

Bewildered, he shook his head. 'Nobody knows—'

'I do!' she cried and then, with a sheepish smile, she added, 'At least, I usually have a good idea. Not the specifics, of course, I would avoid the hardships if I could. But I can usually sense what is to come…in the same way you might know of an approaching storm by the chill in the wind, or know that a day will be sunny and bright by the colour of the dawn. I *just…know* and I have always found comfort in it. Even the dream of the dragon. Yes, as a child I found the dreams frightening, but then I became a woman and…'

'And?' he pressed, not realising his breath was held until his lungs burned to breathe again.

A blush flushed her cheeks, but her eyes were unwavering when she stared into his. 'I thought the black dragon *might* symbolise my future husband.'

Was that why she had asked if, *he alone,* was the black dragon?

Had she hoped for someone else?

'How so?'

She sighed. 'When I was younger, I decided to cast runes with my sisters. We asked the gods to tell us about the kinds of men we would one day marry. Part of me must have known my dream's significance, because I put in a bone with the black dragon drawn upon it…much like the one on that medallion you wear…' she said, pointing at the bronze pendant that sat on his chest. 'My sisters all drew ordinary runes. Valda picked Laguz—a water rune, Brynhild, the warrior god Tyr. But I had the dragon.' At his frown, she added, 'Then again, Brynhild calls marriage another kind of death—so it could very well mean that one day you will kill me and I was never destined to marry anyone.'

'No,' he said vehemently shaking his head, more horrified by that statement than by anything else she had said. Yes, he'd threatened it, but he'd not meant it and now he felt utterly ashamed for doing so. He stared into her pretty eyes, hoping to convey his sincerity. 'Your family may be my enemy, but please know that you are safe under my protection, even as a hostage. To hurt you would only dishonour me.'

'I thought so, too. I am glad you agree,' she said lightly, plucking some cheese from the platter and popping it in her mouth to chew on it thoughtfully.

What had he agreed with?

That it would dishonour him to harm her, or that her family was his enemy? Both were true.

He watched her mouth work, suddenly transfixed by the delicate pink curves of her lips. When she swallowed, he stared in fascination at the movement of her throat, almost too distracted to hear her next words.

'I have no plans to seduce you, whether you are my future husband or not. Regardless, your virtue is safe with me—is that what you Christians call it, or do you say virginity?'

'I am not a virgin!' he scoffed, his pride bruised by the mockery in her eyes.

'I always find that so strange,' said Helga as she ate more of the food and he drank more than his fair share of the wine.

'What is?' he asked in spite of himself.

'That men desire maidens for wives, but do not offer their wives the same courtesy. It is the same in my culture. Although, if a woman is a man's concubine she is not shunned as Christian women are.'

Rhys thought about his own father and the shame he'd faced at court as an illegitimate son. How his family had been shunned for it for at least another generation if not more. 'It is not fair, on anyone, especially the children. But marriages are based on more than love, especially in noble families. And, although it is a relief that you have no plans to seduce me, I am exhausted and long for sleep.'

'Oh, yes, of course, although if anyone were planning on a seduction tonight it was you. You were the one that insisted we sleep together.'

'There are two beds. I knew that from the last time I passed through here!' Rhys replied, a little offended by the suggestion that he would try to seduce her—he had more integrity than that...or did he? Wasn't he admiring the curves of her mouth only moments before? 'The Abbot was being overly cautious.'

'I see. Can you pass the wine?' Helga asked, and he swapped the platter for the jug, filling his mouth with food to avoid further discussion.

After they finished their meal, they prepared for bed, each deliberately ignoring the other. Helga slept fully clothed, wrapping herself in one blanket before lying down on the straw pallet, while Rhys removed his weapons, outer tunic, and cloak first before settling down.

At first, Rhys worried he would be unable to sleep in his hostage's presence, but found himself drifting off almost immediately.

The sound of the monks singing lauds woke Rhys from his slumber and he struggled to wade through the last fog of sleep as he sat up in the guest house and rubbed his face.

The fire had burned down to ash, but the light from around the door suggested it was a bright dawn.

He glanced at the pallet beside his head and leapt from the bed with a start when he realised it was empty.

Where the devil was she?

He threw on his outer tunic and stumbled out into the brisk morning, hopping on alternate legs as he tried to simultaneously put on his boots and make his way down the path.

She couldn't have gone far, he told himself, but his heart still raced like a wild horse.

His men were positioned outside the gate and his guards were vigilant—she would not escape easily. Still, he couldn't stop the worry that clawed against the inside of his chest with every passing moment that she was missing. He looked towards the walls—they were tall, but not insurmountable.

It was then he realised she had not taken his weapons. They were still where he had left them. She could have easily taken or used them against him, but she hadn't. His gaze swept around him in full circle, his erratic breathing jolting to a halt when he finally saw her.

Calmly sat upon a bench in the cloister gardens, Helga seemed oblivious to his alarm. An array of plant cuttings was spread around her and she looked up as he approached, her cheerful smile fading when she saw the fury in his eyes.

'I did not give you permission to leave!' he barked, more annoyed at his own incompetence than her disregard for his authority.

'You were asleep.'

'Then you should have woken me.'

'Why? I didn't go far, as you can see.' She gestured at the bench and then towards the entrance of the cloister gardens, which sat directly in front of the guest house. He scowled, realising she might have seen him hopping into his boots only moments before. 'I gave you my word I wouldn't try to escape, remember?'

'You cannot just leave without telling me where you are going. You might have been hurt!'

'By whom?' she asked, throwing her hands up and scattering a few leaves in her exasperation. 'Abbot Cuthbert? Your own men? The hens?'

She had a point. In truth, Rhys was amazed by his behaviour as much as she was. When had he ever lost control like this, especially about something so insignificant?

He forced himself to breathe normally and ran a hand through his sleep mused hair.

Her eyes softened. 'The last few days have been gruelling on you. Learning of your sister's disappearance, the rowing and riding—all without rest.' She gathered the plants from the bench and patted the seat next to her.

'Why should you care about such things? I am your captor,' he said, sitting. The tranquillity of the garden eased some of the tension in his shoulders.

She shrugged. 'I can still sympathise with your hardships while bearing my own.'

'Not many would agree with you.'

Helga smiled and began to bundle a bunch of herbs together with a strip of linen.

Pointing at her handiwork, he said, 'I would hide those and quickly—the Abbot may not appreciate you pulling up plants from his gardens.'

She shrugged. 'He gave me permission to take as much as I wished. I saw him walking here just before his morning prayers and spoke to him about the herbs. This is a place of healing—did you know that? The Abbot kindly gave me this sack and the lengths of linen, too.' She tapped the small linen bag with her foot.

'Why do you want them?' he asked curiously. 'You may be staying at my fortress for many weeks. What use could you have for them? I have an herb garden there… Or are you thinking to poison me?' The last was said in jest, but her eyes snapped to his with a look of hurt that made him regret his poor attempt at humour.

'None of these are poisonous. You can ask the Abbot if you do not believe me… I mean…' She paused, biting her lip in consternation. '*Some* might make you sick if ingested in too large a quantity, but many healing plants are like that. I would *never* seek to cause unnecessary harm with my infusions.'

'I believe you,' he said quietly, understanding now how seriously she took her vocation.

'Good. But if you must know, I enjoy collecting and learning about different plants. As it is autumn, many of these have seeds that I may be able to plant in my own garden one day.'

'You have a garden in Jorvik? I thought you lived in a hut,' he asked suspiciously.

She laughed, as if he'd made a great jest. Oddly, the sound was as refreshing as the gentle breeze that ruffled his hair. 'It's more of a patch, really. But Brynhild and my mother have plans to own a farm one day, and I will have a much bigger garden then. I will grow vegetables, fruits and herbs. I hope it will be near a settlement so I can offer my cures and infusions to the community.'

'You would give them as charity?'

'No, Brynhild would never allow that—she says I am too soft hearted as it is—but I would accept a fair trade for my skills. In Jorvik the tanners always gave us good prices for our pelts. Others would offer goods or services and I would give them cures or fortunes in return. Sometimes people were too sick or poor to pay and I would accept an offering to the gods instead.'

'What kind of offerings?' Rhys asked, shifting uncomfortably at the thought.

'Carvings or objects mostly.'

He eased back against the bench with a sigh of relief and she laughed.

'You thought I meant blood sacrifices?'

Crossing his arms over his chest, he replied, 'I have heard Vikings regularly make such sacrifices...murder even...'

'Kings and Jarls have been known to make human sacrifices. But not ordinary folk. Even if an animal is sacrificed the meat is always eaten; we do not waste food or life. We also do not drink the blood or eat the flesh of our god like you do.'

'Do you mean the sacrament?' He laughed. 'Mass is a symbolic gesture. Nothing like a Viking sacrifice.'

He must have poked the bear within her, because she suddenly snapped, '*Our* sacrifices are symbolic, too! A gift, in the hopes of receiving favour from the gods. *And...*' she said pointedly, spitting out her fury with hissed words, 'you really should stop calling us *Vikings*. I am Norse!'

'They are the same thing, are they not?' he asked mildly, enjoying sparring with her.

'Are the Cymry the same as Saxon? Is an abbot the same as a farmer? Some of us call ourselves Danes, others Svear or Rus—it changes depending on our origin—but we are all *Norse*!'

She glared at him and he couldn't help but admire her spirit.

'I apologise,' he said with a bow of his head. 'You are right to correct me.'

She blinked, obviously shocked at his apology, her mouth hung open.

He smiled. 'Why so surprised, Helga? You made a good argument. Do you really think me such a tyrant that I would not admit when I am wrong?'

But even as he said the words he wondered if it were true. Was he sometimes too fixed in his own beliefs that he had become blinded by them? Maybe he should try to be more open minded? Not enough to make him believe in snakes encircling the sea, of course, but enough to make him reconsider his own assumptions about Helga and her people.

Helga shrugged lightly, her anger gone as quickly as

it had arrived. 'Thank you. Our differences can seem strange, but that does not mean we cannot live in peace. I have nothing against Christians, most of their values seem sensible to me. But...'

'Go on,' he prodded when she paused and bit her lower lip.

'I think your Jesus wanted people to live like him. Not worship him.' Pointing over at the abbey's chapel, she added, 'Father Cuthbert said he is here to live a humble life...' She leaned closer to Rhys and whispered conspiratorially, 'But it does not seem very humble to me... they own a lot of land.'

Rhys smiled in spite of himself as he reminded her, 'They heal the sick.'

'Yes, that is true.'

'They are better men than me, that's for certain.'

She frowned at that and tilted her head with a questioning expression. He ignored it and looked away, regretting his loose tongue.

'You know,' she said thoughtfully a moment later and, as if he were pulled by a rope, he turned back to her, 'I do not believe in *all* of the old sagas. They vary from place to place and I could never agree with some of our traditions. But when I am in nature, surrounded by trees and plants...I feel as if I am closer to divinity...to peace.' She blushed. 'You must think me strange.'

His thoughts turned to his own land. 'There is a waterfall within my walls. Surrounded by a coppice and wild flowers. Even in the dead of winter—when the trees are barren and the water is freezing cold—it is still beautiful. When I am there, I can easily forget the time because it is so quiet...that is the only place where I am...relaxed.'

She smiled softly at his description. 'It sounds lovely.'

He cleared his throat, embarrassed. 'It sounds as if

lauds has ended. We should go to the refectory and eat. We have another long day ahead of us.'

'I am ready,' she answered, putting the last of her precious bundles into her sack and rising to her feet.

Chapter Eight

Helga's whole body ached. Mostly with pain from another long day of riding. But now as the sun began to drop, hunger pangs twisted her stomach into rumbling knots.

They'd eaten a large meal with the monks at dawn, but had only stopped occasionally to feed and water the horses. Rhys was pushing himself and his men to the brink of their limits and it only emphasised the great threat that followed closely at their heels.

She wondered about the herbs in her sack from the abbey. Her choices had seemed odd, even to her. But the previous night, she had dreamt of a lady carrying a bunch of pennyroyals in her arms and Helga never ignored visions like that. Pennyroyals could be used for chills or sores, but mainly they were used by women to bring on or regulate their menses.

Why she needed pennyroyals wasn't clear. Her own menses were regular and had only just finished. But, deep in the marrow of her bones, she knew she had to take plenty from the Abbot's gardens. Of course, she took other healing herbs, too, ones that seemed more suited to the aftermath of battle, like willow bark, moss, hemlock and thyme.

The food they'd received from the abbey was being rationed, so she'd not complained about her hunger, and to stay ahead of Ulf's army they could not stop to hunt. But she had seen Ulf's horde of warriors and would not wish to face them out in the open with only Rhys's *teulu* for protection. They might be skilled fighters, but that made little difference if you were outnumbered on the road.

At least they were ahead of Ulf. They'd seen no signs of a large army passing through before them and they'd confirmed it with locals whenever they passed through a settlement.

The hills and valleys they rode through were lush and fertile, with many farms along the way. But Mercia had always been a land of plenty, which was why their rulers defended it so fiercely. Most of this region was still being fought over, with large swathes falling under Mercian law, leaving only a few small Danelaw settlements remaining—such as Ulf's—in the northern borders.

Was that why Ulf sought to take Rhys's land? Because he feared the creeping power of the Mercian Queen? It made sense—hadn't Rhys mentioned the Saxons as a previous threat to his own land?

A chilling drizzle had begun to fall and Rhys draped his cloak more fully around her head and shoulders to keep her dry. The kindly gesture diminished slightly when he murmured into her ear, 'Do you still like the rain, Helga, or has it lost its charm?'

Why did he always needle her and, more importantly, why did she enjoy it?

She had to admit, he no longer seemed quite as bad as she'd first thought. He'd apologised regarding some of his earlier assumptions and had treated her with respect since with the exception of some light teasing—and how could she deny him that when it seemed to lighten his mood? She sensed a deep sadness within him and the healer within her sought to ease his suffering, if only in a small way.

'I never said I *liked* it. Only that I do not mind the rain because it has a purpose. Something your questioning seems to lack. Will we be riding much longer? It will be dark soon…'

'We will make camp at a small lake just beyond this hill.'

Helga breathed a sigh of relief. 'Good, it will be a relief to stand on my own two feet again. How many days will it take to reach Ulf's fort?'

'All being well, we should reach it before nightfall tomorrow.'

A grim resolve settled in the pit of her stomach as she thought about the upcoming conflict. 'Can I bathe in the water?'

He paused a long time before answering, 'Are you sure you would not rather wait until we are back at my fortress? I can arrange for a hot bath to be drawn and fresh clothes to be made for you. Or why not wash with a pail of water like the rest of the men? You can use my tent and will at least be assured some privacy that way.'

Disappointed, she gave a quick nod of agreement, but said nothing more. As they crested the hill the lake shone with the golden hue of the setting sun, receding to a dark indigo at the outer edges.

Helga sighed wistfully at the peaceful landscape spread before her. If she'd been with her sisters and mother, they would have gone swimming. They never missed an opportunity to enjoy a proper bath in nature, especially before a battle, when Freya and her Valkyries might be coming for them.

To be covered in the blood of your enemies was one thing, but to be smelling as bad as a pig was quite another!

However, it seemed she would have to wait a little longer before she enjoyed a bath, or even a quiet moment of peace. She only hoped that if she died, she would at least have had the chance to wash her face first.

Rhys felt bad that he'd denied Helga's simple request. But he did not have the time—or even the strength—to stand guard as she bathed. He could trust any one of his men to watch her, but he knew that he would not allow such a thing...*couldn't.*

It had been three days since he'd captured her. He had no clean clothing for her, hadn't even thought to offer her a wash until now. But then, he'd not cared for himself either, or for the comfort of his men, and for good reason.

Life was more important than comfort. His recent actions had ensured that much at least. God willing, they would reach Ulf's fortress well before him and proceed with the next part of his plan.

Helga didn't know it yet, but she would be glad not to have bathed beforehand. It would be a wasted exercise. After all, there was miles of crawling through mud ahead of them.

In the meadow beside the lake the men began to dismount and prepare the camp. Rhys was pleasantly surprised with how well Madoc managed them.

Helga dropped down from his horse and he noticed her wince. She wasn't used to long journeys on horseback, it seemed, and her body seemed stiff and hunched. Despite his cloak, the drizzle had seeped through and saturated her hair. Her lips were also a little blue from the cold and she looked utterly wretched in her filthy dress.

Dismounting quickly, he took off his cloak and wrapped it around her.

By the tilt of her jaw, he could tell she was too proud to thank him or complain about poor treatment. As it was, she accepted his cloak without comment and untied her sack of herbs from the saddle—her only possession. 'What would you like me to do?'

That startled him a little. 'Nothing. Wait here and I will let you know when the tent and your water is ready.' He turned to walk away, but she stopped him with a hand to his arm.

'I would rather be useful than be a burden.'

'Why would you think you are a burden? You wouldn't even be here if wasn't for me.'

She shrugged, a flush high on her cheeks, and he wondered if her family treated her as a burden. He certainly hoped not. Helga was obviously a skilled and capable woman.

'If you insist, come with me.' They walked towards Madoc, who was handing out supplies to the men in charge of cooking.

'Madoc, give Helga a task to occupy her until our tent is ready.'

'She can prepare vegetables...' Madoc said, a little startled by the request. He handed her a bag of turnips, a board and a knife. She lowered herself elegantly to the ground, his cloak wrapped tightly around her as she began to work. Rhys made a mental note to ensure the small knife was returned after she'd used it, then he tried his best to ignore the guilt such a lack of trust gave him.

Hadn't he survived this long by never trusting others? Why should he take a risk now?

'Madoc, we have much to discuss.'

Moving away from her so that he could think more

clearly, he spent the next hour in careful discussion with his second about their battle plans.

When he returned, the sun had long since set and his men were at campfires, eating fish stew. Helga was sat at exactly the same place he'd left her, an empty bowl in her lap, her body swaying slightly from exhaustion. 'Come, Helga,' he said, offering her his hand.

She took it and he helped her up on to her feet. Even in the firelight he could tell she was exhausted. To be fair, the last three days had taken a toll on him as well, although he'd done plenty of travelling beforehand to get used to the initial soreness.

He glanced at the ground, the empty board with the bowl on top of it. Perversely he decided not to mention the missing knife, as he led her to the centre of the camp. For some reason he didn't believe she'd use it against him, which sounded like madness even inside his own head.

'You will sleep in my tent tonight. It offers some shelter from the rain, but little else, I'm afraid.' The tent was small, but big enough for two to sit upright within and two piles of bedding were laid out on the floor covering, with the supplies he'd requested in the middle.

Helga knelt in front of them. There was a simple oil lamp with two wicks, creating just enough light to see by. A comb, wash cloth, chunk of soap and large bowl of steaming water waited for her. All gathered from his own supplies. He'd also requested some hot stones to be put beneath her blankets to help warm them, but she would discover them later—maybe when she was hiding her knife, he thought dryly.

'Take your time. I will be right outside. Call for me when you are done.'

He left without waiting for her response, closing the

flap and stepping to the side. Unfortunately, he very quickly realised that he could clearly see her silhouette against the waxed cloth.

She unwrapped the cloak, revealing the soft curves of her body, and then began to untie the apron dress at her chest. She dipped the cloth in the water and began to stroke it along her face and neck, her spine arching like a bow. He began to imagine how she would look—eyes closed, mouth slightly parted—and his body responded with a fierce intensity that stole his breath.

Would she make that same moan of pleasure that she'd made when drinking the wine? Hot desire shot through him, making his back stiffen and his fists clench.

What would she do if he went in there? Gripped her face in his hands and kissed that open mouth of hers?

Forcing himself to regain some of his threadbare control, he spun on his heel to face the rest of the camp. Some of his men's eyes flew guiltily away when he did so. Throwing a dark scowl at them, Rhys remained where he was, folding his arms over his chest and deliberately blocking her from view—including his own.

What was wrong with him?

Ever since he'd first set eyes upon her, he'd been obsessed. Keeping her close. Riding and sleeping next to her, despite the obvious effect such closeness had on him.

He should create distance between them, but instead he tortured himself like a moth to a flame. Allowing her to fill his every thought until he was drunk on her and unable to focus on the important challenges ahead.

No, he would overcome this! He must!

His attraction to her was only a fleeting passion, brought on by a pretty face, his own long-term abstinence and the stress of the battles to come. Once he was home, things would be easier.

'You can come in now.' Helga's breathy voice sounded like a lover calling him back to bed and he inhaled sharply to cast the lustful thoughts from his mind.

He must remember his sister, how her life depended on keeping Helga hostage. Currently, he had a right to be cautious and to keep his captive close. But when they were safely behind his walls, he would have no such concerns and he could forget his inappropriate feelings towards her.

When he entered the tent, Helga was laid on her back, wrapped in her bedding and ready for sleep.

'The hot stones are lovely, thank you. I have put one in your bedding and used the other for my feet.' She squirmed further down into the blankets with a pleasurable sigh.

She looked radiant with her freshly washed face; her combed hair spread around her like a fleece of gold.

'I am fine without stones,' he grumbled sourly. It was almost painful to look at her, knowing that she could never be his.

'But it is more pleasant with,' she argued with a teasing smile, followed by a wide yawn.

He took off his mail and helm. He'd taken to wearing his full armour since leaving the abbey, in case they were attacked on the road by Ulf. If the worst happened, Helga would either have to run to her uncle or hope he could protect her in the chaos.

It was a grim thought.

Next, he took off both of his tunics, his belt and sword. Soaping up the cloth, he began to wash the worst of the sweat and dirt from his face, arms and chest. The water was now cold, but it was still welcome and refreshing after so much time on the road and he was grateful Helga had asked for it. Sometimes he forgot to look after himself; Alswn and Efa always used to chide him for it.

Glancing over at Helga, he expected her to turn away from him, but was disturbed to notice her watching him intently, her head just peeking out over the folds of her blanket. Her pupils were large in the dim light, ringed by only a slim band of sky-blue. Her mouth slightly parted and full of temptation.

His heart thundered in his chest and his body immediately warmed and hardened with lust. In irritation he tossed aside the wash cloth.

Helga's eyes darted to the roof of the tent and a crimson flush flooded her cheeks.

Her embarrassment gave him some comfort, although not enough to cool the frustration building within him. Focusing on settling down for the night, he moved the warming stone down to his feet as she had done. He was about to extinguish the lamp when he remembered something.

'I wonder…will I have a pleasant sleep tonight…while you still carry that knife?'

There was a soft gasp and then silence. He turned his face to look at her, oddly calm despite the tension rolling back and forth between them.

'I didn't take it to use against you,' she said, staring up at the canopy overhead.

'Why did you take it? Neither myself nor any of my men will harm you.' They might look, as he was also guilty of doing, but they would never do more than that. 'You are my guest…at least, until your family releases you.'

She chuckled at the word 'guest', but nodded, meeting his eyes for the first time. 'I know. But we are to attack Ulf's fort tomorrow evening, yes?'

Realisation hit him hard. She had taken the knife to protect herself during the battle. It made sense, but stung his pride a little. 'I will protect you with my life. You may not even see any fighting…' Initially he'd planned on her not seeing any, but something she'd said about her being useful in trickery had plagued his thoughts ever since she'd said it and she'd already proven herself skilled in defending herself.

He might need her help…

With an easiness that surprised him, she said, 'I have been on the edge of battle before, waiting to learn who is the victor. My role was to guard the families, give them time to run, but I have always prepared for the worst, just in case. If I am to die, I would rather be at my best and have a weapon with me…but if you sleep better without my possessing one…' She sighed and sat up a little, dragging the sack of herbs to her from the corner of the tent.

Strangely, it comforted him to know that she didn't have it beneath the blankets. Not because he felt threatened by it, but it showed her trust in his word.

Withdrawing the knife, she placed it hilt first on the ground between them. 'Then take it. You will need your rest if you are to win.'

'Is that why you wished to bathe? To be at your *best*?' he asked, stunned by the revelation. She was braver than most men to talk of death so calmly.

She laughed. 'It is vanity, but, yes, I wanted to look my best, just in case, and I could not stomach my grubby appearance a moment longer. Saxons may not care to bathe regularly, but we Norse do!'

He looked at her glowing beauty and couldn't help but admire her. Feeling as if he should defend his own lack of bathing, he replied, 'Usually, we Cymry are the same, but we have a long journey ahead before we reach the safety of home.'

'And one battle,' she reminded him.

'I am hoping it will be over quickly.'

She tilted her head, her curiosity obviously piqued. 'How so? Do you have a plan?'

'You will see,' he replied dryly, taking an odd pleasure in keeping her guessing. 'Now, I must sleep because, as you say, I will need my rest if I am to be victorious.' He leaned forward to extinguish the lamp, holding her gaze for a moment with a teasing smile before he snuffed it out.

Deliberately, he left the knife where it lay.

If it gave her comfort, he would not take it from her.

Chapter Nine

When Helga woke the following morning, she had been surprised to discover the knife had not moved from where she'd left it. She was alone in the tent, a soft light shining through the canvas suggesting dawn hadn't fully broken. But she could already hear the clatter of the camp being dismantled around her and shuffled over to the tent flaps, still wrapped in her blanket, to take a peek outside.

Rhys stood a few feet away talking with Madoc, using hushed tones and serious expressions, the kind her family often wore before battle.

Rhys rarely smiled, she realised, not even with his friends, which Madoc and the rest of his men appeared to be by the way they spoke so freely with their leader.

It was strange, mused Helga, for a man so privileged to be always so…sad. It was only one of her *feelings*, part of her strange intuition, but she knew in her heart that Rhys was unbearably unhappy and, more oddly, she wished she could help. Which felt like a giant leap from her previous views of the man.

As if he could hear her thoughts, he chose that moment to look over at her and she nearly jumped out of her skin as his eyes immediately locked with hers.

He walked towards her with long, purposeful strides. 'Eat this, but hurry, we leave soon.' It was only then she realised he was holding out a bowl of pottage. He must have seen the disgust on her face because he pushed it towards her again, forcing her to take it from him.

'It will be your only hot meal today. I suggest you eat it. *All of it*,' he warned.

'Fine,' she grumbled, 'but your men are poor cooks. I wish they had let me handle the stew last night—it was full of bones.'

'But you are my *guest*,' he said, his lips curving ever so slightly. It made her glad to see it—he deserved a little respite from his troubles and she smiled brightly up at him.

Rhys blinked as if startled by her pleased expression and then said coldly, 'Leave your tent as soon as you can, we need to dismantle it.'

'Of course…*my lord*,' she replied with mock severity and ducked back inside.

The full day of riding that followed was far less amusing for Helga. They passed around bread and cheese as they rode, but no one mentioned stopping once, unless it was to water their mounts. The pace was relentless.

The terrain had quickly become more dramatic over the course of the day. Gone were the soft emerald hills, gentle rolling fields and forests. The landscape was now bold and unforgiving. Mountains rose from the rich earth, their rusty peaks surrounded by dark rainclouds.

Late afternoon Madoc came cantering towards them and she felt Rhys's hold on her waist tighten. She sat up in her seat, sensing a change in the mood. By the tight expression on the men's faces and the way they scanned the horizon for enemies, she knew they were close to Ulf's fortress.

Madoc and Rhys spoke together in Welsh. Anticipation hung thick in the air and her heart began to pound like a war drum.

Then Rhys gave a long speech to his men and, even though Helga could not understand his words, she knew by the gruff nods of agreement rippling through his warriors that the time had come for them to fight. She looked out at the horizon, but saw only a large sprawling peak covered with trees ahead. Around its base the road forked, the paths leading in opposite directions around its base.

As they approached the crossroad, the column of warriors split in two, the bulk moving one way, while a small group including her and Rhys went another.

Would he not fight with his men?

That seemed a cowardly decision and did not sit well with the man she'd come to know.

'Why are you separating us from the rest of your warriors?' asked Helga, confused as she watched the majority of Rhys's force move west while they and a handful of warriors headed north.

'We are going to Ulf's fortress.'

'Is that wise? With so few men?' He didn't respond. 'Are you not planning to take it by force then? Will you be using me in some other way? To gain entrance with trickery, perhaps?'

'No,' he answered, although there was a flicker of doubt in his eyes.

'Then why bring me with you?'

'I may have use for you, and if not, then I will keep my hostage close in case things go badly.'

'I will need to know more than that! And it would

probably be wise to explain to me now, rather than in the thick of…whatever action it is you plan to take.'

He sighed grimly. 'There is an old gold mine close to Ulf's fort. One he is most likely unaware of, as it has been empty for some time. We have been using that mine to dig a tunnel to his fortress. I plan on entering with a small force, releasing the hostages and then setting fire to the fortress. As they struggle to cope with the fires, the bulk of my army will attack the gate.'

'Is that why you had hoped for more delays to your sister's marriage with Halfdan? Because you were hoping to rescue your aunt through this tunnel?'

Rhys nodded. 'We encountered many problems during the dig and, as we didn't want to draw attention to ourselves, we had to work slowly. It could have failed at any time. The risk of cave-in was great and if that happened—all would be lost. Honestly, it was a desperate plan that I am surprised has even borne fruit.'

Helga understood more clearly what he meant when they arrived at the mine. It was concealed within dense woodland and down a steep ravine. They had to climb off their horses and clamber down on foot to reach it.

The entrance was little more than a hole and only one man could pass through at a time. The clearing outside the cave mouth was almost hidden from above by the overhanging moss-covered rock. She would have thought it nothing more than an animal den and would have avoided it.

Even though Rhys had reassured her no beasts were inside, her body still recoiled as she entered the darkness and the heavy smell of damp earth clawed at her throat. Hurrying closer towards Rhys in front gave her a small sense of comfort. Despite having to walk slightly hunched due to the height of the tunnel, he walked with surprising ease through the cave, holding his torch out to banish the endless darkness ahead of them.

Rhys said something in his native tongue and she saw the shadows ahead shift, as if they were alive. Her soul nearly leapt from her skin when a voice from the darkness answered and two eyes blinked in the firelight.

She swallowed a scream as the wall to the side of her shifted, revealing another tunnel and man within. Like the other, this man's face and overgrown beard were so dirty he almost blended into the walls.

After a short conversation in Welsh, they were ushered down a warren of cramped passages to a larger room that seemed to serve as the diggers' home. Lit by only a couple of torches, she could just make out the sleeping benches pressed against the cave walls and the array of supplies scattered around. It was a grim existence, but the men gathered in the small space grinned as they spoke to Rhys, pride and triumph shining from their filthy faces.

They must have been down here from the beginning, after the hostages were taken and the negotiations with Ulf began months ago.

Helga whispered to Rhys, 'They are good men to follow your orders in such hard conditions.'

'They volunteered. They are from a village not far from here. Many of the people taken hostage were their kin: daughters, nieces and nephews.' Rhys's voice was filled with pride.

Helga understood now and nodded. 'I would have done the same.'

Sapphire eyes caught hers in their firelight. 'I imagine you would.'

They were taken down another passage, this one far narrower than the last, so that they all had to walk hunched over and in single file. Rhys took the lead in front of her, a warrior at her back. Nervously she reached forward and lightly gripped Rhys's cloak. He wouldn't feel her touch, but it gave her comfort to have him close. She hated darkness at the best of times and this was blacker than night.

They walked for what felt like miles and it probably was, passing stone or wooden chambers filled with dirt and little wheelbarrows. That's how they had dug out so much without alerting any outsiders to their presence, she realised, by filling old chambers with the dug-out soil. It was a clever plan, even if it was full of risk. She glanced up at the roof of the tunnel, shored up with stone and wood taken from the surrounding forest. She swallowed hard and prayed to Odin, Frey and Freya to help keep them safe.

The tunnel became smaller and Rhys had to stoop even lower to follow the miner. They were on hands and knees now, as they crawled up and on to a narrow ledge.

They extinguished the only remaining torch and Helga instinctively gripped Rhys's cloak tighter. She hadn't realised how close she was to him because she felt her hand brush against something warm and solid. Then he leaned back, his fingers curving gently around her wrist.

'Are you well?' he whispered and she realised he'd leaned closer.

'Yes,' she whispered.

His hand smoothed down the back of hers in a caress that had her heart fluttering wildly. She was sure he had only meant it to be reassuring, but it sent a bolt of lightning up her arm.

Ever since she'd seen him washing the previous night, she'd been all too aware of her growing attraction to him: the strength of his body, the protective way he wrapped her in his cloak when they rode together, the care he took in making sure she was well fed and rested.

He might believe himself ruthless, but his actions betrayed him. If things were different, might there have been a future for them? Had the runes told the truth?

Maybe, it was the darkness heightening her senses, but a shiver of longing passed through her at the thought.

Was she mad to think such a thing?

Even if he did desire her, he was obviously fighting his attraction. He did not want her really; she was his enemy—at least in his mind.

Rhys let go of her hand and it dropped limply at her side. She shook her head to clear it. The darkness, the fear and tension of what was about to happen had done strange things to her mind and she refocused her attention on staying sharp for the danger ahead.

Ahead a man shuffled and grunted, as if he were struggling to pull something down. The darkness shifted slightly, from pitch black to a dark grey, and Helga blinked as she saw the miner ahead climb up and out of the tunnel, followed quickly by Rhys, who immediately stuck his hand back through the opening for her to help lift her up.

Cool night air tickled her face, a welcome caress against her clammy skin. She sucked it in, grateful to see the stars above their heads once more and to leave the stifling closeness of the tunnel behind. She understood now why rabbits risked leaving the safety of their burrows. Too long in the darkness twisted your senses and made you imagine outrageous things.

She clambered out, helped by the firm pull of Rhys's arm. The remaining warriors followed and she took a moment to look around her. They stood between two wooden buildings, an array of baskets and discarded rubbish surrounding them and sheltering them from view. It was quiet, the sounds from the mead Hall a gentle hum in the distance suggesting they were too far away to be noticed.

How had they managed to dig their tunnel up into such a fortunate place? It made her dizzy to even think about how someone might calculate the distance in the darkness and even know the best place to rise up.

She gave the miner an appreciative nod and he grinned back at her, his white teeth shining like pearls in the moonlight. Rhys clapped him silently on the shoulder, the only indication of his own appreciation. As they were in the den of their enemy, any sounds could lead to ruin.

Rhys circled his finger in the air and with a nod the man hurried around the back of the building.

All the warriors were out of the tunnel now and the wooden board used to shield the entrance was kept open. They wouldn't be staying long then, Helga mused.

Rhys moved to the front of the group and led them slowly to the front of the building. They stayed close to the shadows, placing their feet carefully and thoughtfully.

There was a pause and a blade glinted in Rhys's hand, then in a rush of shadows he was gone and Helga swallowed the ball in her throat, anxious for his return. There was a strangled gargle of sound and then a thud, followed quickly by another. As she and the other men turned the corner to the front of the building, she saw the head miner and Rhys dragging the bodies of two guards inside.

A metal brazier sat at the entrance to warm the guards, but she could see no fire from within. Not even a glimmer of light came from the open doorway, nothing to suggest anyone was inside. But then she heard a hushed murmur, like the soft breath of wind through the branches of a willow. The waning moon peeked from around its curtain of clouds and she saw pale and haunted faces looking back at her from shackles and ropes, the poor wretches squinting against the weak light, as if it hurt their eyes. Her stomach flipped when she realised some of them were young children and any pity she might have felt for the guards quickly flew from her heart.

Rhys spoke with the hostages and then gave quick instructions she couldn't understand.

The miners began to work on freeing the hostages from their bonds, while two warriors donned the cloaks of the Norse guards and took up positions outside the doors so that, at a distance, no one would realise what had happened.

Taking her hand in his, Rhys guided her away from the building's entrance and leaned down to whisper in her ear. 'The hostages have told us that my aunt is being kept in a room at the end of the mead Hall. There is a window in one of the storerooms towards the back of the feasting tables and we will enter from there. But...' He paused, as if his next words pained him. 'If you enter first, you can ensure the path is clear for us. They will not question a woman in their stores, especially a woman dressed in Norse clothing. However, if you do not wish—'

'I will help you,' Helga whispered, squeezing his hand in reassurance. 'These are not good men and they deserve to be punished.'

Rhys nodded, his eyes almost black in the darkness. 'No, they are not.'

'And...I feel safer with you,' she added, unsure of why she had confessed it.

He sucked in a deep breath, then released it in a slow exhale, his eyes trailing for a moment down her jaw and neck in a caress that caused a shiver of excitement to run down her spine.

She *was* safer with him, wasn't she?

His fingers tightened around her hand. After a glance up at the palisade he was pulling her along with him towards the golden light of the mead Hall, using the shadows of the buildings to hide their progress. Only one other man came with them to guard their backs.

Outside a barn, Rhys suddenly pulled her down to hide behind a pile of barrels. Two warriors passed within view of them from the fortress palisade and Helga held her breath as the men continued on their patrol without even glancing in their direction, their heads turned towards the land beyond the wall, oblivious to what was happening within their own home.

As they approached the large Hall, she could hear the raucous noise of the evening meal from within—the low hum of men's voices, the occasional crack of laughter or thud of fists as men drank, wrestled and feasted.

Maybe they had heard of Ulf's approaching army and sought to enjoy themselves before the inevitable battles began. Either that, or they were an unruly lot, prone to enjoying themselves at their absent Jarl's expense no matter the occasion.

Both seemed possible.

They moved along the outside of the feasting Hall carefully, remaining hunched low as they passed by any open windows. Towards the back of the building they stopped. Rhys easing up the shutter of a window just enough to peep inside. Satisfied with what he had seen, he nodded to the warrior who'd come with them. The man kept the shutter open while Rhys took hold of Helga's waist and lifted her up like an offering.

She grabbed the frame and hauled herself up until she was sitting on the ledge, and able to swing her legs over, Rhys's fingers only moving away once her feet had touched the timber floor of the storage room. There were several barrels, clay pots, and sacks filling the room. On a nearby work bench sat an array of bread and fruit. The organisation was chaotic and with a heavy heart she realised it had been stolen from nearby villages and settlements.

Rhys and his warrior followed her, one after the other.

'My aunt is being held in one of the rooms towards the back,' Rhys reminded her in an urgent whisper. 'See what it is like outside—but avoid the feasting Hall. If any rooms are guarded or locked, then do not linger. Come straight back and we will make a plan.' Rhys stared at her hard and she felt herself drowning in the blue of his eyes. So sharp and intense, as if he were looking into her soul and measuring the value of it. 'Do not betray me.'

She wet her lips, burning beneath his gaze, and then smiled slowly, enjoying the frown that darkened his face.

'Of course not!' she whispered and grabbed a jug from the counter, as well as a loaf of bread as she slipped out of the storeroom.

The heat and smell from over a hundred unwashed men hit her nose, and she wrinkled it in dismay. Turning immediately from the open entrance of the feasting Hall, and the drunken carnage beyond, she made her way to the back of the building. No one was around, the passageway empty and silent.

The corridor was long and narrow, some rooms were timber like the storeroom they'd entered through, others divided by woven screens. Opening doors and little gates as she passed, she saw that they were all storerooms, or chambers for the fortress's leaders—thankfully currently empty, as their occupants were too busy enjoying themselves.

A timbered wall was at the far end, and in its centre was a large wooden door. Interestingly, there were two crude hooks hammered into either side of the doorway and a large plank was propped up on one side. She wondered if it was normally used to bar the door. If so, it could be where they kept Rhys's aunt.

But why was the door no longer barred? Had someone gone in to speak with her, or let her out to eat in the feasting hall?

She needed to know the answer because if it were the latter, the hopes of rescuing her were slim.

If she were wise, she would hurry back to the storeroom and leave Rhys to discover the truth for himself. However, she seemed to lack wisdom recently and decided to follow her instincts instead.

Tentatively Helga walked to the door and pressed her cheek against the wood. She could hear the voice of a man beyond, low and commanding.

'Jarl Ulf will arrive soon. Let us hope you learn to be obedient for him!' The voice grew louder, as if he were approaching the door.

Gasping, Helga sprang away in a panic and ran back down the corridor. She heard the door creak behind her and she dived into the nearest room—it was one of the private chambers. Unfortunately, her leg caught on a discarded cup and it clattered and rolled across the floor.

'Who goes there?' barked a deep voice and Helga silently cursed.

Chapter Ten

There was no escaping it.

The man must have heard her. But maybe he hadn't seen her as she ran into the chamber?

Perhaps he would think he had imagined it and go back to the feast...

There was silence for a while, so long that she almost allowed a sigh of relief. But then the door opened and a blond man with a meaty face stared down at her. He filled the doorway, blocking the light from the passageway lamps.

'Has Kalf been keeping you from us, little one?' he sneered and she gripped the jug and bread tighter.

'He told me to wait for him,' she said lightly, hoping that Kalf was bigger and more frightening than this man. It might be the only thing that saved her. 'He doesn't like me to spend too long in the Hall.'

The man laughed and it was like hearing a bear laugh, deep and throaty. He took another step into the room. 'Really, he doesn't wish to share with his good friend Sven?'

'I should probably go see where he is.' She went to

walk around him, but his hand snapped out to grab her shoulder.

'I have not seen you before,' Sven said thoughtfully, his fingers pinching deeply despite the lightness of his tone.

'Oh?'

'No, and I make it my place to know all who live behind my walls.'

So, she'd managed to run into the commander of the fort. The Norns that had woven her fate must truly be laughing at her. She swallowed hard and gave a weak smile. 'I am not very memorable.'

His hand released, but only to smooth down her arm. Next it slipped like an eel to the curve of her waist.

'I disagree,' he said and the jug trembled in her hands.

'Why do you carry an empty jug?' Sven asked, flicking the jug with one of his dirty fingers.

She blinked and then took the opportunity to take a step away. 'I forgot to fill it! Kalf will be so annoyed with me. I must go to the storeroom…but I'll be right back.' Trying not to show her alarm, she tried to move past him for the second time. She almost made it to the door before a hand lashed out to grab a fistful of her hair.

She yelped as Sven dragged her back, her scalp screaming in pain. Instinctively, she dropped what she was holding and reached up to grab his wrist. It lessened the pressure on her head at least, even if she couldn't force him to let her go.

'My lord, please!' she whimpered and her fear was only half-pretence. She could fight him, but what if the sound of it drew men from the Hall? She had her knife, but she would have to catch him by surprise to use it properly.

He was moving her towards the bed, directing her

with the painful grip he had on her hair. Her free hand went to her waist, but found only an empty leather sheath.

'Looking for this?' he snarled and cold steel pressed against her neck.

Grappling for anything that might help her, she gasped, 'Please, I would not want my man to find us together. He would be very angry with *both* of us!' It was a weak threat, especially as she had no idea about the importance of Kalf, only that he was worthy of a private chamber.

In response Sven thrust her forward. 'Do you think I give a shit what Kalf thinks?'

She landed on the bed face down. But at least the knife was no longer at her throat. She tried to twist around, but his heavy hand pressed her back down, while his other fumbled with her skirts.

Helga's thoughts flew around her mind like a trapped bird before settling on the only option left to her. She went limp and whimpered pitifully. Feigning defeat and waiting for the moment when he would have to use his hands to untie his own clothes.

That's when she would strike. Kick back with her legs and hit his stomach, or hopefully his crotch, and then run.

The hand against her back pulled away and, as she twisted, she raised up her legs to strike. But as she did so, the shadows behind Sven shifted and then the air sang with steel. A blade flashed in the darkness and Helga rolled to the side, falling off the bed and on to the floor on her hands and knees.

Sven's attention was so focused on his prey, on Helga, that she doubted he'd even realised Rhys had entered the room. There was a loud wet crack followed by two thuds, as first his head hit the floor, and then his body hit the bed.

Instinctively Helga closed her eyes and scrambled across the floor to avoid the hot spray. Tripping over her skirts, she fell forward and then rolled on to her back, her heart pounding wildly.

Rhys sheathed his sword and offered her his hand, his breathing shallow and slightly laboured. 'You are safe now.'

She was grateful it was dark. She did not wish to see the fate of the commander too closely. As it was his big shape was slumped forward over the bed, his trousers down in a most undignified position. His head probably lay somewhere in the darkness, sightlessly watching.

Good. He deserved to stand before the gods looking ridiculous.

'Thank you for coming for me,' she whispered, then placed her hand in his. It touched her that he would worry for her, come to protect her even. He lifted her up with surprising gentleness, reaching around with his other hand to hold her at the small of her back to steady her.

'I should not have let you go,' he said, his voice husky and full of regret.

'It was fortunate that you did. He would have raised the alarm if he had seen you.' Avoiding the mess on the floor, Helga took a deep breath to steady her nerves and focus on the next task at hand. 'Your aunt is in the room at the end of the corridor. I think she's alone. There is only a bar on the outside of the door, so it should be easy to rescue her. All the men are in the Hall, no one is with her.'

'Excellent. Their arrogance will be their downfall,' Rhys murmured as he led her to the door and out into the passageway. The merry sounds of feasting continued to fill the building, as if nothing had happened, and the door at the end was now barred on the outside, confirming Helga's suspicions.

They moved swiftly to it and, after another quick glance around them, they opened the barred door and stepped inside.

The room was well lit by a large oil lamp on a raised stone plinth in the centre of the room. The furniture included a big wooden bed box and a table with a bench to eat at. It was a room fit for a great jarl, with sumptuous furs, blankets and tapestries. But it had a strange mix of decoration that seemed thoughtless. More stolen goods, she presumed.

On the bed sat a woman with masses of dark curly hair. She wore a wine-red gown that must have been beautiful once, but now hung torn and loose around her shoulders, with crude repairs.

The woman raised her head as they entered. Brown eyes locked on to Rhys, then widened with recognition. The lady was much younger than Helga would have imagined his aunt. No older than five and thirty winters and still very much in the prime of her life.

The relief on Rhys's face when he saw his aunt made Helga's heart swell in her chest. For a moment the ruthless, hard edges of the man were gone, and in their place was the face of a boy who had been terrified to lose another member of his family.

Sweeping forward with long strides, Rhys rushed towards his aunt, who flew into his arms and wept, her knuckles white against the dark cloth of his cloak as she clung to him. His head bowed over hers as he gathered her tightly to him.

Helga smiled. As she'd suspected, he was not as callous and unfeeling as he claimed.

'Forgive me, Rhys,' his aunt gasped, her voice broken and muffled against his chest.

'Why would I *ever* need to forgive you, Efa?'

'I…I…should not have gone to the villages. You warned me and I refused to listen!'

'I am the one to blame, not you.'

'Has the King finally come to help us—is that why you are here?' she asked swiping away her tears.

Rhys shook his head and Efa sighed with disappointment. 'When will he realise you are not his enemy!'

'It does not matter. Did they harm you?' he asked.

Efa shook her head vehemently. 'No, I was too valuable a hostage.' Her answer seemed too quick to Helga, too dismissive.

The bed was rumpled, some of the blankets torn, and she thought she saw a piece of rope attached to one of the legs. After her own attack by the commander called Sven, she knew all too well the kind of man that had ruled in Ulf's place.

Efa caught her eye and the woman glared at her sharply in warning. Helga dropped her gaze. It was not her place to say anything and Rhys seemed reassured by his aunt's words.

Noticing the exchange but not fully understanding it, Rhys said, 'This is Helga, my own hostage. She has proven quite useful, so far.'

Helga's stomach dropped as the cool dismissal stung her pride and her heart. Such a statement made her feel foolish for imaging more in his tender touches and shows of concern. She was nothing more than a tool to him and his words had proven it.

'Now, let us leave and quickly.' Rhys ushered them towards the door, but before he left, he pulled a blanket from the bed and dipped it into the oil lamp. The wool soaked up the flaming liquid and he tossed it on the bed. In the blink of an eye, thick smoke billowed up to the rafters, followed by a ravenous fire.

Not finished with his handiwork, Rhys pushed the oil lamp over the side of the plinth and on to the timber floor. Burning liquid flowed across the room, the flames rushing to match the oil's pace, greedily consuming everything in its path.

Efa smiled at the sight and Helga knew for certainty that in this room, the lady had suffered far worse things than she would ever be willing to admit.

No one saw them as they returned to the store. Rhys had hoped the fire would spread before the Norse men realised what was happening and as he helped Efa and Helga down from the window he saw the back of the building was already smoking heavily through the gaps in the timber roof.

'There are more hostages!' gasped Efa, pointing towards the building that had held the villagers.

'We have them,' Rhys reassured her. 'But we must move quickly.'

Rhys's warrior dropped down from the window last and then all four of them hurried through the shadows and back towards the tunnel.

The head miner met them as they approached, carrying two unlit torches.

'Are they all out?' asked Rhys.

The man nodded, 'Yes, my lord.'

'Good. Let us burn this nest of vipers to the ground.'

The head miner grinned and lit the torches in the brazier outside the prison. Handing one to Rhys, he ran into the shadows, and like a river of gold, the barns and workshops of the fort began to ignite in his wake.

'Get them out of here!' Rhys ordered one of his warriors, and the women were hurried to the tunnel's entrance as chaos erupted within the fort.

Rhys used his own torch to light the thatch of the prison, the flames devouring the dry roof hungrily. Finally, he tossed it into the roof of the adjacent building.

'Fire!' shouted a Norse man from the palisade. It was followed quickly by more shouts and the banging of swords on shields. Men from the battlements began to rush towards the Hall, its back now clearly aflame.

A cold satisfaction washed through Rhys. He'd sent men to bar the door of the Hall and the Norse men inside were now locked in a dangerous cage. He doubted it would take them much effort to escape, what with their fellow warriors already rushing to help, but it would waste precious moments. Time his men outside needed to break through the gate.

Crouching low in the darkness, he patiently watched his carefully laid plans unfold with beautiful precision. He would guard the tunnel until he was certain enough time had passed to ensure the women's safe return.

Men ran desperately to and from buildings, trying aimlessly to put out the flames and grab their weapons.

A war horn sounded, a low and forlorn lament, too late to be of any use as several more buildings began to light up with flames, including the palisade towers, this time from flaming arrows that rained down from beyond the wall. His army had seen the signal and had attacked according to his command. Already there was the bang of a battering ram against the gate.

Rhys's men gathered around him with unsheathed swords to await his next order.

'Let us welcome our friends into the fight! To the gate and show no mercy!'

Rhys charged forward with his sword held high, a battle cry booming from his throat. There was no doubt in his mind as he led his men. Tonight they would be victorious against their enemy.

Chapter Eleven

Helga and Efa stumbled through the darkness of the tunnel, their bodies hunched and their hands groping the earthen walls for balance as they chased after the flickering light of the guard who was moving briskly ahead of them. The thundering chaos of the battle overhead rained soil down upon them and Helga feared a cave-in might very well be a possibility.

Efa slipped and fell to her knees with a whimper. Rhys's aunt had been struggling to keep up and so their guard hadn't noticed the gap stretching between them.

'Take my hand,' Helga said gently, fumbling in the darkness for her.

'I cannot see anything. Oh, God, where has the torch gone?' Efa cried, before calling out in Welsh, but no one answered.

Keeping her voice calm and gentle so as not to frighten her further, Helga said, 'Do not worry, they have only gone round a bend in the tunnel. We will catch up with them shortly. Come, take my hand, I know the way.'

Efa made a retching sound and an acrid smell hit Helga's nose as she bent to comfort the woman.

Helga rubbed her back in a soothing gesture. 'Shall we rest a moment?'

'I feel a little faint, that is all…' Efa said, rising to her feet and gulping in air at an alarming rate. They continued to hold hands as Helga guided her forward a few more steps.

Wondering how best to help this woman—who had been through so much already and, if her suspicions were correct, had more difficulties ahead—Helga decided to focus on calming and reassuring her. That would be the best way to get her moving forward more quickly.

So, Helga said lightly, 'Later, when we are safely out of here, I can make you a camomile infusion to calm your stomach. I am good with herbs and can make all kinds of remedies… If you ever need my help, do not hesitate to ask… It is always best if I know *sooner*, rather than later.'

There was a moment of silence and then the guard must have noticed their absence, because the torch returned. As the flickering light illuminated Efa's face, Helga saw the painful understanding in the woman's eyes. The possibility she might be pregnant seemed to have only dawned on her at this moment and it obviously troubled her greatly.

Helga couldn't understand what the guard said, but she imagined he was telling them to *hurry up* by the way he nervously glanced at the trembling ceiling. The tunnel was hotter than before and she had a horrible feeling they were beneath one of the burning buildings.

'We are coming,' Helga said cheerfully and the man looked at her as if she were mad. She didn't care as long as it eased the lady's panic. Bunching her skirts into one fist so she could move quicker, Helga gestured at Efa to walk ahead of her.

After a long and stooped walk through the narrow tunnel they finally made it to the entrance of the mine, and the cool forest that awaited them. The few warriors that had been left behind to guard stood at points around the top of the ravine, keeping watch with the horses.

A small campfire was burning and the poor wretches from the barn were huddled around it for warmth.

'I wonder if we have any food to give them?' Helga asked.

'Yes! Food—they have not eaten well for months,' said Efa, with a renewed energy now that she had a task to focus on. Immediately she began ordering the men closest to her and they jumped into action at her command.

'I can cook and I have some healing herbs with me. Shall I ask if anyone needs aid?'

'Yes,' Efa said firmly.

'And I presume it is too late to travel? If we need to wait for Rhys's men to return from battle, then should we not organise places for people to rest? We do not have all the tents and equipment with us, but maybe if we see what the miners have available?'

Efa nodded and smiled warmly. 'Thank you, Helga. I am glad you are here. You are a good woman.'

Helga patted her arm. 'If you do not help when you can, then what is the point of living?'

Efa shook her head with a chuckle. 'You Norse have odd ideas. But tonight, I am grateful for it. We have a lot of work to do, so I hope you are strong.'

Helga lifted her arms and flexed them with a grin.

Efa laughed.

When Rhys returned, he was surprised at how well ordered the miners' camp was. He'd expected to spend at least another hour preparing shelter and food. After all, the only orders he'd given had been to protect them until after the battle.

But it appeared Efa had been busy, or at least…Efa and Helga, he suspected, by the way he saw his hostage confidently weaving through the people offering bowls of food, then rushing back and forth to get more, too distracted by her tasks to notice his arrival. The rest of his men were up at the top of the ravine, encircling it with their horses and taking turns to rest.

Efa approached his side and he threw an arm around her shoulders in silent greeting. She had been more like an older sister to him growing up, as she was closer in age to him than to his mother and had always lived with them until she was married.

Efa had been widowed at the invasion attempt at Anglesey. She'd begged Rhys to let her remain unmarried and he had loved her too much to deny her—in his eyes, she had already fulfilled her duty to Gwynedd.

'Is it already dawn?' she asked, looking at the amber glow filling the sky just above the tree line.

'No, that is light from the fires.'

'How did it go?'

'Better than expected. There will be nothing left.'

'Good,' Efa said and he blinked at the callousness of her tone. His aunt was normally a gentle and kind soul. But maybe the months in captivity had changed her. There was definitely a hardness to her eyes that had not been there before and it twisted like a blunt knife in his gut to know that his failure to protect her had caused it.

'You have done well in my absence,' he said, dropping his arm from her shoulder and folding them across his chest. He studied the well-ordered camp in front of him. The villagers were resting peacefully, some with clean bandages and fresh clothing.

'I did what I could, but Helga is to thank for most of it. She knew what needed to be done and even in what order. I would have been lost without her.'

His eyes strayed to his hostage; she was handing a bowl to a young man who looked up at her as if she were an angel.

'Helga has experience of warfare. She is a shield-maiden—their women sometimes train as warriors. She used to stay behind and protect the camp while her family fought—she was the last defence.'

'That makes sense.'

'Sense?' He'd expected her to be surprised, horrified even.

Instead, she shrugged. 'I have never known anyone like Helga. She is so calm and dignified... And why shouldn't a woman fight to protect her family? I only wish I knew how.'

He looked towards the glow of the burning fortress. War was bloody and cruel. He would not wish his family anywhere near it. Previously, he would have seen Efa's comment as a criticism on his own ability to protect her. But after meeting Helga, he now realised how useful such defensive skills could be.

Hadn't he seen her take down four men with his own eyes? Even earlier, when he'd arrived and thought her defeated by that brute, she'd actually only been preparing herself to fight back. It was impressive, yet she still considered herself less capable than her sisters.

'I am sure Helga would teach you if you asked. I would offer, but I think my training would not help you in quite the same way.'

Efa's eyes brightened. 'Maybe I will.'

He didn't doubt Helga would help her; it seemed an intrinsic part of her nature to care for those around her.

What had she said the other day? How she hated to be a *burden*. He only hoped her family appreciated her and didn't value her contributions less just because they were different from their own.

'She reminds me of you,' Efa said quietly:

'Me?' he scoffed. Helga was a wild and untamed creature who danced through life without fear. He admired her for it, but could not imagine anyone *less* like himself.

Helga was so *free*.

Efa nodded firmly, ignoring the doubt in his expression. 'I know she is young, but there is something very wise and measured about her. You have always been the same, older than your years.'

Bitter regret coated his tongue. 'I do not deserve such praise... Alswn and Hywel are missing.'

'Helga told me.' Efa sighed wearily. 'Let us hope they return safe and well. But, in the meantime, promise me you will treat your own hostage well. You are not a tyrant like Ulf.'

'I know,' he said, offended by her words.

'Then remember it.'

Efa walked away, leaving him alone with his thoughts.

Unable to help himself he moved towards Helga. She was settled on a log with a blanket around her shoulders and a bowl in her lap. Everyone else had already been fed, except for those returning from battle like himself. It didn't surprise him that she would choose to eat last and only made his admiration for her grow.

She glanced up as he approached and a bright smile— one which nearly cut him down at the knees—bloomed across her dirt-smudged face. 'You're alive!'

Warmth flooded his chest to have her greet him like a cherished friend, although he refused to show it.

'As you can see,' he grumbled. 'Why are you so happy

about it? Surely if I were dead, you would be one step closer to your freedom?' Even as he said it, he knew how ridiculous and petulant it sounded.

She frowned and waved his words away like a bothersome fly. 'Freedom? Believe me, I would be much better off with you than Ulf...or are you teasing me?' She stared up at him, her head tilted and eyes narrowed. 'It is difficult to know with your face so covered in soot.'

He rubbed at his face self-consciously and saw the black come away on his already filthy palms.

Casting aside her blanket, she got up and handed him her bowl. 'There is plenty to eat, take mine.'

'No, it is yours.' He tried to hand it back, but she ignored him.

'Nonsense. I can get another. I will also get you a cloth and some water.' She hurried away before he could protest a second time.

Ravenously hungry, he dipped the spoon in the porridge and took a large bite. He sighed with pleasure. There were blackberries in it and the texture was surprisingly creamy despite the lack of milk. Then again, maybe it was delicious because he was so hungry and exhausted. With a bone-weary sigh he sat down, his back braced against the log as he ate a few more mouthfuls.

Helga returned with a bowl of water and a long strip of linen.

'Where is your food?' he asked guiltily, as she sat down beside him.

'I will eat in a moment.' She wetted the cloth and then squeezed out the excess, the gentle sound a balm to his ears after the fiery screams of battle. She reached for his face, taking his jaw tenderly in her fingers, and gently gliding the cloth down his cheek.

'I can wash myself.' But it sounded weak even to his own ears and the cool freshness felt heavenly on his skin.

'Stop whining and eat.'

He couldn't eat, he could barely breathe, what with her intoxicating scent filling his head. She smelt of aromatic herbs, fresh blackberries and warm earth. Her skin glowed in the firelight, and he wanted to wrap her silken hair around his fingers to feel its softness.

But, most of all, he wanted to kiss her. To wash away the terrible darkness of the last few hours and feel alive once again.

Unable to do any of those things, he remained perfectly still, letting her wash away the brutality of war from his body with tender strokes. She began to hum a soft melody and he closed his eyes, allowing the peaceful tune to ease his muscles and unwind the tension at his temples.

'Where did you get all the cloth from?' he asked, not wanting to disturb the moment, but finding his curiosity getting the better of him. He'd seen a few people wrapped in bandages and he knew they had very little in their supplies.

'Some of the villagers had little to no clothing. I asked the warriors to offer whatever they had spare and your men were generous. They gave all that they had, even the cloaks they were wearing and their spare woollens.'

'I would expect nothing less and you should not have had to ask them. They should have known.'

Helga wiped his brow with the cloth, her sweet breath mingling with his own. 'They are good men. But they had other concerns, like keeping watch. I am sure they would have moved on to clothing and injuries eventually... There!' Another blinding smile dazzled him. 'There's your handsome face. I thought I would never reach it!'

She took his hands then and began to wash those as well. He should stop her, insist that he could wash himself, but it felt so *damn* good. No one had ever cared for him like this, not since he was a child at least.

And had she called him handsome?

Why did that please him?

Sex had never been difficult to find; women seemed to like his face and body. Intimacy, however, had always been a struggle for him and he had chosen his partners accordingly. Willing women who did not mind his remoteness and desired no entanglements of the heart.

But those dalliances had grown less frequent over the years as his responsibilities weighed more heavily upon him, and he'd grown less approachable as a result. It did not matter to him that his days of frivolity had been short. He was aware of his priorities and his own heart was not one of them.

But, in Helga's tender care, and after the way she had so joyfully greeted him, he could almost imagine what it would be like…to be loved. The hollow ache inside of him eased a little in her presence.

'Are these family rings?' she asked smoothing the cloth over his fingers. There were three in total, one on each of his smallest fingers, and a blue gem on the fourth of his right hand.

'They were my mother's, except for this one…' He pointed out the gem. 'My grandfather gave this to my father as a symbol of our royal lineage. It is a sapphire and very rare. It came from the East and the gold was mined from Gwynedd.'

'Have you always worn them?'

'Since my parents' death.'

Memories of the Anglesey raid filled his mind. The smoke and chaos, much like the battle tonight. He'd been too late to save his parents. He'd found two Norse men—presumably their killers—trying to strip the rings off their lifeless fingers. He'd cut them down in a furious rage and had put the jewellery on his own hands before re-joining the fray. He'd never taken them off, with one exception—the ring he'd given to Alswn before she'd left.

'Ahh.' Helga nodded with sympathy, as if she could see into his memories and knew the horrors of what he'd seen. 'I knew they meant more to you than mere trinkets. You are not the type of man to wear pretty things for the sake of it.'

'No, they have meaning.' Removing his hands from her light grip, he picked up the bowl in his lap and offered it back to her.

'I am not that hungry. I think I would rather sleep.'

'Neither am I,' he lied. 'So, share this with me.' He offered her a spoon and she opened her mouth for him. His body tightened with longing and he immediately regretted his offer, but like a bee drawn to the flower he could not keep away.

He fed her until Helga held up her hand. 'Honestly. I cannot eat another bite.'

Satisfied that she'd had enough, he ate the rest. 'We will need to ride as soon as dawn breaks. Otherwise, we risk meeting Ulf, or allowing those who fled time to regroup.'

Helga nodded and gave a sleepy yawn as she curled up tighter in her blanket. 'There still should be enough porridge for those who are hungry at daybreak. We cleaned out one of the miner's barrows to make it in.'

He looked over and chuckled at the sight of the makeshift vat. 'Clever. You should sleep, Helga, We've at least another full day's travel ahead.'

She rested her head lightly against his shoulder, believing in him to hold her steady as she slept, her trust as boundless as her kindness and ingenuity.

She had seen what needed to be done and had worked tirelessly to accomplish it. The blackberries must have been picked from the brambles at the edge of the clearing, the water and oats scraped together from both his warriors' and miners' supplies. There was only one cauldron and kettle over the fire, so she must have had to continuously add the hot water to the large barrow of porridge. He was sure she would have had help, of course, but the resourcefulness and order of the camp had her mark all over it.

The bundles of cloth, the hot infusions of calming herbs passed around, even the sweet smell of healing balms that drifted from the now well-tended villagers. How had she 'known' to collect so many herbs? Because it was fortunate that she had.

It is not fortune telling! he berated himself silently.

She knew there was a battle ahead. There was no magic behind her preparations, only common sense.

Still, it was impressive foresight and what surprised him the most was that she had done all of this for her enemy. And that no one—not even his aunt, who had been a captive of the Norse herself—had questioned Helga's authority.

She was a remarkable woman, the kind he would have been proud to call wife.

Why had he thought that?

The realisation unsettled him, but not because it felt wrong—because it felt right.

'How long until we reach your home?' Helga asked, her voice soft and sleepy.

'At least another full day of riding before we reach the base of Cadair y Ddraig.' It would take time. With so many sick and wounded, each horse would need to carry two riders.

'What does it mean? Cadair y Ddraig?'

'You pronounced that well,' he said with a smile. 'It means Dragon's Chair. It is said that long ago a dragon clawed out that ledge so that it could have a pleasant place to lay in the sunshine and sleep. Then, one particularly cold winter forced it to crawl deep into the heart of the mountain for warmth and, in the darkness, it forgot to wake. Eventually, its fire dimmed and its scales turned to rock. Sometimes, on very hot days you can hear it… snoring.'

Helga giggled through a yawn. 'What does it do on all of your cold and rainy days?'

'It growls, but only very softly. You see…it does not realise it is asleep.'

'How sad,' Helga whispered, all merriment gone from her voice.

'How so?'

'To not even realise you are asleep…to never be truly living… I hope his dreams are sweet.' Her words drifted away as she succumbed to sleep herself, but they had pierced him like a knife.

To never be truly living...

Why did those words cut so deep? Because…sometimes he felt like that, numb to all emotion except vengeance, his duties and responsibilities almost suffocating.

He had to admit—despite the worries plaguing him— with Helga he had laughed and smiled more than he had in months. Yet, shouldn't he distance himself from her? His attraction and admiration for her was growing daily, but she was still his hostage.

It would be dishonourable to think of her as anything more, especially as there was no future for them. She was his enemy and always would be. Besides, he had accepted long ago that he was better off alone. Even if the loneliness sometimes felt hard to swallow.

He spent the rest of the night wide awake, watching the true dawn paint the sky above his head with warm yellows and milky blues. Hoping for some clarity of thought regarding the woman who slept so peacefully at his side.

He never found it.

Chapter Twelve

Helga found the next long day of travel a miserable experience in more ways than one. Not only was the terrain hard, but they rode through burned-out villages and farms, one of which was the settlement the villagers had been stolen from and the low sound of weeping had filled the air as they passed the charred bones of their homes.

'What will happen to the villagers? Where will they go?' she asked, her voice quiet out of respect for those in mourning.

'They will live at Cadair y Ddraig until it is safe to rebuild. They *will* return and it will be a better life than the one they lost.' It was a vow, she realised, one he had sworn to himself, and she believed without question that he would fulfil it.

When the village was long behind them, she said, 'I will be glad when our journey is over.'

'The journey has been hard on you.'

Offended by what she viewed as a criticism, she replied, 'This kind of riding…I do not enjoy.' Although that wasn't entirely true as she'd not minded being wrapped in Rhys's arms. 'But I do like horses. In Francia, I used to do tricks on horseback to entertain my sisters. I could even ride while standing on the saddle! But…long journeys are tedious.'

'You must have done a lot of travelling in your youth. If your mother fought with Rollo…'

'We did.'

Rhys spoke quietly, as if he were making a confession. 'The furthest I have ever been is Jorvik. That must sound laughable to you. However, my life and duty will always be here and I would never question that… But sometimes, I wonder what it would be like to travel to distant lands.'

She smiled at his unguarded admission and relaxed against his chest. 'Valda likes to travel. She loves adventure and new experiences. Our mother did, too, when she was younger. But Brynhild and I, we are not like them. We long for a place to settle, to lay down our roots and thrive. I will say this about travel, it makes you appreciate stillness and what it is to have a home. Nowhere has truly felt like home to me.'

'But…you will. You spoke of owning a farm with your mother one day.'

'Yes, maybe we will, or maybe that opportunity has already passed.'

'Passed? How so?'

Helga looked out at the dusky mountains around them. It was everything she loved in nature. Wild, bold landscapes, a peaceful wind sliding through the heathers. The only thing missing was her family at her side. 'I do not know. It is just…a feeling.'

Before nightfall, they arrived at the base of a large and sprawling mountain with a lake beneath. A high-up waterfall fell from its peak into woodland, then came back out again further down the mountainside, draining into the lake below, which narrowed to a river in the distance, no doubt meandering out to sea.

All water returned to its mother eventually.

Helga missed her family terribly today.

No matter all their bluster and protestations about feeling responsible for her. She knew they needed her just as much as she needed them.

Who would tend to her mother's wounds? Or feed and reassure Brynhild—who was far more sensitive than she would ever dare admit. And who would help Valda with the birth of her child, if Helga was not there?

Rhys paused at the water's edge and allowed his horse a drink.

'Tonight, we will stay at my farm. But up there…' He pointed up to a ledge on the mountainside where the waterfall first fell into the treeline. Squinting, she saw only the tops of a few guard towers, some flickering lights and peaceful tendrils of smoke rising up, suggesting a large settlement hidden within.

'That is Cadair y Ddraig…my home.'

After a short ride through the forest, they entered a flatland filled with fields and orchards. There was a large farm with a low wall surrounding it and several barns and buildings within, all made of timber, or a combination of stone and thatch.

As they passed through the open gate, they were greeted by an elderly lady with smoky hair and dark eyes the colour of clay. She smiled up at Rhys and spoke to him in Welsh. She was introduced as Gwenllian and she managed the land.

Rhys swept down from his horse, then turned to help Helga down.

Efa and three village women moved to her side, their

eyes pained but determined as they looked towards her. Efa spoke first, her chin raised high. 'You said to tell you...sooner rather than later.'

She looked at the nervous villagers, their fingers knotted in their skirts.

These were the brave ones.

'Gather the women. I wish to speak to all of them. I will prepare a remedy, meet me in the Hall.' With a nod the villagers hurried away.

Helga reached for her sack of herbs and was about to untie it from Rhys's mount, but he had already beaten her to it and held it in his hands. Only the pennyroyals were left inside.

Rhys looked between Helga and Efa with a confused frown. Helga said nothing and would have left it that way—for it was not her heartache to tell.

But then Efa fixed Rhys with a hard look. 'Women were raped. Myself included. I do not wish to have a babe and Helga can help us avoid that extra pain...'

There was silence as the truth struck home.

'I am so sorry.' His voice was rough, his eyes filled with unshed tears. 'Is there anything I can do to help?'

Efa's face softened. Stepping forward, she cupped his face in a motherly gesture, and kissed his cheek. 'You asking that is enough.' Taking a deep breath, she turned and walked away.

Rhys handed Helga the sack, a helpless expression on his face. 'Is it safe?'

Helga nodded, determined that she would take extra special care with the tonic's preparation and check on all of the women regularly. 'I have made it before, with no problems. But it does not always work.'

'How did you know? That you would need these...'

'You probably won't believe me…but that night in the abbey…I dreamt of them.'

To her surprise, he only nodded. 'Thank you. If they need anything more, do not hesitate to ask.'

Curious, she asked, 'If a woman does not wish to take it, will you…as their lord, help them with the care of the child?'

Rhys answered without hesitation, 'Whatever they want to do, they will always have my protection and my support.'

Taking his hand in hers she lifted it to her lips and kissed it. Rhys looked as if he had been struck by a bolt of lightning, but she did not care. 'You are a good man,' she said and then turned and strode towards the Hall.

Later, Helga was fetching water from the well with Gwenllian and Efa. The abortive had been made and given to all women who had requested one. She had spoken with them all, telling them what Rhys had said. Some had chosen to refuse the offer, while others accepted it gladly.

All appreciated being given the choice.

She'd warned all of the women to come to her if their bloods failed to come, or if they felt more pain than normal. But as there were only a couple of women obviously carrying, and both of those had decided to keep the babe, she didn't fear any difficulties. For many, it would be a welcome precaution.

Now, her attention was focused on preparing a hearty evening meal. Anyone that could work had to work as there was still harvesting, milling and the transportation of supplies to organise. When they retreated to the fortress, nothing could be left here to sustain Ulf's army.

'Who are they?' asked Helga curiously, as she pointed

out a group of men who stared at her as they passed. Long chains were attached to their hands and feet, impeding their movement. But they were all tall, powerfully built men, and even though their clothing was torn and dirty, it was distinctly Norse in style, like her apron dress.

Efa spoke to Gwenllian and then began to translate for her. 'Yes, Gwenllian says they are Ulf's men who were captured in the first raids. Rhys has used them as hostages ever since, but with little success,' Efa explained.

'Ulf won't care if they live or die.'

The older woman continued in Welsh and Efa listened intently before translating. 'Indeed, Gwenllian says Ulf told Rhys to do whatever he liked with them because he didn't care either way. Rather than execute them, Rhys decided to put them to work in the fields. They have been surprisingly good workers.'

'They will work hard because they fear death otherwise.'

'I thought your country men were unafraid of death?' asked Efa.

'They do not fear a *good* death. Dying without a weapon in their hands is considered demeaning.'

'And yet they surrendered?'

Helga nodded, 'We do not like to lose. They will have surrendered because they will hope to live and fight in a better battle in the future. My people are brave, not stupid.'

Efa stared at her in surprise, then they both laughed. Gwenllian must have asked Efa what they were talking about and after she translated the conversation, all three women were chuckling good naturedly.

'I think I would like to learn your language. Would you help teach me, Efa?'

'If you wish. Although…are you sure? You may not be

here that long—Rhys said your family were due to return for you within a month.'

'I enjoy learning new things,' she answered with a shrug, but in truth she had to wonder if it *was* worthwhile. Strangely, she now felt conflicted about leaving Rhys, whereas before she would have been glad. But now she had seen glimmers of the man behind the cold exterior and was even beginning to wonder if she should once again trust in visions. After all, when had they failed her in the past? However, that would mean giving up and disappointing her family, and she could never do that.

Efa smiled. 'Then I will gladly teach you. I myself only learned Norse from Old Aneurin, although my months in captivity have definitely improved it. I should introduce you to him. He is a good teacher, if…odd. He was once a travelling bard and has been to many distant lands. Rhys always enjoyed his tales growing up—his mother believed a wide knowledge of the world was a powerful tool.'

'She was right. What was she like, Rhys's mother?'

'Beautiful, kind and clever. It was impossible not to love my sister. She was everyone's greatest joy.' Efa's bittersweet smile was telling and spoke of great loss. 'I am sorry you have been brought into this, Helga. I know what it is to be a captive and I would not wish it on anyone!'

Helga patted her arm, hoping to ease her distress. 'Rhys has treated me well. Soon, my mother and sisters will come for me and I am sure Lady Alswn is safe, and will be returning with them as we speak.'

'You are too forgiving, Helga. I would have tried to scratch out his eyes by now.'

Helga chuckled. 'Maybe I will one day.'

They returned to the hall kitchens, where they made flat breads, and cooked them on the lid of the enormous cauldron. The stew inside was made with salted pork, grains, root vegetables and apples, the delicious aromas bringing people to the main hall well before it was ready.

The hall was probably only ever used for the field workers, and what with Rhys's *teulu* and the freed villagers it was packed to the seams with people. But nobody minded the crush.

'Where are the Norse men I saw earlier?' asked Helga. 'We're nearly out of bread and, before I offer seconds, I want to make sure I have enough.'

Efa wasn't sure and so repeated Helga's question to Gwenllian. The translated response had Helga fuming. 'They do not eat with the free folk. They are considered too dangerous and are chained in with the pigs tonight. Whatever is left is sent to them after.'

'Have they hurt anyone since arriving here?'

After Efa translated the question, Gwenllian shook her head.

'Then I shall take them their food,' snapped Helga, ladling stew into a smaller cauldron and putting some bread and dumplings into a basket.

Efa and Gwenllian exchanged worried looks, which she deliberately ignored.

'Ask one of the men to take it,' said Efa. 'It is dark and Gwenllian says they are fierce and terribly strong. It was why their food was rationed, so that they would not have the strength to break their chains.'

'Nonsense.' Helga huffed, picking up the basket and cauldron. 'I understand they need to be punished…but starvation? They need to eat to be able to work.'

'I shall speak with Rhys—I am sure they are not being starved. Please, Helga, do not go, especially *alone*…' She looked anxiously at the door to the hall, as if a great beast loomed over the threshold. 'I cannot go with you… I…'

Helga's temper cooled at Efa's distress. 'I will ask Madoc to come with me. Do not worry.'

Except, when she went to look for Madoc, she could not find him and none of the other men seemed to speak enough Norse to understand her when she asked for help. It was frustrating and only reinforced to her that she needed to learn Welsh.

Maybe he was with Rhys? He'd not returned for the evening meal and, as no one had seemed concerned about this, Helga had refrained from mentioning it.

The hall was now filled to breaking point with so many people jostling for space and, stepping outside, she breathed a sigh of relief.

A few braziers and torches were dotted around the entrance of the farm's buildings, lighting the way. A quick glance around her confirmed that both Madoc and Rhys were nowhere to be seen.

Should she go back inside? Ask Efa to translate her request to another man?

Loud singing began to rumble from the hall, putting her off the idea. It was hard enough to be heard as it was and she couldn't face the heat again so soon.

Besides, if these people were so intimidated by Norse men, then surely they would have guards? So, why would she need more men? Especially as she was only bringing food and they were already chained up…

No, she would be perfectly fine.

Hoisting up her cauldron and basket a little higher, she headed towards the animal pens, convinced she was doing the right thing.

Chapter Thirteen

It didn't take her long to identify the pig pen. Not only from the fully armoured guard sat on a bench outside, but also from the snorting of the swine. They hadn't even *bothered* to remove the pigs!

Irritation flared into anger and when the guard didn't understand, she simply shook the food at him and sauntered past.

There was little light cast by the guard's brazier, but she could see it was still better conditions than the hovel the villagers had been kept in, although not by much. It was a pig pen, after all, with a leaky roof and damp-stained walls.

Five men sat on a long bench, the manacles around their feet and wrists having left the skin red raw and bleeding. Each of them was tethered by ropes to a hook in a rafter above their heads and though they each had a blanket, there was not enough room to lie down. Their only option was to sleep sitting upright.

One of the men in the centre of the row looked up as she entered, he met her eyes with a disarming smile. He was older than her by at least fifteen winters—if not more. It was difficult to tell because he was quite handsome and still had plenty of strength and vigour despite the grey in his beard.

In fact, all the men appeared to be healthy, so they could not have been starved. A few smaller, less nourishing meals perhaps, but nothing cruel. Her rage lowered to a steady simmer.

'I have brought you food,' she said, setting down her cauldron and basket on the flattest patch of mud she could see. She was about to hand out the bread, but frowned when she noticed the earth caked on their hands.

There was a water trough, but she suspected it was their drinking water, so it would be unwise of them to use it to wash their hands. Taking the clean square of linen that covered the bread, she dipped it in the water and offered it to the first man. 'You will want to clean your hands first.'

He was the youngest among them and at least three winters younger than herself, judging by his patchy beard. He blinked up at her in surprise, but did as she had said, handing the cloth to the next man afterwards. On it went until each man had cleaned most of the obvious dirt from their hands.

Then she started to hand out the bread from her basket. When the youth immediately raised it to his mouth, she gasped, 'Oh, no, not yet! I didn't bring any bowls for the stew so you will have to use the bread as your trencher.'

'Patience, Egil, have you forgotten your manners?' She could tell from the command in the older man's voice that he was in charge of the group.

'Thank you, lady,' Egil said, a little red in the face as he ducked his head.

Helga gave him a reassuring smile as she continued down the line. 'Do not worry, Egil. My sister is the same when it comes to fresh bread. She would sooner burn her mouth than wait a moment longer than she had to.'

As she handed the leader his bread, he asked softly, 'What is your name, sweet lady? Are you a Dane, like us?'

She chuckled at the man's flattery, but she instinctively sensed nothing vicious behind his sweet talk. He probably hoped she could help them escape. After all, she was unchained and had more freedoms than them.

'My name is Helga Þorundóttir. My mother is from Skane originally, but I have spent most of my life with my mother and sisters in Francia—they fought under Jarl Rollo's banner.'

'Jarl Rollo? Impressive…' He eased back with an admiring smile and Helga continued down the line handing out the bread. 'Were you unfortunate enough to be captured too, sweet Helga?'

'I am a…guest,' she said, unwilling to share too many details until she fully knew the measure of them. She would not forget the pale faces of those villagers so easily and, if these men had anything to do with that, no amount of flirting would help her forgive them. 'And you are?'

'Harald Olafson, and these are my brothers.' He pointed out each man in turn, who gave her a polite dip of their heads. 'Egil, Sten, Toke and Arne. We were captured last autumn.' That eased some of Helga's concerns as she knew the villagers had been taken in the spring. Harald leaned forward. 'Why is a guest feeding us? Not that I am complaining—it smells delicious—but I wonder why the Dragon Lord has had such a sudden change of heart regarding us…'

'I made the stew. It is only fair that I have a say in who it is given to.'

Harald nodded thoughtfully, but she did not miss the flare of respect in his eyes at her stubborn spirit.

Returning to pick up the cauldron, Helga then began to ladle the stew out on to the men's flat breads. It was thick enough not to run and the bread soaked up the juices greedily—as did the men. 'They say you raided his settlements,' she said.

'We did as Ulf ordered. He said it was to open negotiations,' Harald said stiffly, obviously not pleased regarding Ulf's methods.

'And you believed him…why?' asked Helga curiously.

Harald gave a deep and appreciative laugh, before answering, 'Ulf promised me land if I helped build his fort and secure his alliance. I did not care about his methods—as long as they worked.'

'You raided despite your own misgivings? That seems dishonourable to me,' she pointed out, hoping her disapproval was clear.

Light amusement flashed across his face and he nodded. 'We did, although we were captured before we did any real harm. Ask anyone, they will tell you the kidnapping and slaughter only happened *after* I was captured. Sven, the new commander of Ulf's fort, is far more ruthless than I. We only took some livestock and grain.'

Sven…the man who had attacked her.

'And why were you so generous?' she asked dryly.

'If, in the future, we were to farm the land here, it would be better that we had no bad blood running between us and the locals. That can cause problems later on…with finding wives, for example…'

'You should not have trusted Ulf at all. He rarely delivers on any of his promises. I doubt you would have received any land from him. He has none to give, except that which he steals.'

'It seems you have better wisdom than I. Ulf said the raids would encourage an alliance between himself and the Dragon Lord, that such tactics worked with the Saxons. But I understand that alliance has already crumbled?'

Helga shrugged. 'It has and the fortress you helped build no longer stands.'

All of the men stopped eating. Frustration twisted Harald's features into a snarl of resentment, as he cursed beneath his breath. Then he sighed, staring down at the meal in his hands with bitter defeat. 'Is this to be our last meal, then?'

'No!' Helga gasped, immediately feeling terrible for worrying him. She did not know him well, but from this short conversation she had decided to trust in Harald's words. It seemed he only wanted a better future for himself and his brothers.

How could she blame him for that?

And, if it were true that he'd only stolen some supplies, then she would not hold it against him. Her family had done similar in Francia.

Stepping forward, she placed her hand gently on Harald's shoulder to comfort him. She wanted to reassure him that he would not die. But it was not her decision to make.

'At least…I do not think so and I will do all that I can to help you,' she said.

Rhys entered the pig pen and glared at the sight before him. Anger slithered through his body like a green-eyed serpent, stealing all reason from his mind.

Helga had her hand on Harald Olafson's shoulder and he'd never hated another man more. Harald had a silken tongue—Gwenllian complained he regularly charmed and distracted the serf women from their chores—and had been responsible for the first raids, a fact Rhys would never forget, or forgive.

The man was almost old enough to be Helga's father!

Still, she had more in common with Harald than with him. They were both Norse, held similar beliefs and traditions. The realisation only unsettled him further.

'What is the meaning of this?' he barked.

Had she been about to free them?

They remained in chains, with food in their laps—so possibly not. The guard had also been watching them closely from the doorway when Rhys had arrived and he hadn't seemed overly concerned.

Efa had said that Helga had taken it upon herself to feed them. His aunt had turned pale with worry when she'd seen him with Madoc, saying that she feared for Helga's safety.

She needn't have worried, he thought bitterly. It seemed Helga was more than happy to spend time with swine—both man and beast!

Stupidly he'd allowed her the same freedoms as before, not thinking about the potential consequences. But with Helga he reacted without thought or reason.

Rather than look ashamed, Helga had the gall to place her hands on her hips and began to scold him as if he were a child!

'I would have thought you *Christians* would treat your prisoners better! Forcing them to sleep with the pigs? With only one blanket and no fire…and *manacles*!' She pointed at the red marks around the men's wrists and ankles. 'These wounds will fester if not treated!'

Harald smirked at him from across the room. He was obviously enjoying the tongue-lashing Rhys was receiving.

Clenching his fists to stop himself from drawing his sword, he snapped, 'Come away from them, Helga.'

She frowned as if his order were ridiculous. 'They are chained. What harm can they do me?' Deliberately, she continued to ladle out stew. Each man thanked her softly like timid lambs and when she was done, she stepped away. One eyebrow raised as if to say, *See!*

They glared at each other, both unwilling to back down.

He tried to reason with his temper.

Why should he care about the gentle and familiar way she'd touched Harald? She was his hostage... They were barely even friends...

Because you are jealous, whispered an inner devil.

Which was ridiculous! There could never be anything between them. To think that he'd begun to believe her fortune-telling dreams. *What a fool!* Her tender touches and sweet words were meaningless. She was his enemy and would always place her people and family first.

As would he.

Gwynedd binds me.

But the oath did not comfort him as it once had.

'These *men* are no better than swine! They have committed crimes against my people.'

'We stole some bags of grain and a few sheep,' Harald said, rolling his eyes insolently.

'Your brethren have done far more than that!' he snapped. 'Villages burned; so many lives ruined, countless people slaughtered in their beds. Women and children!'

Harald eyes narrowed. 'Not I and not my *brothers.*'

'Only because you were captured before Ulf ordered it. I'm sure you would have done the same—behaved like an obedient dog for your master!'

Harald ignored him, which was even more infuriating than the usual denials. Instead of pleading his innocence, he looked towards Helga. As a slow, deliberately roguish smile spread across his face, Rhys was convinced it was purely to goad him.

'Delicious…' he said, and after too long a pause he added, 'The stew…is delicious.'

Rhys had never regretted not killing a man more.

Helga gave a polite nod, then began to gather her empty basket and cauldron. She passed Rhys on her way out like a haughty queen, uncaring of the scowl he threw her way.

Before he followed her out, he turned to Harald and warned, 'Be careful, Harald. Soon it will be winter and I will need to decide if you and your brothers are *still* worth feeding.'

Harald's gaze turned to steel. 'Release us and you will never see us again. Save your food. If Ulf is coming, you will need it.'

Catching up with Helga in only a few strides, Rhys took the cauldron from her. 'Never speak to them again.'

'How could you treat them so harshly?' She thrust the basket into his chest. 'You can carry this, as well!'

He took the basket and tossed it to the side of the path. The cauldron quickly followed. 'Would you prefer chains, too? Continue to berate me and I may consider it!'

She squared up to him, completely unafraid. 'I am not a dog for you to train and neither are those men. They came because they wanted land of their own. Sons do not equally inherit, as they do in your land. We are like Saxons in that regard—the eldest son gets *everything*. How else are they to make their fortunes unless they look further away from home? I believe Harald. He and his brothers had no real intention of hurting your people, I am certain of it!'

He snorted. 'You are naive to believe that. They are dangerous men and you should avoid them for your own safety.'

'You are not the first to think that of me!' Her eyes glistened with anger and frustration. 'But I am not stupid, or weak. Those men could be an asset to you, if only you opened your eyes. They know how the Norse fight and they are not bound to Ulf by blood. They would just as easily swear loyalty to you. If you treated them kindly, let me tend their wounds and gave them back their dignity, they would gladly fight to the death for you. All they want is some land to farm. A place to settle and call home—'

His rage boiled and overflowed. 'They are *raiders*!' he shouted, hissing the last word like a curse. 'Do you think a raider values life? They do not! Did you not see the burned villages? Did you not hear the weeping? You are the one that is blind. Raiders want to rape, steal and kill. *Nothing more!*'

She shook her head. 'Are there not Saxon men who would do the same? Or even your *own* countrymen? I may be young, but I have seen war. Some people are cruel, no matter what land they were born in, or which god they follow.' She touched his arm, her words full of sympathy that made his skin itch. 'They stole from you and I understand they must be punished, but—'

'You understand nothing!' he spat, jerking away his arm. '*You* have never had to defend your home and family from invaders. You have never had to step over the bodies of your parents, just to hold back the tide.' He lifted his hand, his rings glinting in the weak light of a nearby torch. 'These are all that remain of them and I had to pull each one off their dead fingers. Do not presume to tell me what is, and is not, a fitting punishment.'

His breathing was heavy as he finished his tirade and she stared at him. Not in horror as he would have imagined, but with a pity that burned his flesh to the bone.

Cursing, he began to walk away, but quickly realised that if he did, she would be left alone. He stopped, stared at his feet in the mud, and waited. Even now, his honour came first.

She joined him at his side and now that he was a little calmer, he muttered, 'They are only sleeping there tonight. Usually, they sleep in the barn, but tonight it is filled with the villagers and my *teulu*.' He refused to look at her, feeling as if he had ripped out his heart in front of her and now couldn't bear to watch her judge it.

'I misunderstood… Rhys…' She touched his arm and he met her eyes. 'I am sorry…for your parents.'

He stiffened, shrugging off her sympathy. 'It was a long time ago. But do not think I have shown those men mercy. I have worked them hard and will continue to do so. They will regret stealing from me!'

'You will not kill them, then?' She appeared relieved and it was like a knife in his gut.

'Why waste strong backs?'

Her head tilted in that knowing way of hers. 'You do not *want* to kill them. There is no shame in that.'

'I would rather work them to death first!' he snapped. 'At least then we will gain something by their presence.'

'You wouldn't do that.'

'And how do you know? Did you *dream* it?' He sneered, he saw the way she flinched and hated himself for it.

'No… I just…know *you*.'

Her words broke him and he shook his head in denial. 'You do not.'

'Not everything...' she said, her words hesitant and gentle. 'But I want to know more if you'll tell me...' She took his hand in her own. 'Rhys, there is a bond between us. I see it...even if you do not.'

All of his arguments for why they could never be together scattered into the night sky and, as if drugged by her words, he dipped towards her, reaching with his free hand to cup her face and tilt it towards the light of the torch.

He longed to kiss her. To feel her heavenly skin beneath his feverish body. The temptation to abandon all duty and to indulge in carnal pleasure was overwhelming.

She smiled as he leaned closer, then closed her eyes in expectation.

She had dreamt of a black dragon stealing her away from the family she loved and what could he offer her? *Nothing.*

Hesitation twisted into doubt and he stepped away, releasing her, horrified at what he might have done, at what he *still* desperately wanted to do.

'It is late,' he said, avoiding her eyes, 'I will see you back to the hall.' He began walking and she hurried after him.

At the hall, Rhys held the door open for her as they entered. 'You will sleep with Gwenllian and Efa in the back room.'

It was quieter now as people had found benches or spaces on the floor to lay their bed rolls.

'Goodnight, *Lord Rhys*,' Helga whispered coldly. Lifting her skirts slightly, she began to weave through the slumbering bodies, careful not to disturb them.

Rhys remained by the door, watching her progress. He would sleep somewhere else tonight.

The firelight caught in her hair like glistening rivers of gold and his heart clenched as if it were being squeezed by a fist. *Her fist*, for she had surely imprisoned him.

He turned away and walked back into the night.

Chapter Fourteen

Helga stared up at the fortress as they approached.

It reminded her a little of Jorvik, with its mighty wooden palisade above a heaped earthen defence, but that's where the similarities ended. Firstly, the air was fresher, the smoke of the workshops and homes snatched away by the brisk mountain winds.

She still rode with Rhys, which had surprised her after their argument and near-kiss the night before. But she supposed it would have seemed odd for him to suddenly no longer ride with her for the final part of their journey.

Last night, the revelation about his parents' deaths had gone a long way in helping her to understand him. When he'd bent as if to kiss her, she had thought the wall between them had fallen. She'd been mistaken, but she had gathered the moment with all of the others, as if they were feathers she could use to line a nest for him in her heart. A secret wish that waited only for his acceptance.

Of course, she wasn't sure if he would ever accept her, he'd turned cold, pulling away from her as he always did, his hatred of her people too strong to ignore. It had been humiliating in the extreme. Standing there, waiting in expectation for a kiss that had never come.

*Was she mad to believe there was more between them?
And did she really want a man who hated everything
about her family and her past?*

As they rode through the mighty gates, Helga saw yet
another wooden wall just beyond. Two lines of defence. It
was an intimidating prospect for any attacker…except…

'So few men?' she asked, disheartened at the lack of
armed warriors walking the walls.

'My *teulu* is the bulk of my force… That and the serfs.'

Helga grimaced—the serfs weren't like her countrymen, who spent all their lives training to fight and raid. A
Norse farmer used his axe for both wood and blood. She
wasn't sure the serfs of Rhys's land could say the same.

They passed through the second set of gates and entered the very large settlement beyond. Many stone and
timber roundhouses with thatched or turf roofs filled the
plateau. In the distance she could see a great waterfall
streaming down the mountainside, the water falling into
a woodland towards the back of the fortress.

Proudly stood in the centre was a very large timber
building, which looked a little like a grand longhouse,
except more rectangular and topped with a golden roof.
Several smoke holes were along its back, the white tendrils disappearing into the bright blue sky above.

Many smaller buildings surrounded the impressive
hall and they stopped at a stable to dismount. The rest
of Rhys's *teulu* had already stopped at the inner wall and
only a few of them had joined them through the gate, including Efa, who rode with Madoc.

Rhys helped Helga down from the horse and gestured
towards the hall.

There were dark smudges beneath his eyes and the
tightness of his shoulders told her he had not slept well.
Locking away her sympathy, she kept her words cool,

stepping away from him as soon as he had helped her down. She would not beg for affection—she had more pride than that.

No matter what the runes foretold, she would not accept a man who hated the very essence of her being and called her family liars. At least Brynhild and her mother would return soon with Lady Alswn and Rhys's doubts about her family would be proven wrong. Although she wondered if that would make any difference to either of them. His hatred of her people was so strong.

But could she leave him behind to face Ulf alone? Deep in her bones she knew that *somehow* Rhys could not succeed without her. It was clear that he would need more than a few serfs to hold Ulf's force back.

Maybe it was hopeless and she should leave him alone to his fate?

She glanced at Rhys as they entered the hall. There was a grim determination on his face, a cold intelligence that allowed no room for warmth. But she had seen beneath the frozen surface to the wounded man beneath. She longed to heal his pain and see him smile once again.

'Welcome to my home.' Rhys gestured at the hall, the lines of his brow deepening when he realised she was staring at him, rather than at their surroundings.

Slowly she looked away from him, refusing to be intimidated by his scowls.

The hall was divided with large wooden screens, elaborately carved with Celtic knots, and painted in bright greens, whites and golds. Silk-embellished tapestries hung on the walls, depicting impressive scenes she presumed were from Welsh history or the Bible. She would probably spend a lot of time admiring them in the days and weeks to come.

Turning full circle to take in the sheer splendour of

her surroundings, she noticed a large gold and silver crucifix above the entrance, as well as ornate benches and
long elaborate feasting tables, probably where his *teulu*
ate. The kitchens and pantries were just visible behind
the screens at the sides of the hall, including an impressive clay oven. The Hall was very well lit with many oil
lamps and braziers, as well as the main fire in the centre
of the feasting tables.

Unable to help herself, she teased, 'You *are* a prince.
This is a palace.'

Rhys looked around him with a critical eye. 'It is as
good as King Anarawd's court, I suppose.'

'You have a throne,' she said dryly, trying not to laugh
as she pointed out the raised dais at one end of the hall.
The chair upon it was intricately carved with what appeared to be dragons, the beasts coiling around it like
Jörmungandr—the serpent that encircled the world.

'My parents encouraged and supported the local
craftsmen, they made it for them in thanks.' He paused,
a sombre expression growing on his face. 'There are two,
but I have use for only one.'

Until he marries a Welsh lady, Helga thought bitterly.

Staring at the dais, she tried to imagine herself sat on
an identical one next to it. She could not see herself on a
serpent's throne and her earlier humour died at the thought.

She moved her gaze away from the lonely chair to
the equally lonely man. 'When did you become Lord
here?' It felt a safer question than asking him when his
parents had died.

'After the failed invasion of Anglesey ten years ago.'
His words were clipped, devoid of feeling.

'You were a child,' she said, horrified.

'I'd seen fourteen winters.'

'Even my sisters did not fight in battle at that age—let

alone lead men! Not until they were older and my mother deemed them ready.'

'How old were you?' he asked and she wished she'd not said anything at all.

'My mother never deemed me ready.' She smiled at him, but it felt tight and brittle. 'I would stay behind, remember? It suited me.'

His head tilted as if he were trying to see past her words to the truth beneath and she was grateful when Efa came to stand beside them.

'Efa, will you organise clothing and supplies for Helga, while I show her to her room?' he asked lightly.

'Of course,' said Efa, although her mouth went slack as she watched them walk towards the back of the hall.

Helga followed him past the throne and behind a large screen that almost filled the width of the hall.

The room beyond was large and divided once again into sections, with an area of comfortable seating around a firebox, surrounded by smaller chambers to the side that were quite sparse in comparison to the rest of the hall's furnishings. They appeared mostly to be for storage, with only a few chests and furniture present—many of which were covered with linen cloths.

It was a sad-looking space, absent of personality, as if the furniture were tucked up in bed asleep, waiting for the time when they could be useful again.

At the back of the room beyond an elaborately carved dividing screen was a large bed, covered in woollen curtains to block out the chill.

'You will sleep in my bed,' he said, so coldly she wondered if he hated the idea, but if that was the case, then why offer it?

'And…where will you sleep?' she asked, glancing quickly at him out of the corner of her eye.

'I will have a pallet moved into another chamber.' Then, with a roll of his shoulders and a firm nod, he added, 'I will leave you. If you need anything, ask Efa.'

'Wait!' she said and he paused at the doorway. 'What do you expect of me?'

'Expect of you?' He turned, his frown deep with confusion. 'Nothing. Within the fortress walls you are free to go and do as you please, but you are not allowed past the inner gate.'

She nodded and it irritated her that she had to keep reminding him of it. 'I gave you my word. I only meant… what can I do? I do not like to be idle.'

'You do not have to work to justify your place here.'

Her breath caught in her throat.

Did he know that was what she feared, being a burden and a disappointment to those around her?

With false pleasantry, she replied, 'Then I will do as I please.'

For some reason she wanted to torment him. Maybe it was because his sympathy had stung her pride.

She strode towards the bed, turned and sat down upon it with a deliberate bounce, as if to check the firmness of the straw. She sank a little instead, realising it was stuffed with feathers and down.

Of course it was!

Brazenly she stared back at him and smoothed her hands over the soft blankets. Leaning back a little, she enjoyed the way his eyes flowed over the lines of her body, taking delight in teasing him, and testing his rigid control. 'How luxurious! I will enjoy sleeping in your bed, *my lord*.'

A muscle in his jaw flexed and his eyes were bright as he gave a curt nod. Then, turning on his heel, he strode from the room.

Helga flopped back on her back with a heavy sigh.

'That man is made of stone!' she grumbled to the empty room. She lay only for a short time, though, before deciding that she would rather be anywhere than in this soulless room.

Efa was busy in the kitchens, organising the food stores and preparing the evening meal, the serfs buzzing around her in a whirl of activity.

Helga offered her assistance and Efa welcomed her gladly. 'Thank you! I will definitely need your help with the evening meal, there's so much to do, and supplies are constantly arriving, both through the gate and over at the cargo pulley, I don't know which to bring in first, what we should use and what we should store. I am a little overwhelmed, to be honest!'

'It is a worrying time,' Helga said sympathetically.

Efa nodded sadly and it was as if a heavy cloud had settled over her, stealing the light from her eyes. 'I could not bear it if Cadair y Ddraig fell... I cannot go through it again...' Her voice broke, as if the words were too terrible to utter.

'You do not have to speak of it,' reassured Helga, placing a hand on her arm. 'But if you do wish to, then I will always listen.'

Efa sucked in a deep breath and closed her eyes. After a moment she seemed a little more composed and patted her hand gently. 'There is no need. The King will send aid and this fortress will not fall.'

'Why has your King not sent aid before now?' asked Helga curiously. 'Surely he was informed of the raids?'

Efa shook her head grimly. 'He fears our family's power... Always has. Rhys's parents were a love match, though many did not believe it at the time—including the

King. Tewdwr and my sister, Nest, were from two great houses. Tewdwr received this fortress and a settlement on the coast by marrying her, as well as his rightful share of land from his father, King Rhodri. Tewdwr wasn't a natural fighter, he had no desire to increase his share, or rival the King, and he and Nest were content to ignore politics and live a quiet life, encouraging learning and artisans instead. But when Rhys grew up and showed signs of becoming a skilled warrior and leader, the King grew concerned that their son had the will to do what they could not. He demanded Rhys swear loyalty to him at Anglesey and renounce any kinship as a Prince of Gwynedd.'

Understanding twisted like a knife. 'Was that when the Vikings invaded?'

Efa nodded, her eyes clouded with tears. 'Most of our family went to show our support of Rhys: parents, grandparents, my husband…but only he returned. Alswn—thank God—was here with me.

'Rhys was only a youth at the time, but he fought as well as any full-grown man. He was a hero that day, but it only seemed to worry the King further. He does not realise that Rhys is driven by duty and responsibility—not a lust for power like some men.' Her smile became bittersweet. 'Gwynedd binds me.'

At Helga's confused frown, she explained, 'It is an oath. One all the family swear by. To put the land first above all.'

Everything about Rhys's behaviour suddenly made sense.

'Please, do not think badly of him,' Efa continued. 'I know Rhys can seem blunt and inflexible at times. But it is only because he cares so much and is so afraid to do the wrong thing. Our family has suffered so much loss and *every* time he blames himself for it.'

Helga's pity for Rhys bloomed like a bruise on her heart. 'I understand…but surely the King won't risk another invasion?'

'No, but so far it has been small raiding parties. I suspect the King is hoping that Rhys will be weakened by such continuous assault and any ambitions for power curbed.'

'But…Ulf's army is on its way right now!' Helga cried in outrage.

'Rhys will have sent a messenger to the King, informing him of it. He will send help this time.' Efa slapped her hands together, as if dismissing the worry from both their minds. 'We must stand firm until aid arrives. In our case that will mean preparing the stores and a hearty meal for our returning men.'

Helga nodded. 'Then let us set to it!'

They worked well together and once the evening meal was fully prepared, they walked into the settlement and headed to the head seamstress's home so that Helga could be measured for new clothes.

Helga had been worried that she had been burdening the woman, but Efa had reassured her. 'Think nothing of it, as she said, she has a few shifts and gowns almost ready for me, and she can alter one to fit you before she makes the rest. Besides, you helped her aunt and young nephews. They were prisoners at Ulf's fortress. She considers it an honour to serve you.'

As they left the seamstress's home, Efa took her by the elbow and said, 'Come, let us go for a walk. There are two very important people you have yet to meet.'

Chapter Fifteen

Stepping out into the autumn air was blissful after so much work. The sky was clear, with a brisk wind coming in from the north. She could almost imagine nothing bad would ever happen.

But Ulf loomed in the distance and she had to wonder how her mother and Brynhild were managing. Had they found Alswn? Were they even now coming for her? Part of her felt ashamed that they had to save her. Did they curse their luck in having someone like her as a member of their family?

Someone who needed to be rescued…

Sighing, she pushed the dark thoughts from her mind. There was never any point in worrying over the future, she reminded herself. Her fate was set. She might not understand or know the path, but neither did anyone.

As she began to learn more about Rhys, she wondered if they would walk it together. Something about him called to her and it was more than just dreams now. She had begun to want him, even though it made no sense.

But in his mind, there was nothing between them. His childhood had not been filled with dreams of her, he had cast no fortunes to learn her name and he had already rejected her once…humiliatingly. So, she would not offer again.

As she and Efa walked through the log-lined walk-ways, many of the serfs and townsfolk smiled at them as they passed.

'See, the people are grateful to you, Helga.'

'But I did so little.'

Efa smiled. 'Helping people with kindness when they are at their lowest is always remembered.'

'Do they not hate me for being Norse?'

'Why should they? You have proven you are not like them.'

Efa's words did not comfort her. Helga was Norse and she was not ashamed of it.

At her silence, Efa continued, 'Has Rhys been harsh to you? You know…it is not about you really. He is worried, and he blames himself, for Alswn. But he shouldn't. She disappeared with Hywel, yes?' Something in the way Efa asked the question made Helga suspicious.

'They left together of their own accord. I have tried to tell Rhys this many times. My family are not to blame. Was there something between Hywel and Alswn? Is that why they left without telling anyone where they went?'

'I know nothing for certain,' Efa said quietly, a guilty look flitting across her face before she reined it in.

'If you suspect something, you must tell—'

Ignoring her words, Efa interrupted her by calling out to two bent figures up ahead. 'Aneurin! Tangwystl!' She picked up her pace and Helga struggled to keep up, de-ciding to question her later about the mystery of Hywel and Alswn's disappearance.

The two people Efa had called out to did not move forward to greet them. They merely stood from where they had been bent over some plants. That's when Helga noticed the garden around them.

Initially she would have thought it a wild meadow. But as they approached, she realised there was an order in the seemingly chaotic planting. Groupings of specific herbs and flowers that flourished in the full sun, while in the dappled shade of the woods she could see tumbles of rocks with moss-covered ledges and all manner of mushrooms. All grouped together in a way that would allow all to flourish and thrive. It was the chaos of nature, but not scattered far and wide as it would be normally. Instead, it had been carefully planned and cultivated with meticulous care.

The same, sadly, could not be said about the two people stood within it. Hunched with age and gnarled bones, the man and woman stared at them with deep frowns. They were the wildest and most unkempt creatures Helga had ever seen.

The woman—Tangwystl—spoke first, her voice as cracked and as splintered as a dried-out ship. Helga couldn't understand what she'd said, but it sounded sharp and full of disapproval.

Efa looked helplessly at her feet and then jumped a little to the side. This only caused another lash from Tangwystl's throat. Suspecting what the issue might be, Helga took Efa's elbow firmly and guided her friend to another patch of the meadow. 'I think you were standing on the mugwort.'

The man's gaze snapped to hers. 'The little Viking girl knows her herbs, then?' he said, speaking in the Norse tongue, but with a similar accent to those of Rhys and Efa.

'Your herb garden is beautiful and very well stocked. I would love to learn more about the plants you use. Perhaps we can exchange knowledge? My name is Helga Porundóttir.'

'Ha!' cackled Aneurin. 'As if a child like you could teach Tangwystl anything!'

The old woman spoke to him impatiently, then a heated exchange of words took place. Helga looked to Efa, who was trying her best not to laugh. Eventually Aneurin turned back to her to say, 'Tangwystl says you have the look of the Tylwyth Teg about you.' He tilted his head and squinted up at her. 'I suppose you do, with that golden hair and those strange pale eyes of yours. You good with flowers?'

Helga smiled. She had no idea what the Tylwyth Teg was, but she presumed it was some sort of elf, or spirit of the forest, because she had been described as such many times. 'I like plants and they seem to like me.'

Aneurin must have repeated this back to Tangwystl because the woman then reached for her, gripping her hand with surprising strength and tugging her over to where she was working. She handed her a pair of shears and pointed at the plants in front of them.

Helga looked at them and saw one herb full of seeds that needed harvesting. She clipped it and handed it to the old woman who nodded with approval before taking the cutting from her fingers, and flinging it into a nearby basket. Then, Tangwystl prodded at another plant and Helga frowned. 'No,' she said, shaking her head, 'you will want the flowers of that one, but not until the spring.' She used her free hand to demonstrate a flower blooming.

The old woman gave her a gum-filled smile and then snatched the shears back from her. Picking up her basket of cuttings, she waddled away, back towards the settlement buildings. Confused, Helga looked up at Efa and Aneurin.

The old man gave her a nod of approval. 'You are welcome here. Bring your knowledge with you...if you must,' he said, before he followed Tangwystl back home.

'Well, it looks as if you passed their test,' said Efa. 'Consider yourself lucky!'

'Is this the Aneurin that taught you both Norse?'

'Yes, Old Aneurin taught us many. Norse, Saxon, Latin. He has an ear for them, he says.'

'And Tangwystl—she is your wisewoman?'

'I suppose so. The priest puts up with her because she's lived here for so long. They both have. Old Aneurin was a travelling bard in Rhys's grandmother's time, you see. Then he met Tangwystl and came to live here.'

Helga smiled as she watched the old couple shuffle into a little round hut at the edge of the meadow. It was on the outskirts of the settlement buildings, a little detached from the others, but older, as if the other buildings had grown up around them, never daring to encroach too closely on the couple's home. 'How romantic! He left his life of travelling behind to live with his one true love.'

Efa snorted with laughter. 'True love? I have never really thought of them in that way. They have always been ancient and bad-humoured, even since I was a child.'

'Do they have any children?'

'No.' Efa shook her head. 'Which is a pity...for all their odd ways, they are always kind and patient to little ones.' They were almost at the hall now and Efa took Helga's arm, a cheerful smile on her lips.

'Maybe our clothes will be ready when we return? I am going to order a hot bath drawn.' She arched her back with a wince. 'I can feel your remedy beginning its work.'

'I could grab you some willow for the pain?' asked Helga with concern.

'Do not worry.' Efa smiled, squeezing her hand. 'And

thank you…for understanding and for giving me back my freedom and my future. I want to forget the past and move forward, and I could not have done that without your help. Now, enough talk of such things. Would you like to bathe? Rhys has a bathing tub, but he will not mind us using it.'

Helga squinted at the dipping sun. 'If my new shift and gown are ready, I will take them out to the waterfall to bathe. It is not full dark yet and I think I would prefer the freshness of the cold water. I have been inside for too long.'

Efa shivered with mock horror. 'Rather you than me! That water is freezing!'

Rhys watched at a distance as Efa and Helga walked into the hall. He turned and walked towards the waterfall instead.

He could not do it. Face her again so soon and act as if her presence did not affect him.

At this time of day, he knew the pool would be empty as water was collected first thing and bathing and washing of clothes were done at midday, when the sun was at its highest.

A wash in the freezing water would help him collect his thoughts before the evening meal, before he saw *her* again.

Since leaving her that morning, she had infiltrated and consumed his every thought. Her expressions, her arguments, and how she had *teased* him. The press of breasts against her gown as she leaned back in his bed. The way she had whispered that she *knew* him, as she held his hand. The softness of her touch as she washed his face and, worst of all, the brightness of her smile when she saw the man beneath.

It was enough to drive him mad and then a messenger had arrived from Porunn, pleading with him not to harm her daughter and informing him that they had no connection with Ulf, or his plans to wage war against Gwynedd. She wished to reassure him that she and Brynhild would do all in their power to ensure the safe return of Lady Alswn. They believed his sister and her guard had left of their own volition as lovers and were in no danger as far as they were aware.

Lies!

Why her mother had sent such a message he could not understand. It was so obviously false. Did her mother not care for her at all? It struck him as a delaying tactic, a way to keep Helga alive until Ulf broke through. And even if they did keep their word and brought Alswn to him, he wasn't sure if he could give her up. Not to people who did not value her as he did.

Rhys stripped off his clothes as he reached the clearing surrounding the waterfall.

The water came from the mountain's rocky peak and combined with rainwater to flow in a steady stream into this pool below, only ever freezing during particularly harsh winters.

The pool was deep and surrounded by black slate. It drained back into the mountain, only to come out again, further down. As a boy he had tried to search the bottom to find the secret entrance into the mountain. What he would have done with such knowledge still remained a mystery to him, although he suspected he would have enjoyed the personal triumph of finding it.

When had he last felt any pleasure in his accomplishments?

Even the destruction of Ulf's fort had felt like a hollow victory. Nothing satisfied him any more, because he knew yet another problem would await him around the next bend.

Were Alswn and Hywel even alive?

Should he not be lighting candles in the chapel for them, instead of hoping for a miracle? He hated not knowing.

His vision became blurry and he walked into the icy water without hesitation.

Chapter Sixteen

Helga wasn't alone. A pale shadow shimmered beneath the silver spray.

She'd heard the waterfall before she'd seen it, the coppice surrounding the slate pool sheltering it from view of the settlement, a pocket of tranquillity in an otherwise bustling fort. Thick, ancient trees crowded around the clearing, their trunks covered in dark green moss, their leaves heavily gilded with crimson and gold.

Her hand rested against the bark of a nearby oak and she sighed with disappointment, her basket hanging limply from her elbow. It was filled with her new clothes, a comb and a chunk of wood ash soap.

Would they be long? she wondered.

She was desperate to wash the days of travel from her skin and feel the bliss of fresh linens once again.

Just as she was about to return to the Hall, the pale figure moved through the shimmering curtain of water.

She sucked in a sharp breath. Even if she had not recognised the regal movement of his body, she could not miss the wide shoulders or long limbs as belonging to the Lord of Cadair y Ddraig.

Rhys's dark curls were heavy with water, but refused

to be restrained. They fell in his eyes, causing him to sweep them away. Tilting his head back into the spray, the water crashed over raised arms and splashed over his smooth chest.

Helga had felt those muscles against her back as they'd ridden together, but now she saw them in their full glory. He was slim and elegant in build, the strength of a warrior clearly defined in each ridge and sweep of his body.

Her eyes lowered curiously to below his waist. She wasn't disappointed by what she saw, but she could feel the heat of a blush on her cheeks and she looked up, feeling a little ashamed of herself…

Bright blue eyes met hers and she gulped down a gasp of shock at having been caught admiring him so openly.

There was no embarrassment in his expression. Calmly and deliberately ignoring her, he walked out of the spray and dived into the inky pool below, his body cutting the water like a blade and causing waves to lap against the pool's edge.

For a moment, she considered leaving, but his haughty and dismissive reaction to her presence only forced her feet forward, and in no time she was stood on the slate edge, looking down at the man below.

He frowned up at her, swimming to the edge of the pool where he was able to stand waist deep in the water.

'Be careful, the stone can be slippery. You wouldn't want to fall in,' he said coldly, although she saw the worry in his eyes as he studied the black rock beneath her feet. Then he looked up at her. 'You should go back to the fort.'

She slipped off her shoes, and stood barefoot upon the rock, placing her basket beside her. 'I came here to bathe.'

'Go back to the hall, I have a wooden tub you may use. The pool is too deep and dangerous—' He paused. 'On the boat… You said you could not swim.'

'I said, I could not swim *away*. Which was true, as where would I have gone?'

'Born of ash and elm, you said, not the sea.' He shook his head with a frown, his voice filled with dry humour as he sat on an underwater ledge and rested his back against the side of the pool, his arms draped casually over the edge of the rock.

'I let you presume I couldn't swim because I was worried you would never untie me and…the rope was beginning to hurt.' Embarrassed about her admission of weakness, she snapped, 'Are you leaving soon? I would like to wash before it gets dark.'

'I'm sorry, I never meant to hurt you.' She glanced up to meet his eyes and saw only regret within them. 'I was…distracted. So much had happened.' He sighed, tipping his head back against the stone and closing his eyes, tension clear in the lines of his brow and jaw.

'I forgive you,' she said lightly. She sat down on the ledge and dangled her feet in the cool water. It wasn't as bad as she'd thought it would be. Cold, but refreshing. 'Has something happened? You seem worried.'

He smiled softly, opening his eyes to regard her thoughtfully. 'No more than usual.' Before she could reply he said, 'It will be dark very soon. You should go back now. The path can be deadly for those who do not know it well.'

She frowned, considering for a moment whether she should heed his warning. Then on a wild impulse she shook her head and pushed away from the rock, leaping out and into the water.

She'd braced herself against the cold, but the playful dip with her feet hadn't prepared her. An icy blanket wrapped around her and she had to force herself not to gasp. Breaking the surface, she inhaled a shattered breath and then laughed.

The weight of her apron dress and shift was dragging her down, but she managed to tread water enough to keep her head and shoulders above the surface. Rhys had moved forward in alarm.

'Did you mean to do that?'

The bewilderment on his face made her giggle even more. 'Yes! I won't miss another opportunity to bathe in nature and you can lead me back. Although, I probably should have removed this first!'

The woollen apron was pulling at her and she began to struggle with the ties.

'Christ's toes, woman!' snapped Rhys, ploughing forward into the water and lifting her by the waist to place her on the ledge he'd previously been sitting on.

Their bodies were close, his hands not budging from her sides as he stood before her, waist deep in water. A light steam rose from his torso and into the cool night air.

She shivered, but not from the cold. Unable to help herself, she slipped her hands around his neck, fingering the soft curls at his nape. Their eyes locked and she lightly pulled him closer. There was a moment when she thought he might pull away and she held her breath, stopping before their lips could meet.

'I will not beg,' she whispered. 'You either want me, or you do not.'

'I want you,' he confessed. 'But I should not…'

'You worry too much,' she teased, although there was a painful certainty behind his words, and so she added, 'I am not your enemy.'

He closed his eyes, his arms tightening possessively on her waist, as if unwilling to let go. 'I know,' he said, his voice husky and filled with torment. 'You are so beautiful. I am not worthy of you.'

'Let me decide that for myself.' She pressed a light kiss against his mouth, then eased back, waiting for his response. He opened his eyes and stared at her with a hunger that caused a shiver of longing to run down her spine.

In the dimming light, it felt as if they were alone in the world, the rustle of leaves and the crash of the waterfall the only things keeping them company.

He took another step closer and she widened her legs to allow him to step between them. His hands smoothed down her hips and thighs to rest lightly on her knees beneath the water.

She gasped as his fingers gripped them and he kissed her.

His tongue tasted her, gently, almost hesitantly, as if he expected her to reject him, even now. Her fingers threaded through his hair and her spine arched like a bow, desperately wanting more of him, and his kisses deepened.

Feverish despite the chill of the water, Helga's heart raced and she gasped for air beneath his increasingly urgent kisses. Her face and neck felt hot and she fumbled with the ties on her apron and shift, eager to get rid of the barriers between them because, more than anything, she wanted to feel the roll of his muscles beneath her fingertips and the strength of his desire.

She tugged both layers down to her hips, not caring when she heard seams rip. Wrapping her arms around his shoulders, she pulled him into her, her hands roaming all over him, demanding more. In response, he pulled her closer. Her breasts crushed against him and they both moaned with pleasure, intoxicated by their passion for one another.

Rhys began to trail kisses down her face and neck, his hand moving to cup her breast. She squirmed in her seat, her legs hooked around his hips, the fabric of her gown swirling around them.

Then he stilled, and his shoulders tensed. 'What is that?' he gasped, his chest heaving with exertion as his bright eyes flicked to hers.

Drunk on her passion for him, she stared down at her body, confused. Then his thumb brushed over the blue ink above her heart, as if he were checking it were real.

'A tattoo,' she said, realising now what had unsettled him.

'It's...' He stared in awe and horror at the symbol branded to her skin.

'Your dragon,' she answered for him. 'I drew it everywhere. In the end, my mother offered to tattoo it on my heart.'

Rhys stepped back and the cold of the water began to seep into her bones as the passion between them seemed to fade, as if it were a fire and someone had thrown a buck of cold water of it.

'I cannot deny that I want you,' he said grimly, as if he found the words bitter. 'But I think it would be better if we go no further...'

Shame and humiliation crept through her slowly as if the pool had begun to freeze around her. He thought her prophecy foolish, her visions the wild imagination of a silly girl. Her family probably thought the same and only indulged her because they loved her. After all, she wasn't good enough to join them in the shield wall.

Rhys was still talking, but she barely listened, praying that the pool would crack open and pull her down into the darkness.

'I do not mean to insult you, Helga. You are a beautiful and kind woman. But it is wrong of me to take advantage of your beliefs… We must both want each other for the right reasons and I am sure I will only disappoint you later on. We are very different, you and I, both in temperament and in upbringing. It would be a mistake to begin something that could never end well.'

There was no colour in the sky now, only the white stars and thumbnail moon saw them, and she hoped he could not see the tears in her eyes. She gathered the wet fabric around her and stood.

She clambered up the rock to her basket with wide steps, water falling from her in streams and splashing against the slate.

She refused to cry in front of him and focused on dressing herself in her new clothes, bitter that the pleasure she'd previously anticipated in wearing fresh linen now felt hollow and stupid. She hadn't even washed with soap or combed her hair. He'd even stolen that joy from her.

She spat her fury like arrows. 'Do not worry, *Lord* Rhys. I am not so *pathetic* to hold this *mistake* against you. Have no fear, I will *never* humiliate myself like this again. Even if you begged me on your knees!'

He rose from the water and she concentrated on packing her basket, thrusting the wet clothing in and not even bothering to wring out the water first.

'I am truly sorry,' Rhys said quietly. 'I should never—'

'Fine!' she snapped breezily, hoping that indifference would be a more dignified retreat than anger, which at this moment only made her want to scream and wail at him. 'In fact, let us pretend this never happened at all.'

She lifted her basket, silently cursing the sopping

weight of it, and was about to walk away when he called out to her.

'Wait for me…please. I do not want you to trip in the darkness.'

It is too late, she thought miserably. *I have already fallen.*

Chapter Seventeen

The next morning Helga found the hall in better order than the day before, so rather than spending her time inside, she decided to go to the wild garden to restock the herbs in the pantry instead.

She needed to be in nature if she was going to forget the terrible embarrassment she'd had with Rhys the night before. Apart from the obvious heartache and humiliation, she'd also been left deeply frustrated. The passion between them had been overwhelming and she'd spent a fretful night screaming into the feather pillows of Rhys's bed in frustration, wondering why she had the misfortune of falling in love with one of the few men wedded to their honour.

Love. Bitterness coated her tongue just thinking of that word. How stupid she had been to long for it! It was a brand on her heart that burned brighter with every passing day.

At least she wasn't fully alone in her torment. No matter what he said, he could not wash away the heat of his kiss. She had not imagined his desire; it had rolled off him in waves, growing stronger with every touch.

Maybe he just needed more time? It was a comforting

thought, if a little frustrating, and she swore she would not forgive him easily. His rejection had stung bitterly and had needled at the old wounds she carried; That she was never good enough, too odd and weak to be of any real use.

Her Aunt Freydis had once said, *'The dandelion offers us a lesson. Its seeds are as light as feathers and its flowers just as fragile. It is bare of thorns, yet its roots run deep. If it is pulled or plucked it returns again and again. Be like the dandelion, remember your roots and you will always return.'*

Helga sighed, taking comfort in her aunt's words. Even when no one else believed in her, she had to believe in herself. If she and Rhys were fated to be together, then they would be—she had only to be patient. If not, then the true meaning of the vision would eventually reveal itself.

Better to fill her days with labour to keep her mind and hands busy, she decided, and she would prefer to do that outside before the weather turned and forced her inside. She could offer Tangwystl and Aneurin some of the seeds from the Abbot's garden. Maybe then she could take some cuttings of their rare plants with her when she left?

If she left.

As she weaved her way through the meadow she leaned into her feelings, exploring what they could possibly mean. It was something she had done regularly in the past, when she was unsure of the message her intuition was trying to give her.

Will I never leave here?

She looked to the trees and some of the browning leaves fell. They did not catch the wind, but fluttered lazily to the tree's roots.

Is this my new home, or will I die here?

The winds stayed silent, but then, she'd asked too

much. Fate did not appreciate being hounded for its secrets. If it were to be her new home, then wouldn't a death
here be inevitable?

Helga did not fear death, she saw how natural and useful it could be. How life always slept through the cold
winter and returned in the spring. Death would be another adventure for her—one she hoped not to experience
for some time—but that was not her decision to make.

Instead, she feared an empty life, like that of the
dragon beneath the mountain. She did not want to sleep
through her days alone and unloved. She wanted to feel
the full warmth of the sun on her skin and experience
all that life had to offer.

Spending the rest of her days here would not be a hardship as long as she was loved and valued.

Cadair y Ddraig would make a lovely home, the land
rich and wild, but with enough people to suit her temperament. She liked to talk to people, to make friends and
build a community. She had done it in every place her
family had lived, not only to ease her loneliness while
her mother and sisters trained for battle, but also because
camp life depended on sharing skills and resources.

If Helga were to thrive here, she had to first tackle
her greatest obstacle—language. Thankfully, Efa had
given her the key to conquering it. Old Aneurin could
be her teacher and in exchange she would help with the
harder labour of the gardens, or anything else he needed
doing. It would be a good trade, she decided, and as she
approached the old couple, she hoped they felt the same.

All of the harvest and serfs were now safely within
Rhys's walls. It should have been a relief but now he felt
imprisoned in his own home.

It had been two nights since that evening at the waterfall and he'd spent his time down at the farm, ensuring he was far from Helga and the temptation of her in his bed.

His decision to leave had had the unexpected benefit of allowing him to get to know Harald and the rest of the captured Norse men better. Something he really should have done before now if he were honest with himself.

Helga had been right—they were willing to swear under his banner and were led by a desire for land and wealth. They had no loyalty to Ulf, whom they viewed as a dangerous and petty jarl, one they had followed only for the promise of land.

Harald was charming and clever, but there was a strength of character behind his easy smiles that reflected the man's ability to lead and command men in battle. Rhys had watched him interacting with his brothers, ordering them with a lightness that was only possible through mutual loyalty and respect.

Harald was driven by the need to protect and look after them and that was admirable. He had already offered to teach Rhys's men how to defend against the infamous shield wall, in return for better treatment for his brothers. And there was definitely a greater understanding between them now that Rhys was able to think clearly without his hatred of their heritage prodding him like an angry bear.

That did not mean Rhys trusted Harald and his brothers. But at least he no longer feared them behind his walls. If he had to separate them from the youngest, Egil, to ensure that, then he would, although for some reason that made him far more uncomfortable than it should.

Rhys entered the fort with them on foot, the horses heavily packed with supplies, grain and fruit. Soon they would separate as the guards were leading the brothers towards the waterfall. Each man carried a fresh bundle of clothing and a chunk of soap. He would see how well this kinder treatment encouraged them.

Gwenllian had wrapped linen around the men's wounds, cushioning the shackles and stopping them from rubbing any further. Tonight, they would sleep in one of the barns. Their guards would remain, but he was still undecided about the shackles. There was a limit to his trust.

He noticed Harald's eyes roaming the fortress walls. 'Something of interest to you, Harald?' asked Rhys dryly, already sensing what the man had noticed.

'There are not enough men, my lord,' Harald answered directly, although he kept his voice low.

'It will be enough until we receive reinforcements.'

'Hmmm,' murmured Harald and he tilted his head thoughtfully, before shrugging. 'I suppose it will have to be. Either way, you should free us of these shackles, we can—'

Something caught the man's eye, cutting him off mid-sentence. Harald's jaw became slack, his eyes widened and he inhaled sharply, as if he'd previously forgotten how to breathe. It was the first time Rhys had ever seen the man appear shocked by anything.

Curious to see what had captured Harald's interest, Rhys followed his gaze, only to have his own breath catch—although, he suspected, a different person had caught the man's attention, for he had met Helga before.

Efa and Helga were walking back from Tangwystl's gardens, their arms overflowing with herbs and flowers. Efa's head was thrown back as she laughed merrily at something Helga was saying and the veil on her head was slightly askew, some of her ebony curls falling out from beneath the cloth and bouncing around her face.

Normally it would have warmed his heart to see Efa so happy as she had had so few pleasures in her life, especially recently, but turning back to Harald he knew what the man's awestruck expression meant—he knew because he'd felt the same when he'd first seen Helga.

'Do not even *dare* to dream,' he growled, leaning in so that the women would not hear his threat as they approached. He would not spoil their happiness even to reprimand the arrogance of a Norseman and, oddly, he'd felt something akin to relief when he'd realised the man's infatuation was definitely aimed at Efa and not Helga.

What that said about his own weakness was troubling, to say the least.

'Keep moving!' snapped Rhys, shoving Harald forward. The man stumbled a few steps before he righted his balance and walked on, his stare not faltering once from Efa's face, like a man spellbound. As she passed, Efa finally noticed him, her amusement fading as she frowned at Harald's intrusive attention. Dismissing him with a disdainful wrinkle of her nose she looked away and Harald—the lunatic that he was—*chuckled*!

'Keep away from them,' Rhys warned Efa, concerned that she would become frightened by Harald if he continued to make cow's eyes at her.

Efa's spine stiffened with irritation. 'You do not have to remind me, *Nephew*. I am well aware of what they are capable of!' she replied curtly. She always called him *nephew* when she thought him too overbearing and it pleased him to see the old defiance spark in her eyes once again. He'd been worried something had died in her after her imprisonment, but now he could see her stubborn nature returning, bruised but not broken.

Helga cleared her throat and Efa blushed with horror as she realised the insult she'd given her friend. 'I am sorry, Helga, I did not mean…'

Helga shrugged. 'You have good reason. Do not be sorry.'

Rhys's irritation caused the back of his neck to itch and he scratched it with a scowl.

Why did she forgive Efa for saying such things and admonish him so soundly when he did the same?

Immediately he felt like a maggot—it was because Efa had suffered far more than he could ever imagine. He should ask Helga if she would mind teaching Efa how to defend herself—she might feel a little braver if she had those skills. Then again, maybe he should leave that to Efa to decide...

As if she were shaking off her earlier discomfort, Efa brightened and prodded Helga forward. 'Practise on him.'

Helga looked a little uncertain, but then said, 'My name is Helga. Did you have a good day?'

'What?' he asked, confused at first by the introduction and question until he realised, she was speaking Welsh—with an infuriatingly perfect Gwynedd accent, he might add.

'Forgive me,' she continued. 'Your tongue still feels strange in my mouth... But I am learning.'

Efa giggled at her phrasing and Helga looked adorably uncertain.

'Language,' he corrected, gulping down the lump that had formed in his throat at her innocent words. 'You speak it well.'

'"Language",' she repeated, smiling brightly. She switched to Norse. 'I am a quick learner, but I am afraid I have not learned much more than that.'

His stomach clenched and he felt a desperate need to be anywhere but here, in front of Helga and his aunt discussing tongues.

'Pah!' Efa flicked her wrist dismissively, 'You have

learned a great deal! You'll be fluent by the time your family come for you.'

Helga grinned with delight and a hollow pain ached inside him. His short time away from Helga had done nothing but carve an even deeper hole in his heart. 'I have duties to fulfil. I will see you at the evening meal.'

Rhys walked away as fast as his long legs could carry him, hoping his cowardice would go unnoticed.

Chapter Eighteen

After another long day of learning and gardening with Aneurin and Tangwystl, Helga was pleasantly surprised to see Harald sit down at one of the feasting tables with his brothers when she arrived for the evening meal.

When he reached for the jug of ale, she saw that his shackles were gone and she couldn't help but smile at the sight. It seemed that Rhys had relented. *Was this another example of his hard heart softening?*

Harald and his brothers wore clean tunics and trousers in the tighter-fitting Welsh style. It cheered her to see it, but then she noticed something a little strange.

'Where is Egil?' she asked, frowning. She could not see the youth along the bench or even in the hall for that matter.

Harald held up his bare wrists, still marked by his previous shackles, but healing well. 'It is a condition of our release. One of us is to be kept prisoner at all times.'

'What?' cried Helga, horrified.

Harald's expression softened. 'It is fine, Helga. I agreed to it and we shall each take our turn. If the people here trust us more for it, than it is a good thing. We are sick of being chained like dogs.'

'But where is he? I should check on him, ensure he is being well treated.'

'I do not know. But I have been assured of his welfare.'

'But poor Egil…he's so young—'

Harald's voice was gentle, but firm. 'The deal is done. There is no need for you to worry over it. Every month one of us will take our turn, youngest to eldest, and if it makes these people more accepting of us, then I am glad of it. Maybe there is a future for us here.'

'Do not worry, fair lady. Egil could do with a rest.' Sten laughed.

'Our brother is not used to hard work.' Raising his arm, Harald flexed it and gave it a sharp slap. 'He doesn't have our muscles yet.'

His brothers all chuckled in agreement, but Harald's attention suddenly shifted elsewhere.

'We all know what keeps your arm strong, Brother!' sniggered Toke.

Toke yelped loudly as if someone had stamped on his foot and all eyes turned towards them, including Efa's. She had just entered from her chamber.

'Who is she?' asked Harald, his focus unwavering, even as Efa deliberately ignored him and walked towards the high table set out on the dais behind them.

'Her name is Efa. She is Rhys's aunt and I consider her a friend,' Helga warned tartly.

'Please introduce us,' Harald urged quietly, and at Helga's silence, he whispered, 'Be assured, my intentions are honourable. I would never harm your friend.'

Efa was passing them now and with a sigh Helga turned to her. 'Efa, have you met Harald Olafson?'

'I know who he is.' Efa paused and gave the man an aloof nod, so unlike the woman she'd come to know. 'Helga, come join me at the high table.'

To his credit, Harald ignored the dismissive tone and stood, covering his heart with his fist as he bowed politely. 'My Lady Efa, it is an honour to meet you.'

'I see. Are you coming, Helga?' Efa asked curtly, ignoring Harald completely.

'Will Rhys mind? I know you insisted when he wasn't here, but now that he is back…'

'I am the mistress here and you are welcome at my table,' Efa replied and Helga was once more startled by her friend's sudden coldness. It could only be because of the Norse man's presence.

'Then I will come shortly. I need to change first.' She pointed at her old apron dress and shift. Not wanting to damage her new clothes, she had taken to wearing her old ones while working in the garden.

Efa nodded and walked away without a backwards glance.

'Is she married?'

Helga stared at Harald, wondering if the man's mind was a little loose. 'She is a widow. But I do not think she is interested in remarrying.'

He snorted, as if that idea were unthinkable. 'A beauty like her? It would be a waste.'

Helga frowned. 'Not to her, I think.'

'Any children?'

'You are wearing my patience, Harald. What difference would it make if she did?'

He smiled. 'None. I wish only to know her better.'

The hall was beginning to fill, the smell of food signalling it was almost ready to be served. 'I must go and change, but understand this…' She thudded his chest with her finger and he laughed. 'Efa has already become a dear friend to me… She was a captive at Ulf's fort for several months and will not look kindly towards you.'

The blood drained from Harald's face and his brothers all seemed to pause in their conversations. 'She was a captive under Sven?'

Helga nodded, then asked stonily, 'Does that change your view of her?'

Harald looked her straight in the eyes. 'Yes.'

Her stomach dropped with disappointment; she had thought better of the man.

'Because...' he explained softly, 'she must be very strong and clever to have survived her time there. Thank you for telling me. I will be sure to be respectful in my courtship.'

'Hmmm.' She huffed, unsure whether to cheer or scold him for his arrogant answer. 'Well, I must go, but know this—you will have to answer to me if you upset her in any way.'

Harald smiled and sat back down on his bench with a nod. 'Understood.'

When Helga returned to the hall, the evening meal was already served on steaming trenchers and everyone was eating heartily. Rhys had been hunting and working the fields hard, so there was plenty to eat. A stag had been roasted and stewed. There was salted pork skewers, stewed plums and apples spiced with nutmeg. Braised cabbage with onions, and sausages stuffed with leeks and herbs. Bread was laid out on steaming platters straight from the oven and the ale flowed.

'It is a feast!' Helga said cheerfully as she sat at a stool beside Efa on the high table. Rhys's throne sat empty in the centre, with Efa on one side of it and Madoc on the other.

Efa nodded. 'It will be our last for a while. But Rhys thought it best to remind our men what they are fighting for. It might keep their spirits up in the weeks and months to come.'

Helga's cheerfulness dampened a little at that information. 'Oh, I see.' It was another reminder of the precarious position they were in and Efa patted her hand with a sympathetic smile.

Rhys entered the hall then and her thoughts were immediately silenced by the weight of his presence. It felt as if his eyes sought her out straight away and her body reacted with a low thrum of awareness, as if he were playing her like a lyre.

He strode towards the dais, stopping to speak with Harald, who then followed him as he headed towards the high table.

'Why is he letting *that man* come sit with us?' snapped Efa, her earlier frostiness returning.

'I expect he wishes to discuss tactics with him, my lady,' answered Madoc. 'Harald has proven quite useful in that regard.'

Rhys took his seat in the centre, Harald joining at Madoc's side.

Efa turned to Rhys. 'Surely Helga could help you with tactics. She is a shieldmaiden, after all, and she, at least, has proven herself trustworthy.'

If Harald was insulted by such a remark, he did not show it.

Helga shrugged. 'I could, although my skills are with a bow and managing a camp's retreat. In battle, I'm afraid I would be the weak point in a shield wall.'

Efa seemed to take offence to her words. 'You are not weak, Helga.'

'No,' she agreed, 'But I know where my strengths lie and, much to my mother's dismay, it was never with sword and shield.'

'Good archers can turn the tide of battle. Do you have any advice you could give my archers, Helga?' asked

Rhys, looking her in the eye as he took a sip of his ale, and her heart melted like honey comb in the summer sun at the display of trust and respect he had just shown her. Porunn had never asked her advice in warfare and neither had her sisters. But Rhys had and she could tell by his expectant gaze that he meant it.

'I suppose I could speak with them…if you wished?'

'I would appreciate it. I will ask the archery master to speak with you.'

She nodded dumbly.

Rhys stood and made a short speech in Welsh to the hall, which she could only half follow. He spoke of defending their freedom and homeland, and everyone present from serf to warrior cheered at the end, raising their cups high in salute to their master.

If the feast was to encourage morale, it had certainly worked. The drinking and eating began in earnest, with loud chatter and laughter filling the air.

They discussed defence plans and possible strategies. Helga's surprise turned to shock as Rhys continued to ask and listen to her advice and she quickly realised she knew far more than she thought she did about warfare. She supposed living with her mother and sisters had taught her a lot without her realising. Confidence began to stretch and grow within her, taking root and replacing her earlier doubt.

A quick moving shadow above Helga's head caught her eye and she watched in astonishment as two ravens landed on the head of Rhys's chair.

Rhys glanced up at them with an amused smile. But Madoc jumped to his feet and shooed them away with a flick of a cloth.

'No!' cried Helga, but she needn't have worried. The two birds flapped their wings with a shriek and flew safely to the roof. It looked as if they had made their home high up in the rafters.

'We need more cats, Rhys.' Efa sighed. 'Soon, we will have a whole flock of them up there, dropping their mess down on our heads!'

'But don't you see?' Helga laughed, her excitement making her want to dance across the table. 'It is a good sign!' Her confidence bloomed and she felt as if the birds had delivered her courage to her. The old belief in herself—the one that had been shaken repeatedly—had returned. The black dragon had not been as she'd expected him to be, but how many times had she reassured others that the twists in life were part of the joy of living? She should take her own advice. Trust in her instincts and not in her presumptions.

'Yes.' Harald nodded sagely. 'Huginn and Muninn are Odin's ravens. A pair of ravens making home in your hall can mean only one thing. You will be victorious in the battles ahead.'

Rhys frowned. 'We are Christians here.'

Helga leaned forward, urging Rhys to trust her. 'It is still a good sign. I am sure of it. Leave the birds be— what harm can they do?'

'I would listen to Helga if I were you. Women can see the unseen and it is always wise to heed them,' warned Harald quietly.

'Then they shall stay,' declared Rhys, 'Even if it does mean I end up with mess on my head.'

Efa and Helga laughed and everyone returned to their meal.

Later there was poetry, songs and games. But eventually the revelry began to tire and people started making their way back to their homes and beds.

Harald was entertaining them with one of the sagas. When the story came to an end Efa smiled and Harald's eyes sparkled with triumph at the small concession.

'I am exhausted,' Efa said with a sigh. 'But I really did enjoy your tale, Harald. Your gods sound a mischievous lot. They remind me a little of the old Celtic gods. Do you not agree, Rhys?'

He nodded. 'A little.'

Efa rose and waved the men down when they tried to respectfully rise for her. All men except Harald sat back down. 'I shall bid you all a goodnight.'

As Efa passed him, he gave a short bow similar to the one he'd given her earlier, his hand to his chest. 'Sweet dreams, my lady.'

Helga grinned at the way Efa rolled her eyes as she walked away, but there was definitely more amusement in her countenance and a lightness to her step that hadn't been there previously.

Helga decided to take a chance and leaned towards Rhys. As if he sensed her every movement, he turned to look at her expectantly.

'My lord, may I speak privately with you in your chambers before I, too, retire?'

Rhys's eyes widened, but he nodded and gestured for her to lead the way.

A serf had kindly lit the fire and the room was painted in a golden glow that reflected off the polished wood. She'd not dared to move anything in the room or look at what was beneath the cloths. But she had placed a tray of plants by the shutters and a jug of autumn flowers sat on the table.

'Well?'

'I want to know about Egil,' she said, ignoring the way

he stood with his arms folded across his chest, already creating a wall between them.

Did he fear she was about to seduce him? Her skin prickled with offence.

'Egil is playing dice with Old Aneurin and enjoying his fair share of the feast. Did Harald ask you to speak with me?'

'No.'

'Then be reassured he is safe and well.'

'He is their youngest brother, barely a man. How can you separate him from them? He relies on his brothers.'

'Which is precisely why he was chosen.'

'How can you be so callous?' she snapped, her fists clenched tightly at her side. To think she'd thought him changed by her words!

Rhys's voice snapped like a whip. 'Callous? I am offering them yet another kindness and you dare to criticise me for it?' He stepped closer and she raised her chin to glare back at him, the room suddenly hot despite the breeze from the open shutter. 'Egil will not have to fight on the walls—did you think of that? He will be safely guarded and far from trouble when Ulf arrives. Harald and his brothers will fight better because of it. They will not have to worry about guarding his back and will do as I ask to ensure his continued protection.'

The wind in her anger disappeared and she was cast adrift. 'But Harald said you would change them each month. Why make such a stipulation if—?'

Rhys's expression softened. 'For his brother's pride. Do you think a young warrior would accept captivity willingly, especially if he thought it was only done for his own protection?'

She shook her head, her arguments and outrage falling limply from her fingers as she realised what Rhys had done and why. In one month, the fortress would either be defeated, or it would have stood firm. If they survived, he would know he could trust Harald and his brothers. If not, it didn't matter either way.

'Rhys...I didn't realise... I'm s—'

'No,' Rhys interrupted before she could apologise, pressing a finger to her lips. Then, as if remembering himself, his hand dropped and colour rose in his high cheekbones. 'There is no need to say sorry. Not to me. If you wish it, ask Madoc and he will take you to see him. I only ask that you swear not to tell Harald where he is being kept.'

Humbled by his trust in her, she nodded, 'I swear it.' Her lips still tingled from where he'd pressed his finger and she wet the spot with the tip of her tongue, longing to taste him once more.

Rhys's eyes dropped to the movement and darkened in the firelight.

'Goodnight, Helga,' he said, then he was gone.

Chapter Nineteen

The next day, the weather changed for the worst and Helga decided to work in one of the storerooms, drying and sorting herbs.

Her peaceful work was interrupted by a furious Efa, who stormed into the room with a cluster of bell heather in her fist. The flowers were wilting a little, but still a pretty shade of purple, and she could well imagine why Efa looked so angry.

'Did Harald give you those?' Helga asked, rubbing the ache in the back of her neck.

'Yes, the man is infuriating!'

Helga smiled, holding her tongue from pointing out that Efa had still accepted them.

'And you will never guess what he did with them!' Efa spluttered.

'Tapped them against your cheek?' Helga asked mildly and Efa's eyes widened.

'How did you know?'

'Because they are purple.'

Efa frowned down at the handful of wild flowers with their bell-shaped petals. 'Why should that matter?'

Helga chuckled to herself. 'It is an old Norse tradition.

Quite sweet really, although, if he'd asked me, I could have found better flowers than those for him.'

Efa gave her a stern look. 'Explain about them and *quickly*—before I decide to hit *you* with them. I swear, it won't be a gentle stroke like the one Harald gave me!'

'A gentle stroke?' Helga asked, raising an eyebrow, which caused Efa to smack her arm with the flowers anyway.

'Tell me!'

Laughing, Helga answered. 'The goddess of love, Freya, loves flowers. She uses them as keys to her hall. They unlock secrets, like…how a woman might truly feel about a man. Harald wishes to unlock your secrets.'

Efa paled as all the amusement left her face.

Concerned, Helga reached for her. 'It is a courtship tradition, nothing more, do not be afraid.'

'I am not.' She tossed the flowers on a nearby table.

Placing a hand on her friend's shoulder, Helga said gently, 'You are not ready for such things. That is understandable.'

Efa's eyes moved to hers and there was raw pain behind them. 'I fear I will never be ready.'

'I will speak with Harald.'

Efa's shoulders relaxed and she gave a little nod. 'Thank you.'

As she wasn't working in the garden that day, Helga wore one of her new gowns. This one was a rich blue with an exquisite band of embroidery at the neckline and wrists.

It was fit for royalty. She had almost returned it, fearing some mistake, but Efa had insisted she wear it, saying, 'They are yours, made for you under Rhys's orders. You cannot return them without insulting the seamstress who made them.' She had to admit that she loved it. Loved quite a lot about this place, its people, and its master.

She had not expected to see Rhys until the evening meal, and possibly not even then, by the way he recently took pains to avoid her—eating early and spending much of his time away from anywhere that she worked. So, she was more than a little startled when he walked into the storeroom, his hair and cloak damp with rain.

'Come, Helga. There is something you need to see,' he growled without any introduction. Maybe she should hit *him* with the flowers to unlock his secrets?

'Hello to you, too, *Nephew*,' Efa said dryly and with enough censure that Rhys dipped his head in a respectful greeting.

'Good day, Efa. We won't be long.'

'Take your time,' Efa said breezily. 'But, if you are going outside, she will need her cloak.'

'Be quick,' he said to Helga, and—if only to be contrary—she walked leisurely towards the door.

'You will not want to miss them,' he warned and, with her curiosity piqued, Helga hurried from the room.

Rhys turned to follow Helga out of the door, but was stopped by Efa's despondent sigh. When he looked back at her, he could see she was staring at an ugly bunch of flowers in front of her.

'Efa?' he questioned, stepping forward with concern.

'I am the last person who should criticise you for this…but why do you do it? Push them away?'

'What?' He blinked, unsure of what she was talking about. However, he had an uneasy feeling that he wouldn't like the answer.

Brushing the flowers into a nearby rubbish pail with a sweep of her hand, Efa said, 'I see the way you look at Helga—like a man dying of thirst—and yet you have avoided her the last two days.'

'I had preparations to make—we are about to be attacked!' he snapped and Efa's eyes bore into him even harder.

'That is an excuse. Not that my opinion holds any sway with you, but I think Helga would make a good match.'

His jaw clenched so tightly, he was sure he was about to break a tooth. 'She is my hostage!'

She waved it away as if it were nothing. 'Nonsense. She is our guest and I'm sure she would forgive you for stealing her away—if you apologised properly.' Efa rested her hands on her hips in the same way she always did when she wished to give him an earful of her advice.

'I tell you this as someone who loves you. Court Helga, before it is too late! You are not married and most likely never will be if the King has his way. In fact, he may even approve of such a match—to have a foreigner as your bride would weaken your strength at court. *If* she were to agree to have you, that is. But since your behaviour is as inconsistent as mountain weather, I fear she will not!'

Reminding himself that Efa meant well, he said gently, 'I have known for a long time that I may never marry. The King seems content for our family line to fade or disappear. I presumed Alswn's children—when she had them—would inherit. The family name would end with me.'

'And you would accept that, a life *alone*?' Efa asked, horrified. 'I had thought you were only waiting until you were older and things were more settled...'

'If it protects our people from the King's ungrounded fears, then I will do so gladly. It may even be for the best for everyone... Besides, Helga will be returned to her family soon. God willing, Alswn will also return. It is better if *all of us* do not become too attached to her while she is here.'

'Too attached?' Efa's eyes softened with pity and she shook head. 'Rhys, keeping your distance does not make it easier when they leave. They just wonder what they have done wrong… You pushed Alswn away, too, you know. She only ever wanted to make you proud.'

Guilt squeezed his chest tight. He opened his mouth to deny it, but found he had no words to defend himself with. He *had* always kept Alswn at arm's length, knowing that through marriage she would have to leave him eventually and he'd hardened his heart against it, preparing himself for the inevitable loss. He'd not thought anyone had noticed him doing it.

Had Alswn?

So many of the people he had loved were gone and each time he felt as if a part of him was disappearing, too. If he gave his heart to Helga and she left…would anything remain?

He noticed Helga at the doorway, a cloak around her shoulders and a flush on her cheeks.

How long had she been there?

'I am ready,' she said.

They ran through the woodland towards the boundary wall, their cloaks pulled up and over their heads as rain poured from the pewter sky.

There was a storm in the air and Helga's stomach churned with apprehension.

The boundary of the inner wall was still high at this point in the defences, but the cliff edge and water below served as more than enough deterrent against attack at this point in the palisade. The guard tower was higher than most of the ones she'd seen and it took a while for them to climb its stairs.

'Is someone climbing the mountain? Is it Ulf?' gasped

Helga, as her mind hopped from one thought to another. 'Is he coming by river?'

'No, he will come by land.'

'Then who?'

At the top of the stairs, he turned to her, a grim expression on his face. 'I think it is your sister.'

'Brynhild?' Excitement burst from her throat with a squeal and she pushed past him to the look-out tower's viewing platform.

'Let Old Aneurin and Tangwystl know they might be needed at the gates tonight,' Rhys said to the guard on duty and Helga was pleased with how much she understood—her Welsh was improving.

'The weather is turning. They might not risk the climb in the dark,' replied the man.

'True, but have them ready to translate regardless.'

With a nod the guard left and Rhys came to stand beside her.

'Where are they?' she asked almost breathless, 'I cannot see them. Brynhild will hate this weather!'

'There,' said Rhys, pointing out two figures on horseback far down the valley, trudging against the wind and along the shingle of the lake, the rain pouring down on their hunched backs. They looked no bigger than ants from this vantage point.

'I can't be sure if it's her,' Helga said, squinting at the two dots on the landscape.

'I believe it is,' said Rhys frostily. 'But where is my sister? Both figures are too big to be her, so it must be Brynhild and Erik travelling alone.'

Now she understood the reason for his resentment and she could understand it. He was worried for his sister.

'Maybe my mother has found Lady Alswn and they are merely delivering the news?' she offered.

'Possibly,' replied Rhys, although he did not seem convinced and neither was she. If Brynhild came empty-handed, what did that mean?

Had they not found Rhys's sister, or was she…*dead*?

Her heart broke for him and she wanted nothing more than to comfort him. Rhys's face was pale and troubled as he stared out at the two figures making slow progress towards them. He had a lot in common with them, Helga realised. He, too, was burdened by responsibility and battling elements beyond his control.

Helga stepped closer and placed a hand on his arm. She thought back to the ravens—such a good sign would not come before such terrible news. 'I am sure your sister is alive and well.'

A bitter smile crossed his face, but there was no censure in his tone when he asked, 'Do you know, or is it your instincts telling you that?'

'It is what I believe.'

He sighed miserably, looking out at the bruised clouds and striking landscape of his homeland with apprehension. 'I wish I had your certainty. Alswn is so…young. She's not like you, she knows nothing of hardship. I doubt she would last even a day or two on her own.'

'But Hywel is with her… You trust him, do you not?'

'I did. He was my greatest friend…' Grief weighed down his words. 'He would not have left her alone. No matter what has happened to Alswn, I must presume him dead—he would die to protect her. So…she is either captured, or…she is also lost to me.'

'Hardship and struggle can be a good thing,' Helga said quietly, wanting to offer him some kind of comfort in the darkness. 'A good sword is beaten and tempered with fire and ice to strengthen it.'

A muscle jumped in his jaw. 'I do not want my sister to be beaten or tempered with fire and ice.'

Helga wanted to slap her own head. 'That was a bad comparison... I only meant to say that people are sometimes stronger than you imagine. My mother and sisters always despaired that I would never make a decent warrior. It hurt, knowing that every day I disappointed them. But then I realised that I had other strengths and skills. I took a risk on pleasing myself, instead of my family, and was happier for it. Maybe Alswn did the same?'

Anger flashed in his eyes. 'You think my sister ran away? Willingly left Efa in those monster's hands—just so that she could be...*happy*?'

She stared him straight in the eye, refusing to back down. She didn't know Alswn, but she knew her own family had nothing to do with her disappearance and she was beginning to believe Alswn had indeed run away. 'I do not know what happened to Alswn and neither do you.' She thought of the conversation she'd overheard between Rhys and Efa back in the storeroom. 'But tell me, why does the idea of her running away to be happy so disgust you? Is it because you refuse to be?'

He closed the fragile distance between them, his body pressing hers against the timber of the lookout, his breath stealing hers as thunder rattled in the skies above them.

His words were soft, a gentle warning. 'Happiness is a luxury. My people and land must come first.'

'"Gwynedd binds me." I have heard of your family oath, but how does your misery help them? And why are you so determined to deny your feelings? It is clear we desire one another, yet you push me away.'

He turned as if she had struck him, staring out of the open shutters with a fierce and exasperated sigh. 'Helga! I have one army approaching, a sister missing and my aunt has lived through unspeakable crimes. This is not the time to discuss my future happiness. We may not even live through the upcoming days!'

'There is no better time! If we are to die, is it not better to have at least lived a little before our days come to an end? Do you want to be like that dragon in the mountains? Never truly feeling or experiencing anything?' She sensed him wavering and she went to him, her hand smoothing up his arm, resting on his shoulder to nudge him into turning back to her.

'Helga…' he warned and she smiled, holding up her hands to show she carried no weapon.

'Fear not, I will not *tempt* you further. Besides, I do not believe you will lose against Ulf. You should have more belief in yourself and your own strengths. You are a wise and courageous leader. Rescuing Efa seemed impossible, but you managed it, and even dealt Ulf a terrible blow at the same time. I know it is difficult to trust in yourself when no one else believes in you. I found it incredibly hard. My mother and sisters have always felt responsible for me, as if I cannot manage without them. But they were wrong, they needed me as much as I needed them… For you, it will be easier.'

'How so?'

'Because you are not alone. I believe in you.'

Winded by her words Rhys sucked in a shaky breath. No one, including himself, had trusted in him like Helga did.

Was it true? Did he only push people away out of fear of losing them? For years he had told himself it was better if he kept himself at a distance. That it was the only way he could rule his land well and protect his family.

But the loneliness of it all was killing him. Meeting Helga had awakened in him the desire to feel again, tempting him to take the risk and allow another into his heart.

With the pressures, and uncertainty of the future pressing down upon him, he could no longer resist her.

'I do want you,' he confessed, his throat raw with the admission of his weakness. 'More than *anything*.'

Relief washed over her face and she pressed closer to him, wrapping her arms around his neck. He felt weak in the knees and he gripped the cloth of her skirts, hoping to steady his thoughts, as well as his body.

She rose up on her toes and pressed a tender kiss to his mouth. His fingernails cut into the fabric and he gasped. 'There is no future for us...' The words sounded hoarse and broken on his tongue.

'You might be right,' she said, and her eyes were steady and clear of doubt. 'But I am willing to leave it up to fate because at this moment, it does not matter. All I want is you.' As their lips joined, he sank into her embrace.

Between fevered kisses, she unclasped his cloak and let it fall to the timber floor.

'Helga,' he gasped. 'We should go back to my chamber.'

She shook her head and dropped his belt to the floor. 'No, we have wanted this for too long. I swear I will go mad if you make me wait a moment longer!'

Picking up his cloak from the floor, she shook it out and quickly laid it down a few feet away, followed by her own. She must have seen the hesitation in his eyes because she returned to him and cupped his face, her thumb brushing along his jaw, leaving sensitive tingles in its wake.

Glancing at the doorway, he was grateful to see it was closed. But to be safe he braced his foot on a nearby chest and then thrust it forward. It slid across the floor and bumped into the door with a soft thud, blocking the entrance from anyone who might try to enter.

Helga's eyes widened and then she threw back her head with a throaty laugh that made his toes curl.

'If I cannot offer you a bed, then the least I can do is give you privacy.'

Unable to restrain himself a moment longer, he cupped her face with both hands and kissed her deeply, letting all of his tension, doubts and fears be burned away by her touch. Breathless, they began to undress one another, taking it in turns to unlace and remove a piece of the other's clothing until they were both naked, their clothes mingled together in a heap beside them.

'Are you certain this is what you want?'

In answer she ran her hands up his chest and neck, greedily exploring his body, her eyes bright with desire. 'Yes.'

He leaned down and kissed her neck. She moaned, arching beneath him until her breasts rubbed against him. She stepped back and his hands went lightly to her hips, unwilling to let her go.

Sky-blue eyes stared up at him with trust and affection. She lowered herself to the cloaks on the floor, pulling him down with her, the sweetest grip on his arms.

'Have you—?' His question was swallowed by his pounding heart when her fingers wrapped around his manhood and stroked him.

'Done this before?' she asked. 'No, but I know enough…'

He groaned, her tender exploration buckling him at the knees. Bracing a hand either side of her head, he sucked in a deep breath and tried to concentrate.

Was it wrong to take her virginity like this—on a timber floor?

Her hands drifted up and tenderly pushed aside some

of the curls that had fallen in his eyes. 'Rhys,' she said firmly. 'Just allow yourself to enjoy this with me, won't you? Stop worrying and just make love to me. That's all that I want.'

How could he deny her?

All thought and reason flew from his mind and he gladly surrendered to his desires.

Cupping her face, he kissed her thoroughly, determined that she would enjoy every moment with him.

She tried to reach for his length once again, but he took her wrists in one of his hands and pushed them up over her head. 'I will not last long if you keep touching me there,' he warned and she smiled. This close and with her body under his, he was reminded of the last time he'd held her like this, in the hen house in Jorvik.

He soothed her with kisses this time, his free hand reaching between her legs to find her hot and wet beneath his touch. As his fingers began to circle and tease her needy flesh, she cried out, arching her body towards him, and he took one nipple in his mouth and sucked on it gently. She opened her legs wider, lightly hooking her ankles around his knees, their bodies entwined in a lovers' embrace.

Locked beneath his devoted attentions, he began to coax out her pleasure with light strokes of his fingers. She began to pant and squirm beneath him, her thighs clenching against his with helpless abandon.

'Please, I need you,' she whimpered, desperate for release.

He released the hand that held her wrists and immediately she reached for his hips, trying to pull him closer.

'Patience,' he whispered, gathering her hips in his own hands and ignoring her protest as he shifted further down her body, her heels stroking up the backs of his thighs as he did so. 'I want you fully sated before we go any further. You will enjoy it more that way.'

'I will enjoy it *now*,' she grumbled, although her words ended with a moan as he dropped his head between her legs and licked her with an insatiable hunger only she could ease.

He was determined to worship her with every stroke of his tongue and lips, until he had unlocked the key to her pleasure. Soon, her hips began to buck as her release washed through her. Her cry of ecstasy almost killed him and he gritted his teeth against the desire to thrust into her hard and fast.

Carefully, he rose and positioned himself at her entrance. Helga still trembled from her release, her face flushed with passion. She reached for him, wrapping her arms around his waist. Slowly, he sheathed himself in her body, his eyes watching her face for any sign of pain or discomfort.

To his relief there was none. Sinking into her, he moaned as her warmth enveloped him with blissful pleasure. Melting heat rubbed against his hardness and he began to rock back and forth.

Helga wrapped her arms and legs around him. Unable to resist the pleasure, he began to thrust with increasing speed and Helga moved beneath him in a carnal rhythm that came naturally to both of them.

Helga arched her back for a second time, her release propelling his own forward. Gathering her close, he pressed into her, shuddering against the power of his climax, which seemed to strip the strength from him, leaving him weak and limp.

The mist of their breaths began to mingle in the air between them, the chilly wind from the shutters unnoticed against the burning heat of their lovemaking.

They held one another tightly, their fingers reaching up to tangle in each other's hair as they kissed one another in thanks. The rain continued to beat down on the timber roof above them and a distant thunder rumbled above the mountain, announcing the arrival of the storm.

Moving to Helga's side, he hugged her body to him. He thought he had hardened his heart to her, but the truth was that she had infiltrated it regardless. Shaken by the revelation, he knew that he could never let Helga go. Now that he had tasted true intimacy, he couldn't give her up.

Even an army could not take her from him.

Chapter Twenty

Brynhild and Erik entered the Hall, their big bodies dwarfing those of his men. They were built like oak trees, solid and thick. Helga was so different to them, so beautiful and elegant, he could almost believe she wasn't Brynhild's kin.

But then they would never have met...

He could not imagine Cadair y Ddraig without her presence any more. It would feel empty and cold without her sunshine. He'd left her in his bed, her golden locks spread across the pillow, her body exhausted from their afternoon of lovemaking.

The hour had grown late, and the evening meal had come and gone, all without her sister's arrival. Helga had worried for them and he had reassured her that they must have camped in the forest to take shelter from the rain.

That was not the case, judging by the two titans before him.

They dragged back the hoods from their windswept faces. Both looked pale and tired. Erik slapped his hands as if to warm them, the sound echoing around the timber walls, while Brynhild stepped forward, her face wet and ruddy from the harsh wind and rain.

Rhys refused to feel sympathy for their suffering. Alswn was still missing and these two goliaths had failed him, but more importantly they had failed Helga. The fact that they dared to return empty-handed was an insult to both of them.

Did they not care for Helga's safety at all?

Rage twisted in his gut and he battled to restrain himself. But if they did not care, then that would give him good reason to keep Helga with him.

He must know.

Leaning forward, he focused his attention on Brynhild first. Erik rallied to her side, a protective and possessive gleam in his dark eyes. Erik, whose father had caused so much suffering in his lands, who had killed and stolen from his people. He was surprised he had the courage to face him.

What was it about these women that could possess a man's soul so completely?

Helga and Valda were beautiful, their charm obvious for all to see.

But Brynhild? She was no beauty, yet Erik moved around her like a shadow, permanently connected to her and obviously devoted. He could tell that, regardless of the armed men around them, Erik would fight to the death for her.

'*You* are her sister?' Rhys asked, not because he did not know the answer, but because he wished to remind Brynhild of her duty as Helga's kin. A responsibility she had woefully failed to fulfil by arriving at his gates empty-handed.

Brynhild raised her chin. 'Yes, I am. My name is Brynhild.'

'You don't look like her,' he snapped, wanting to lash out, but also inwardly wincing at what Helga would have done if she had heard. It was lucky that she was still warm and asleep in his bed.

How he wished he had never left it.

'You don't look old enough to be a lord,' she replied, sarcasm dripping through every word, 'yet life is full of surprises.'

He recognised the sharp wit he'd come to admire in Helga's bite. Was this who she'd learned it from? 'You certainly sound like her.'

'May I see her?' Her question was asked gently, but it caused righteous anger to ignite the tinder of his own patience.

'Where is *my sister*?' he hissed.

Erik stepped forward protectively. 'We found her. But she did not wish to return to you.'

'Lies!' Rhys gripped the armrest of his chair tightly, anything to stop himself from lurching forward and strangling them both. 'What of Hywel? Is he dead?'

'Alive and well. He was the one who took your sister north.'

Alive and well.

Relief washed through him, followed quickly by doubt and fury. If they were alive, why would they not return home? 'Now I know you are lying. Hywel would never betray me.' His words were said firmly, but doubt gnawed at his heart.

Brynhild held up a bag. 'Here is your proof, words written by your sister in her own hand. She was not taken, she ran away. I say again, Hywel is the man who has her now, but as you will soon learn, he had her long before…'

Rhys barely had time to process the insult to his sister's reputation before Brynhild struck him with another lash of words that rung true in a distressing way. 'My sister has nothing to do with your petty grievances with Ulf. You behave as if we owe you something when we do not. You stole a young girl from her family—you are the monster here, not us. Why should we have brought another frightened girl to you for punishment?'

Her words stung him, causing his skin to itch. Alswn might have found him overbearing at times, but surely she would never imagine that he would hurt her?

'Give me that!' Striding forward, he took the outstretched bag with a snap of his wrist, ignoring the posturing of Erik who obviously hated the implied threat to his woman. Rhys turned from them both, not wishing to give them any clue to his emotions when he saw their 'proof'.

Inside were two rings and a parchment.

Hywel's family ring—proving the authenticity of the note—and his mother's ring. The one he'd given to Alswn to marry Halfdan with.

The message explained that she was returning it to him. That she could no longer be a daughter of Gwynedd, that her heart was with Hywel, and in turn Hywel had given up his own honour and family name. He was no longer a warrior of Gwynedd; he could not follow his orders and deliver the woman he loved into the hands of the enemy. They would begin a new life with his distant relatives in the far north.

For his part, Hywel admitted he had lied to her and told her that Rhys had already saved Efa so that she would leave with him. It was a moment of madness that he deeply regretted and he could not face Rhys because of it.

Their betrayal was worse than the grief he'd felt for them. He could understand their deaths, but this? Why would they do it? Was love truly so cruel and…stupid?

Because of it they would walk away from their duty, with only a weak apology.

Even if it meant another woman's death?

Efa's death.

Brynhild's hesitant voice carried to him as he stared in disbelief at the words scrawled in charcoal on the back of the marriage contract. It was the same contract he'd written for Alswn and Halfdan. How easily it had been overturned and disregarded by those he considered family!

'Hywel said he was sorry, that he wasn't strong enough…that you would understand.'

Rhys could not speak.

His heart shrank in his chest, as heavy and as dead as a frozen stone. He could not rely or trust on anyone but himself.

They could take Helga from me.

He fought to regain clarity and control, to think and plan. But he felt trapped, as if he were clawing at the walls of a pit. He wanted to retreat, pull those he loved close and shut the doors on the rest of the world.

His men shifted, sensing the unease of their master. 'She seems happy…your sister. They're expecting a babe together.' Brynhild almost sounded as kind and as gentle as her youngest sister and he could not bear it.

Rhys's hand fisted, crumpling the parchment into a ball. He threw it into one of the nearby braziers that lined the path to his seat of power, his cage. 'Hywel is wrong. I do not understand.'

He would keep both Efa and Helga safe, even if it meant throwing out Helga's family and locking the gate. Rhys returned to his seat, sweeping his cloak to the side as he turned to sit and stare back at Brynhild. There was sympathy in her eyes, an empathy he could not bear to witness because it reminded him so much of Helga and her gentle heart.

The woman he could never let go of, no matter what her family told him.

'Helga will be staying,' he said firmly. He gestured with his fingers to the leader of his guard, an imperceptible order to remove them from his hall.

Erik must have realised the finality of the dismissal because his rage was immediate. 'Your sister was taken by your own man! You have no right to hold Helga hostage.'

'Helga is no longer my prisoner. She stays with me willingly. She says I am her *fate*.'

Except would she still accept her fate when she realised her family had come for her and he'd turned them away?

Brynhild's eyes widened with understanding and, for the first time, fear. She knew the stubborn, unflinching confidence Helga held in her beliefs. That it wasn't a trick or a ruse as he'd first assumed, it was faith—*in herself.*

'Let me see her,' she gasped and he felt a pang of sympathy that he stamped down quickly.

'No.'

'Why not?' barked Erik, striding forward. A guard stepped forward to halt him and Erik threw him to the ground with a curse. The Norse were strong and fierce, but their arrogance was always their first downfall. They had no discipline, no sense to consider the repercussions of their actions.

Thankfully, all Rhys had to do was raise a hand to stop his men from cutting them both down where they stood. Always obedient, they paused, their hands resting on the hilts of their swords in readiness.

'Please,' Brynhild begged. 'Let me see her, I need to know that she is safe.'

They don't deserve her, whispered a reptilian voice from within.

Helga was too pure, too good for these barbarians. He would not give her up. He *could* not. 'You will have to trust me when I say that she is well. As I will have to trust *you* regarding the welfare of Lady Alswn.'

'You honourless wretch! How much silver for her return?' shouted Erik.

Always it came back to silver and gold.

The Norse were obsessed with treasure. They did not care for Helga.

Not as he did.

There was no treasure more precious than she and he was harshly reminded of this man's sire, who had earned his wealth off the back of slaves. No different to the raiders who had killed his parents.

Rhys snarled at Erik with cold fury, 'It is time your people learned that a man's soul cannot be bought like cattle. We were here long before the Saxons came to our shores and we will remain long after you have crawled back to your pits. Remind your father of that before he thinks to attack my lands!'

He would fight to the death for her if he had to. It was clear to him now. No matter the distant future, he would fight and protect her at all costs. Her family would not do the same. They'd left her alone in a market square, they didn't value her the way he did. They didn't even know her the way he did.

Helga was strong and resilient and put everyone before herself.

While *they* only saw her as a burden and a weakness.

Erik glared at him. 'Ulf is not my father. He disowned me long before he disowned my brother. We are nothing to him.'

'And yet, *here* you are!' Rhys could barely contain his frustration and anger as it boiled within him. Did it even matter that Ulf was not to blame for Alswn and Hywel's disappearance? No, the result was still the same. His people would suffer regardless. 'In *my* lands, demanding I do *your* bidding! I know Ulf means to attack us again. I will defeat him and burn away your people's plague from Gwynedd.'

Brynhild placed a calming hand on Erik's shoulder. '*Please*. Helga would not want us to worry about her. Let us speak with her, if only to reassure us that she stays willingly.'

'No.' He couldn't trust her to speak with Helga. What if they persuaded her to leave? How would they protect her if Ulf's army arrived? The lookouts on the mountain side of the fortress had spotted the dust cloud of a horde approaching only that morning. They would join them within a day or two at the latest. He needed Helga safe behind his walls and Ulf's son as far away from her as possible. He did not trust him with even one hair on Helga's head.

'Please, I beg you—I cannot understand why you will not let us speak with her! We are her family,' Brynhild cried in desperation and for a moment Rhys almost caved under her demands. It was strange to see such a giant and powerful woman beg. She did love Helga, even if she did not value or protect her as she should have.

'You may stay within the first wall tonight,' he said. He would not throw them back into the storm, Helga would never forgive him if he did. 'But I expect you gone at first light.'

'I will not leave without seeing my *sister*!' shouted Brynhild and he flinched, wondering if the commotion would wake her.

'One night. Now leave me!' Rhys ordered his guards to move with the click of his fingers and they dutifully rushed to do his bidding.

Erik fought hard, even managing to take two swords from Rhys's men, both of which had been embarrassingly flattened with only the use of his fists. It reminded Rhys of his lack of skilled warriors and only enraged him further. Erik didn't attack the remaining men, instead he retreated to protect his woman, twisting the swords in his hands in a flourish that intimidated the remaining guards into hesitating. They looked to Rhys for guidance and he stood, all patience and kindness vanished from his thoughts.

Brynhild's voice soared into the rafters of the Hall, filling it with power and fury. 'Helga is an honoured and beloved sister! You cannot treat her as a spoil of war. She is worth far more than you could ever imagine. You may throw us out tonight, but soon *all* of her kin will come for her. You will see, Lord Rhys! We shieldmaidens will save our sister or die trying!'

If Helga had not woken before, she definitely would have by now. He looked to Madoc and was glad to see the man had already called for reinforcements. He refused to kill or maim them. They were still Helga's kin after all.

The room filled with armed warriors, some with arrows already notched and aimed at Erik. Brynhild stared at Rhys with a cool determination that unnerved him, then she placed a hand on Erik's shoulder and gently squeezed, pulling back her trained wolf with the gentlest of commands.

No wonder these women could command armies.

Erik dropped his swords and the men rushed forward to subdue him, punching him and kicking him with the fury of humiliated men. Erik had barely flinched during the attack, managing to still appear threatening even with his arms held firmly behind his back.

Confident he was subdued, Rhys returned to his seat.

Brynhild didn't fight them. She had the wisdom to save her energy—the sign of a true leader. 'You have made an enemy of us, *Lord Rhys*. You have made a terrible enemy—'

Then her mouth dropped open with shock as she stared at something just beyond his shoulder. Out of the corner of his eye he saw a flash of blue and knew that Helga had joined him. Her small hand slipped to his shoulder, in a display of unity that would have buckled his knees if he'd not been sitting down already.

Triumphantly he reached up to cover Helga's hand with his own and he saw the exact moment Brynhild realised the true depth of her sister's devotion. Her eyes widened in horror, and…pain. As if she knew how hurt and disappointed Helga would eventually be by him. He tried to ignore his guilty conscience that agreed with her.

'I am happy here. Please, do not fight,' Helga said gently, then she turned to him, asking softly, 'May I speak with her?'

It went against his instincts to deny her, but he couldn't risk it.

'No.'

He looked pointedly at his guard and they were shoved outside, Brynhild shouting Helga's name repeatedly as she was dragged away.

'I would speak with you in private, my lord!' snapped Helga, spinning on her heel to stomp back into their chamber.

He suspected he would rather face a hundred Brynhilds on the battlefield than one wrathful Helga in his bedchamber.

Chapter Twenty-One

Helga's fists shook as she stormed into their bedchamber. She would not rage at him in front of his men, but there was nothing to stop her here. After proving her loyalty and heart in such an open declaration, how could he still not trust her?

'Why can I not speak with my sister?'

Rhys folded his arms against his chest. 'She did not do as she promised.'

Teeth gritted, she shook her head. 'I heard enough, Rhys. Alswn and Hywel are both alive and well. There was no reason for Brynhild to force them to return! Do you doubt the missive—is it written in another's hand?'

'No, Alswn wrote it.'

His eyes were pained and she realised how much their lies had hurt him. 'I am sorry that they betrayed you. But my family are not to blame for that.'

He raised his head stubbornly. 'I know that, but we had a deal and they failed to deliver!'

'That means nothing! I am no longer your captive, Rhys. I haven't been for some time—not in my mind at least—or was I foolish to think such a thing? Did I not just prove my allegiance...my *devotion*?'

For the first time his expression wavered from obstinacy to guilt. 'You did.'

'And where is your proof?' she snapped, closing the gap between them.

Had she misjudged him?

He had not said that he loved her.

'What do you mean?'

She reached up and cupped his face. 'Where is the proof of your loyalty and love for me? You treat my family as if they were the enemy. When all they have done—'

'I do not trust Erik,' he snapped.

'But you can! Erik hates Ulf, more than anyone. If you let me explain—'

'I have made my decision.' Rhys walked to the table and poured a chalice of wine.

Helga's anger boiled over. 'I still do not see why I cannot speak with my sister if only to reassure her that I am well!'

'Will they want you to stay here? When Ulf is only days away from launching an attack?'

She frowned and he nodded, as if his suspicions were confirmed. 'Exactly, they will try to convince you to leave.'

'And I will refuse! But at least they will know it is my decision—'

Rhys sighed wearily. 'Helga, please understand. I must presume the worst. I cannot trust the lives of everyone here on the word of two people I do not know!'

Hurt swallowed her anger. 'I tell you they speak the truth and you refuse to believe it.' She stared at him in disbelief. 'You *still* do not trust me!'

'It is your family I do not trust.'

'Then I will sleep somewhere else tonight, *my lord*. For I will not share a bed with a man so blind to the truth set before him. If my sister is not welcome here, then neither am I!' Grabbing a blanket from the bed, she pushed past him towards the main Hall.

He grabbed it to stop her. Trying to force him to let go, she gave it an angry shake, but he held firm. 'Helga,' he said softly. 'I will go. I am the one at fault.'

Hope flickered within her, fragile but bright. 'Then you will call them back?'

'No, too much is at stake. Merely speaking with them could put us in danger. It is dark now, they have not seen our numbers, but in daylight… We could never hide the truth from them. My first responsibility will always be to my people…'

She glared back at him, unwilling to back down, and he sighed. 'Goodnight,' he said and left.

Chapter Twenty-Two

The atmosphere in Cadair y Ddraig the following day had become oppressive, as if the arrival of her sister had reminded everyone of the imminent threat.

Helga was more worried for Brynhild and Erik—what if Ulf found them out in the open when he arrived and hurt them? It tightened the already twisting knots in her belly just thinking about it.

She was determined to speak with Rhys again, despite his stubbornness the night before…if she could only find him.

He'd not broken his fast with the rest of the Hall that morning and when she'd asked the serfs, they'd mentioned him 'training with his men'.

She had gone searching for him, but the archery master had stopped her, begging her assistance, and saying that Rhys had told him to speak with her for advice on defeating Ulf's army. Seeing the fear and worry in his eyes, she had spent a long time discussing technique and strategy with him, as well as demonstrating and practising her skills with a bow.

Then, as she was on her way towards the gate, she saw Rhys striding towards the hall and she hurried to catch up with him.

Out of breath, she managed to reach his side just as he was entering the hall.

'Rhys!' She gasped, 'Please can we talk about Brynhild and Erik? I am worried for them—'

'I have greater concerns than them,' Rhys replied coldly.

Helga continued to follow his relentless pace as best as she could, but he was walking so fast that she practically had to run to keep up. She was not paying attention to where she was walking and her foot kicked into the corner of the dais by accident. She hissed a curse as white-hot pain shot up her leg and she dropped to the floor, clutching her foot.

'Damn you, Rhys!' she screamed. 'Stop for one moment and speak with me!'

He stopped and turned, his eyes wide with shock when he realised she was hurt. He rushed to her side, kneeling in front of her. 'What happened?'

Scowling at him, she snapped, 'I was trying to keep up with you and then stubbed my toe in the process!' She had spent her whole life trying to keep up with others and it was exhausting. Unwelcome tears welled up in her eyes. 'Why will you not *listen* to me?' Her voice cracked and the tears fell, and she covered her face, ashamed by them.

'Leave us!' Rhys shouted, horrified by her distress, and the serfs hurried out as fast as their feet could carry them, the door to the hall closing softly behind them.

Rhys scooped her up and placed her gently on his chair, then knelt at her feet. 'I am sorry,' he said quietly, taking her foot in his hands and gently rubbing her toes in a soothing gesture. 'I know you want me to change my mind, but I cannot.'

Lowering her hands, she stared at him, 'Why must you

make that decision alone? Why can you not discuss it with me first? Talk to me. *Trust* me! I know my sister, she—'

'You cannot know anything for certain… What harm can their leaving cause us? None. But, if they stayed, and one of them betrayed us…'

'Brynhild and Erik would never do such a thing!'

'I cannot take that risk. Already you have convinced me to grant Harald and his men far more freedoms than I thought wise. What if *they* turn against us? How terrible would that be under the command of your sister?'

'That would never happen.'

'There is no point arguing about it. Brynhild and Erik have left already, although they have not gone far. They have made camp down by the lake.' He scrubbed his hand down his face, a weary look in his eyes. 'We have another, far greater threat at our door.'

Dread pooled in her gut. 'Ulf?'

He chuckled. 'Yes, he's still coming. Less than a day away, I believe.' He set down her foot and sighed, then turned so that he sat with his back to her, his forearms draped over his knees and his dark head resting lightly against her knee. 'What is your father's name?'

'Jarl Sihtric, some people call him—'

'Sihtric the Far-Sighted?'

The breath rushed from her body and she gave a nervous laugh, wondering how her father could have any relevance at this time. 'That's right. How did you know?'

'His ships were spotted near the coast of Anglesey. He is headed here.'

'Oh, my mother must have asked for his help.' She thought for a moment and then reached forward to tilt his face up to look at her. 'He might be able to help— against Ulf.'

A muscle jumped in Rhys's jaw and he gave her a weak smile. 'He might, or he might not.'

'He will,' she reassured. 'Once I speak with him, he will surely help us. He lives in Ireland—' Her stomach bucked at a terrible thought. 'But I do not think he was involved on any raids on Anglesey…'

'No, a man called Ingimundr led that raid.'

Helga sank back into the chair with relief, placing her hands back in her lap. 'I have never heard that name connected with my father. But I am afraid I know little of my father's past or present exploits.'

Rhys nodded and dropped his head.

'What is it?' she asked softly. Whatever it was, it had caused Rhys to once again retreat from her if only for a moment. She sensed it was to do with her father's imminent arrival. Did he fear an attack on all sides?

Rhys ran his fingers roughly through his hair and shook his head, as if to banish bad thoughts. 'I am not worthy of you. I know that, believe me. But no matter what I do, the people I love always end up hurt or dead. I am cursed—'

'You are not cursed,' she reassured, her heart aching at the cool manner in which he'd said it. As if it were his fate and he was helpless to change it. 'You are not. I am a witch, remember? I would know if that were the case. All will be well.' She stroked his head, the curls like silk ribbons between her fingers.

'You could die here,' he whispered. 'If you stayed with me and Ulf broke through…'

'He won't! You have to believe that. It is the first step to victory,' Helga said firmly, her mother's words of warning coming to mind: *'Doubt and fear kill more swiftly than the blade on the battlefield.'*

'But what if he did break through? If you left now, right now—with no delay—you might be safe…'

'My place is with you.'

He turned towards her. His fingers wrapped tightly around her hands and he kissed them reverently, resting his forehead against them with a bitter sigh. 'Why do you have such faith in me?'

She smiled. 'Why do you not?'

Rhys rose up on his knees, her hands clasped in his, as he looked her firmly in the eye and asked, 'Will you marry me?'

'What?' she squeaked, confused by his unexpected question. Not once had he spoken of marriage and, when she'd heard him talking with Efa, he'd seemed against even the idea of it.

Silence stretched between them and then he asked, 'Do you want me to beg?'

Her breath burned in her lungs she'd been holding it for so long. With a rough exhale she whispered, 'Maybe…a little.'

An appreciative chuckle rumbled from his throat. 'I am sorry, Helga. For ever doubting you, for being bad tempered and unreasonable. But if you did agree to marry me, I swear I will treat you like a queen.'

'Is that it?'

His eyes widened in the flickering light of his golden hall. 'What more do you want?'

She leaned back against his throne, relishing the power it gave her. 'I want you to apologise again and tell me…' she hesitated, unsure if she were brave enough to ask, and then leapt into the unknown anyway '…that you love me.'

His hands slipped over the polished wood and came down to rest either side of her thighs. She could feel the warmth of his hands through the fabric of her gown, like warming stones.

'*Cariad*—my love.' He pressed a kiss to the top of her thigh. 'Please, forgive me.'

She leaned forward, her hair tumbling forward to brush the tops of his hands and head. 'You will have to do better than that,' she teased, her voice husky with desire and longing. She wanted the battle between them to finally come to an end, in a way that satisfied them both.

'I will,' he promised, his palms smoothing down her shins and locking around her ankles. Gently he pulled them a little wider apart before he stroked back up her calves, his hands now beneath her skirts, trailing up her skin to cup the back of her knees, revealing her lower legs to his hungry gaze. Helga's breath came out in soft pants as she watched him, mesmerised by the sharp lines of his jaw and nose.

After pressing a gentle kiss on the side of each of her knees, his jewelled eyes moved up to hers, his broad shoulders filling the space between her thighs as he wet his lips. Reaching forward, he bunched the material of her skirts around the tops of her thighs. Finally, his teasing fingers reached her hips and he gripped them tightly and jerked her forward.

She gasped, her nails biting into the wood of the arm rests.

Hooking her knees over his shoulders, he dipped his head to kiss between her legs, his tongue tasting the damp heat that already ached for him, and she moaned, her head falling back and her eyes closing as a familiar bliss began to gather inside of her.

Unable to help herself, she widened her thighs wantonly, giving him full access to her most intimate area.

His tongue swirled over the apex of her pleasure in a relentless worshipping of her body that caused her thighs to tremble against his silken head. Her skin shivered with desperate need and she gripped his hair to pull him closer as her hips arched to meet his insistent mouth.

The tightness built until it was too much to bear and then her climax peaked and she cried out, her feet jerking against his back.

She had wanted to draw out her release, somehow make it last longer, but she'd been helpless under Rhys's tongue. Lowering her legs from his shoulders, she took a moment to catch her breath.

'Will you?' he asked, raising his head.

'What?' Her mind was still spinning and she was certain she could see the dust floating like gold in the beams above.

'Marry me?'

'It's your turn to sit,' she said with a sigh that slid into a mischievous smile. Rising on wobbly legs, she then offered him the chair with a flourish.

He took his seat warily, his lust still clearly visible in his eyes and groin. Helga was glad she had worn her apron dress for her chores today. She untied it quickly, letting it fall around her, and then swept her shift over her head.

Rhys's eyes flowed over her body and she savoured his awed expression. She unstrapped his belt and tossed it aside. The seat of the chair was large and, although it was a little awkward, she managed to slip her legs under the arm rests and straddle him.

She palmed his face and kissed him deeply, her tongue stroking his in a deeply passionate caress. His arms wrapped around her and she dragged his undertunic up and over his head.

'Helga?' he asked softly, his eyes searching hers for answers, but she ignored him and instead kissed and licked his chest. Confidently she reached down, and undid the ties around his waist, forcing his hard shaft out and into her hand, pumping him until he was moaning beneath her touch.

Positioning herself over him, she sank down, gripping the hair on the back of his head tightly so that she could look into his eyes as he filled her. He groaned and she melted against him, her hips fitting his perfectly, as if they were made for one another.

Pulling her close, he licked and sucked her breasts until she couldn't take it any more and she had to push him back. She wanted to be in charge. She began to ride him, slow deliberate thrusts that set her pleasure climbing quickly.

He held her gently as she worked her body over him, giving up all of his control into her capable hands. 'Helga,' he groaned. 'Give me your answer.'

'Yes… Rhys,' she panted, gasping for air against the hot pulse of his neck. 'I will…marry you… We will see this through to the end…together, yes?'

'Yes,' he groaned and his own release ripped through him. He threw back his head with a strangled curse. Every muscle in his body clenched as he came and she sagged against him as her own satisfaction rolled through her.

Chapter Twenty-Three

Rhys's head throbbed and each heartbeat felt painful in his chest. There was so much left to do that it left his mind reeling, flitting from one worry to another with no reprieve.

Fear snapped at his heels like a hungry wolf and he had spent many hours training, or working on the defences in the hopes of appeasing it. But nothing sated it.

Worst of all was the guilt.

It tormented him constantly with his past mistakes, promising death and ruin to the people of Cadair y Ddraig, in the same way that he had failed his parents by arriving too late to save them. Images of Efa and Helga falling under Ulf's sword kept him awake at night.

He would do anything to protect them, even if it meant hurting one of them…the woman he loved.

How would Helga feel when she learned the truth?

That the reason for his hasty proposal was political rather than based on a declaration of love?

And he did love her. It was why he could not let her go. Why he risked warfare with yet another jarl to keep her by his side. But it was also why they had to marry… and quickly.

Would she understand? A part of him knew that she would not.

They broke their fast early. Helga gave him a tentative smile that he returned weakly and she continued eating her porridge with stewed plums. The entire hall was sombre, the rumours running like rats from table to table in hushed whispers.

'Ulf is here!'

'Another Viking army is coming!'

'Lord Rhys will have to marry his hostage to prevent war!'

'He has already bedded her!'

No one would tell Helga—they felt sorry for her. Captured and taken from her family, many were sympathetic to her plight. Old Aneurin and Tangwystl thought well of her and that was enough to convince the rest of her good character. She had learned a few Welsh phrases and treated everyone in the fortress with respect and kindness.

If anything, they judged him more harshly and so they should.

Their sour and bad-tempered lord—who had treated his sister like cattle to be bought and sold—was now using his future wife as a power play against his enemies.

But what choice did he have?

As their leader, his duty was to protect them. It did not matter if they liked him for it.

Thankfully, no one had heard the worst thing, which was sadly true…

No one is coming.

Rhys stood and the room immediately hushed. 'Helga and I will marry this morning,' he said and Helga coughed as she tried to swallow a mouthful of fruit.

Efa's genuine cry of delight was the first response and

she wrapped Helga in a fierce hug and squeezed her tight.
Harald and his brothers banged their table with their fists
and shouted their well wishes while a polite cheer rose
from his people, whose smiles were anxious and filled
with side glances.

When things had settled down, Madoc nodded sagely.
'A wise decision, my lord—shall we send a messenger
to the King?'

'Immediately,' replied Rhys and Madoc hurried to
do his bidding.

'Why would the King need to hear of it?' asked Helga
quietly.

'Ulf's army arrived last night at the base of the mountain.'

'But…won't the reinforcements already be on their
way?' she asked with a frown.

Thank God she spoke softly.

'Keep your voice down,' he whispered and then, so
quietly that no one but she could hear him, added, 'The
King denied our call for aid. He is waiting until your
father's ships have safely passed Anglesey before he al-
lows warriors to come here. Do not speak of it with anyone, it will only spread terror among the people. When
the King learns it is your father, and that we are married, he may feel confident enough to send help…but
we should not rely on it. He could believe your father is
here to join with Ulf against me. Frankly, I cannot be
certain that is not the case.'

Helga's eyes widened with horror, but to her credit she
kept her voice low. 'I should go and speak with Brynhild.
I know you still have your doubts, but this is foolish—
they might be able to help.'

'No!' The single word was barked as an order. 'You
said it yourself—you have not seen him since you were

a babe. The Viking rulers of Ireland are said to be ruth-less slavers—it would be foolish to presume otherwise. I suspect he will combine with Ulf to ensure a swift and decisive victory. Your mother probably only gained his help in rescuing you by enticing him with the riches he might win by raiding here.'

Helga shook her head. 'Brynhild and Valda always said he was a good and honourable man.'

Rhys took her hands in his and kissed them. 'You think the best in everyone around you, but we must be cautious. Your father has come with five ships...'

Helga's jaw tightened. 'It is a show of force. A means to open negotiations between you.'

'Negotiations?' He spat the word like a curse. 'He has at least three hundred warriors. With that sizeable a force he cannot possibly be here to merely negotiate—he brings an army to wage war!'

'Is that why you want us to marry?'

Rhys tempered his frustration; it was not Helga's fault. She hoped for the best because it was in her optimistic na-ture to do so. 'I want to marry you because I love you.' He spoke loudly, for the benefit of the room and its rumours, before returning to a whisper. 'But I'm sure when he hears of our happy marriage, he will be content to leave. There are no guarantees, of course, but with you safely behind our walls, he will have no cause to join with Ulf.'

Rhys rose from the table.

Helga also stood. 'I will change first.'

Rhys looked down at the green gown she wore. 'Do you need to?' He thought she looked beautiful as she was.

'I need to gather my thoughts,' she said, her face pale as she walked towards their chamber. Efa followed her—after throwing a dark scowl in his direction.

* * *

Efa entered the room, a worried look on her face, as if she were expecting Helga to cry at any moment. Entirely possible considering how wretched she felt.

In her mind, she'd already picked out her favourite gown to wear. The blue one, because she thought it matched Rhys's eyes. But that had been before.

She took if from her chest, placed it on the bed and stared at it, wondering how she'd gone from happiness to misery in only a few moments.

'I'm sorry, this must seem awfully rushed and unromantic,' Efa said, clasping her hands tightly.

Helga shook her head and cool tears began to slide down her cheeks. 'It's not supposed to be like this.'

Efa dropped on the bed beside her gown and took Helga's hands in her own, drawing her eyes away. 'How was it meant to be? Let me help.'

More tears began to fall and Helga swiped them away angrily. 'You will think me stupid, just like Rhys does!'

'No! He doesn't think that at all! This is how he gets when he's worried. There's a lot to consider and he takes it all upon himself, then acts like a callous *beast*.'

That made Helga sob even harder. 'He doesn't need to do that. He can share the burden with me! But he doesn't trust me. He thinks I know nothing.'

Efa frowned. 'I agree he should consider your opinion before making decisions…but, you have to admit… another army arriving does not bode well for us.'

Helga nodded, but said nothing. No one believed in her, not her friends, or her family—not even Rhys!

'Come,' Efa pleaded, stroking away her tears and tucking her damp hair behind her ears to see her better. 'Tell me, what *did* you imagine for your wedding day? Is there some Norse tradition we could follow?'

Helga shook her head. 'I do not care for those things. I never wanted anything grand, I just…always imagined my family would be with me and that…I…I would have flowers in my hair. It's so stupid!' The sob cracked her throat like an egg and misery poured out of her with each gasping breath. Efa stared at her in alarm, then wrapped her arms around her, holding her tight.

'Do not cry, my darling. All will be well and I am sure I can find us some flowers.'

But Helga already knew the recent storm had trampled the last flowers of autumn into the mud. She stamped down her emotions. She was being childish. Her family wouldn't behave like this, crying over the disappointment of silly dreams. She straightened her spine and sniffed loudly. 'No, there is no need.'

'How about some lavender? I am sure we have some dried bunches that we can use.'

Helga began to undress, pulling off her clothes with savage jerks. 'I am not a little girl any more. I should have grown out of such fantasies a long time ago. I cannot keep believing in…dreams and visions. Besides, Rhys is waiting.'

Efa was quiet for a moment, then she stood to help Helga put on the blue dress.

'He does love you,' she said gently, as she laced the back with tender care.

'Or does he love me because it suits his plans?'

Efa gripped her arm and turned Helga to look at her, her dark eyes full of conviction. 'No, I have known Rhys all of my life and I can tell you, he *does* love you. So much so that he is frightened by it.'

'He loves me in spite of what I am. Whereas I love him in spite of how he treats me. Who is the bigger fool, do you think?'

* * *

Marriage is another kind of death.

Brynhild used to say that and Helga had always laughed at her sister's glum attitude. But now as she walked into a dark stone church devoid of colour and life, she had to wonder if her sister had been right.

Was *this* what she had prophesied all along? The black dragon had come and taken her, and she would spend the rest of her days without family or happiness.

When Rhys saw her tear-streaked face he stiffened. 'I know it is not ideal, but we must make the best of it. You believe we were meant to be together and you were right—that is all that matters, is it not?'

Helga nodded miserably. 'We are. But I had hoped you would want to marry me for love…not to appease my father and your King.'

'For the good of everyone, can we not do both?'

She sighed. 'It appears *you* can.'

Helga understood none of the ceremony and only repeated the strange Latin words when Efa or the priest prodded her to do so. She might as well have been at a funeral for all the pleasure it gave her.

Rhys seemed distracted, tapping his foot nervously and repeating his own words quickly and without feeling. To him this was one of many tasks he needed to complete to ensure the safety of all those within his walls.

At the end of the ceremony, he led her by the elbow out into the morning sunshine. Some of the serfs, along with Harald and his brothers, had gathered to cheer and wish them well. That small act of kindness made her feel a little better and she smiled at them, even though it broke her heart to do so.

'I have to go.' Rhys kissed her mouth lightly, his grip on her biceps firm. 'I love you. Never doubt that.'

She nodded, bittersweet tears pricking once more at her eyes. 'I love you, too.'

He kissed her again, this time the press of his mouth lingering for a moment longer before they parted ways. 'I am sorry, I know this is not what any woman would want. But there is much to prepare.'

'Go,' she whispered and in no time at all he was gone, lost in the crowd as people rushed back and forth preparing to defend themselves against an invasion that was due at any moment.

But Helga was not a woman who could sit idly by while others risked their lives, or wallow in self-pity for long. She was a shieldmaiden and she would do everything in her power to protect those she loved.

Even if it meant leaving.

Chapter Twenty-Four

Helga walked through the settlement unnoticed. A great pile of trees that had been brought in from the forest were being chopped up into smaller logs, the banging of axes filling the air with their steady beat.

From her past experience of warfare, she knew they would be used for the heating of water and the creation of arrows. Boulders had also been collected and they were arranged in heaps along the battlements. They would be thrown at the enemy along with the boiled water.

The storm had drenched the defences, so fire was less of a worry. Even so, waxed skins were hammered to the gates and water poured over the timber to stop flaming arrows from setting it alight.

It was good fortune that this fortress had such easy access to water, as it would be used for many things in the upcoming days—not only to quench their thirst.

Harald and his brothers, except Egil, were walking back from the waterfall and Helga hurried into step beside him. 'Efa once said that not all of the supplies to the fortress are carried up by pack horse. Is that true?'

Harald looked across at her. 'That's true. Some are pulled up by rope…'

'Can you take me to the pulley?' She presumed he would know where it was, as he and his brothers had been used for much of the heavy labour since arriving here.

His eyes narrowed and he set down his buckets with a thud. 'Why do you want to know?'

She looked around her, they were in the shadows of the coppice and away from prying eyes. 'I need your help…to get out. The gates are locked, but I wondered if I might use the cargo pulley. It would also save time… as I wouldn't have to climb down most of the mountain by myself.'

Harald hissed out a curse and looked to the sky as if asking for Odin's deliverance. Then his sharp eyes snapped to hers. 'Why would you, *his bride*, want to leave here on the eve of battle?'

'To save us!'

At Harald's weary sigh, she charged forward with the speech she'd carefully planned. 'I must speak with my family. With my sister and father. They still believe I am a prisoner but if they know the truth, then they will join with us, protecting Cadair y Ddraig from Ulf's attack. We won't last long, Harald, you must know that. My father has at least three hundred men—imagine how easily that could turn the tide in our favour, if we had those warriors behind these walls!'

'But Rhys is not convinced your father comes in peace…and you have not seen him since you were a child.' He rested a hand on her shoulder. 'Would it not be wiser to wait and see?'

Helga shook her head. 'Ulf is at the base of the mountain. Do you think he will be content to wait and see what my father does?'

Harald frowned and shook his head. 'Probably not.'

'Exactly! We must act quickly, or we could lose them.

They will either join with Ulf in the hope of setting me free, or they will die in defiance of him. We must act!'

Harald cleared his throat. 'He has good reason not to trust them, they are his enemy. Your whole family are infamous war leaders and warriors. If he releases you, Rhys may fear they will not let you return, or that if they do decide to join with him, they may betray him regardless.'

'They will not! Joining together may be our *only* chance to survive Ulf.'

'Do not worry.' Harald smiled as he gave her shoulder a reassuring pat. 'Rhys's King has sent reinforcements. They should be here soon.'

'The King's warriors have not left Anglesey. The reinforcements may take weeks to arrive!'

Harald's eyes flared with shock. 'Then you must speak with Lord Rhys, convince him to speak with your family.'

'I have been trying to persuade him to do that since Brynhild arrived! He will not listen because he does not trust the Norse. Most of his family were slaughtered by raiders and they have burned and pillaged his land for the past year. Why would he trust them now? My family will believe no one but me, and I must go now before it is too late. It will take me at least half a day to reach Brynhild's camp, even if I do use the pulley. Please, Harald! I need your help.'

Harald's nostrils flared as he let out a grim huff. 'Egil could be killed, or my brothers punished if I defy him.'

'No, Rhys wouldn't do that—I promise. And besides, he needs every man defending the walls when the fighting begins.' She squinted up at him, measuring the man who had so quickly become a friend to her. 'You will stay here and fight, will you not? For Efa? You wouldn't want her to suffer under Ulf's hands.'

'Yes, even though, as you have said before, she does

not wish for me to court her.' Harald's jaw flexed, as if he were considering whether to go on, and after a moment's hesitation he continued. 'If it goes badly… My brothers will look for Egil and I will take her with me to the pulley, and we will all escape together. That is our plan.'

Helga gave him a disapproving look, but didn't argue it. 'Not before it goes badly, I hope?'

His gaze hardened. '*Before* I thought more warriors were coming.'

'There will be. If you help me.'

Harald nodded with gritted teeth. 'Hurry then, we will need at least one of my brothers to help us.'

It wasn't long until she, Sten and Harald were at the cargo pulley. Not far from the lookout tower, it sat on the side of the fortress that only had one wall defence and a sheer cliff drop as a deterrent.

The pulley was a large timber arm that could be swung over the wall by turning a large bar that worked a little like a steering oar. The rope was thick and strong and had a large round crank like the ones used on the outer gates, to reel the rope up and down with.

'There's already a basket here…' said Helga, as she frowned at the large basket hooked up to the end of the rope.

'Maybe Lord Rhys also planned this as an escape route if the fortress is overrun?' asked Sten.

'Yes, that makes sense.' Rhys would always have another scheme at the ready, even a plan for defeat. She suspected this would be used for women and children only and her heart ached at the choices Rhys constantly had to make.

'We should hurry, before we are missed,' said Harald as he helped Helga climb in, then ran to help Sten with the pulley.

The basket jerked rhythmically and she gripped the sides of the wicker basket tightly. However, that fear was nothing compared to what she felt when the creaking arm was swung over the wall. Swinging from side to side in the mountain wind, she was reminded of her visions of being carried away in a dragon's grip.

The floor of the loosely woven basket was the only thing between her and a terrifying cliff drop and the trees below looked like a carpet of clovers.

She gave a startled yelp as the crank was released. The rope above her head gave a high-pitched hiss and the basket dropped swiftly down towards the ground.

'Where is she?'

Rhys's roar filled the hall and the ravens gave disgruntled shrieks from the timbers above.

Harald and his brothers had been dragged into Rhys's hall with swords pressed against their backs. As usual, their leader's eyes were first drawn to Efa, who stood beside Rhys. It irritated him so much he was tempted to punch Harald.

Efa's hands were clasped tight as she pleaded with Harald. 'You were the last to see Helga. Where is she?'

How no one had noticed she was missing until now still worried Rhys. It was well past noon and he'd only sought her out himself when he'd come to change his sweat-stained tunic for a fresh one and had not been able to find her in the hall. That in itself was not unsurprising as she preferred to work outside, but then he'd not seen her in the gardens either and his worry had begun to eat at him.

Harald eyes moved lazily back to his. 'I do not know for certain.'

'Then what *do* you know?' snarled Rhys.

'That she is most likely back with her family, begging them to give us aid.'

Rhys jumped forward off the dais and grabbed Harald by the throat. The man did not even flinch, but his brothers struggled against the hands that held them and Efa cried out, *'Rhys, no!'*

'If she is harmed because of you, I will cut off your head!' he whispered in the man's ear, his fingers tightening before releasing slowly.

Harald gave a raspy laugh as he tried to clear his sore throat. 'You will thank me when she returns with more warriors to man your walls.'

'She will not return. If her family have any sense, they will take her and sail away. At worst they will attack with Ulf and scorch this place to ash and ruin.'

'Helga would not allow it,' Harald said firmly.

'And you believe she will have any choice in the matter? They will not come to our aid. Now that Helga is no longer with us, Sihtric will have nothing to lose!'

Harald ignored him, puffing out his chest and staring him straight in the eye. 'I do not know Helga's family, but I trust in her. If she says her family will help, then *I* believe her.'

'As do I!' said Efa firmly, pushing between the men and facing Rhys head on. 'You should have had more faith in her! You demand loyalty and obedience, but that trust must be shared. If Helga is hurt, I will blame you, Rhys. I will blame you for pushing her away when you should have been cherishing her. You did the same with Alswn. It is no wonder she was so desperate to fall in love with Hywel—you gave her no independence, no choice in her own life! And now you are doing it again, pushing people into little cages to protect them and refusing to listen to anything they have to say! There is no loyalty without love and respect. I fear you have shown Helga neither!'

Never had Efa spoken to him in such a way. The pain was sharp and piercing, but what hurt the most was that she was right.

He had been blinded by his fears and had treated Helga no better than her family had. They did not trust in her abilities, they did not value her contribution, and he had done the same. He slumped down in his chair, feeling as if his heart had been ripped from his chest.

Which it had.

And he was the one to blame.

Chapter Twenty-Five

The lake was almost in sight, the camp a hive of activity with men unpacking the ships and preparing their weapons for battle.

Despite her exhaustion Helga pushed forward, stumbling ahead with more speed now that the end was finally in sight. The basket had carried her down a good portion of the mountain, but she'd had a couple of hours' walk before she reached the lake as the forest was thick at the bottom of the mountain and she had to weave in and out of the trees and bushes.

A deer burst from the undergrowth in front of her. Startled, she gripped a nearby oak, her fingers clawing into the moss to keep her balance. The young buck stopped and stared at her, its velvety nostrils flaring for a moment before it bounced off into the thicket.

Helga paused, her instincts screaming at her to heed the sign. Closing her eyes, she took a calming breath, listened to the wind rustling through the leaves and—

'Stop teasing me, you beast!'

Helga opened her eyes, unsure of what was the biggest shock. To hear Brynhild's voice so close, or to hear her… *flirting*?

She ran towards the sound and stumbled into a small clearing where Brynhild and Erik were putting their clothes back on after an obvious tryst.

Helga's heart leapt at the sight of her eldest sister, but everything was such a mess and she wasn't sure how she was going to explain it all in such a short amount of time.

'Brynhild!' she called, her voice dry from exertion.

Brynhild turned slowly to face her. 'Helga?'

Confused joy lit up her sister's face and she opened her arms to her in the same way she always did after a battle. A greeting and an embrace all in one. A reminder that everything they did, they did for each other.

A sob escaped Helga's throat as she ran to her. Brynhild's strong arms wrapped around her tightly and she felt like a little girl once again, protected and safe.

'He let you go?'

Helga pulled away slightly shaking her head. 'I ran away.'

'You clever girl!' Brynhild said, pulling her back for another bone-crushing squeeze.

Helga shook her head, pushing away from her.

They still thought Rhys was the enemy!

As much as she loved being reunited with her sister, there was still so much at stake.

'We have to help him!' she gasped.

'Who?'

'Rhys!' she cried and both Brynhild and Erik looked at her as if she had lost her mind.

'Are you mad? The man held you hostage! Why would you want to help such a monster?'

'He isn't a monster!' Desperation clawed at her throat and she wanted to shake Brynhild into believing her, but she knew she had to explain things first. Taking a deep breath, she told her sister the only thing that mattered in all of this. 'I love him!'

Brynhild's eyes widened and then she glanced to Erik who gave her a piteous and sympathetic look. Anger flared and she clenched her fists at her sides.

'I am going back up there, with or without you. I will not let him face Ulf alone.'

'I know you believe he is your destiny, Helga. But—'

'No!' Helga cut the air with her hand as if it were a blade. She ignored the hurt that bloomed at her sister's obvious doubt in her. It hadn't been long ago that she'd doubted herself as well. But seeing Brynhild with Erik had renewed her faith in herself. She had seen it back in Jorvik and here was proof of her abilities. 'It is not even about the prophecy, or fate, any more. It is about protecting innocent families and supporting the man I love. No matter what *he* or *you* say. He is my husband, the man *I* have chosen to spend my life with.'

'You married him? After all that he has done?' asked Brynhild with a dark expression.

'Rhys did not start this, but he has done everything in his power to protect his people. No one else would have managed what he has done—with so little support— and I will stand by his side. You can either help or you can leave! But you will *not* join with Ulf in waging war against us!'

Brynhild let out a surprised huff at Helga's ultimatum. 'I think we should talk this through with Mother first.'

Helga nodded, already walking towards the lake with renewed determination. 'Yes, we do not have time to waste.'

Helga strode across the shingle beach, Brynhild and Erik hurrying in her wake, still tying up their clothing and struggling to do both at the same time. It was a strange feeling to be the one leading the charge for a change.

She could guess where her mother was—at the fishing hut, where the leaders would gather and where her father now stood.

A babe when he'd returned to his family, Helga could not recall what he looked like and only recognised him from how Valda had described him.

'Sihtric the Far-Sighted, with long white-blond hair and a willowy frame. Some have made the mistake of dismissing him as weak, but they are fools and die quickly beneath his clever plans and arrows. They did not see the cunning in his eyes or the wisdom of his actions until it was too late. You are like him, Helga. Skilled with both bow and mind. You see the future as if it were a tapestry, laid out at your feet... That is the gift he gave you.'

As she approached him, she smiled. *'Heill,* Father.'

Sihtric eased away from the wall he'd been leaning against and took in the sight of a daughter he had not seen since she was in infant in her mother's arms. 'Helga...I...'

She placed her hands on his shoulders and pressed a kiss to his cheek. 'Thank you for coming for me.'

Tears clouded his pale blue eyes—so like her own. Then with a sharp inhale of breath he crushed her to him, whispering in her ear the strangely comforting words, 'Tell me, who should I kill?'

She did not hesitate. 'Ulf.'

He pulled away with a questioning look, but Porunn's shout distracted them both. 'Helga!'

She limped forward from the hut with more ease than Helga was used to seeing from her, and it caused a bittersweet joy to burst like a tart berry in the back of her throat. Her mother was happy, not only to see her, but something else had shifted, too. Something that gave her more strength in her step and a sparkle in her eyes.

Helga wrapped her arms around her and hugged her fiercely. Their relationship had been turbulent at times, especially when Helga had given up on joining the shield wall, but at its core there had always been love.

Tostig joined them, a wide smile on his weathered face as he stroked his long white beard thoughtfully. 'Shall I prepare the boats, or do we seek vengeance? I do hope we are still going to fight.'

Helga pulled away to look at the people gathered around. Brynhild, Erik, Sihtric, Porunn and Tostig, the people who had come for her. She was sure if Valda and Halfdan had known, they would have been here as well.

She had never felt so grateful to have a family and friends that loved her. 'I have come to ask for your help in defending my husband's fortress from Ulf's attack.'

'Husband?' Porunn snapped, her eyes narrowing with anger and her hand moving to the hilt of her sword.

'I love him.'

'Are you certain you are married?' asked Porunn gently. 'These Christians have different beliefs to us… There are rumours that he is to marry a princess from a neighbouring kingdom.'

'No,' Helga said firmly, shaking her head, and her family all exchanged worried looks. She had heard from Efa about the rumours that circled the Welsh court and were always aimed at Rhys unfavourably. 'It is a lie, spread by those who wish him to lose favour with the King. He *has* married me.'

Brynhild tried to make her tone gentle—but as usual she had less grace than a bull. 'Oh, Helga, he is not a man worthy of you. He uses the women in his family to make powerful alliances with no regard for their happiness. I am sure it *seemed* as if you did marry him. But he is a serpent. Did you have a pagan ceremony? That means nothing to Christians. He tricked you, so that he could bed you and keep you close.'

'We *are* married!'

'And yet you had to run away from him to come speak with us?' argued Brynhild and Helga regretted confessing that part to her, but how else would she explain her arrival?

'Alone?' asked Sihtric, glancing at Porunn as if to say, *If you wish it, I will help you kill him.*

'No one was allowed to leave the fortress. We are about to be attacked by Ulf's army. He was waiting for more warriors from his King, but they are now delayed because of your ships sailing past his court! Rhys is sorely outnumbered. I beg you, come with me and help him repel Ulf's forces before it is too late!'

Her family looked at each other with doubtful, worried expressions.

Irritation quickly flared into anger, catching fire like a river of burning oil in Helga's veins. 'Do you truly think my judgement so poor? Rhys is a good man and I say that not only from my intuition—which you *know* has never failed me in the past—but also from what I have seen with my own eyes and heard from his people—who, even now, are preparing to die for him. As am I!'

'Why has he not spoken with Brynhild sooner? We have waited here for three days with no word. Is he too much of a coward to face us?' asked Erik.

Helga sighed; this was the part she truly dreaded. 'He is stubborn and mistrustful. But he is no coward. Leaving the fortress would mean a swift defeat and immediate death to his people, so he is using the only tactical advantage he has. His plan is to hold out and wait for help to come. But I fear the fortress will not last long with his low numbers.

'I agree, he should have asked for your help sooner and he should not have turned you from his door, but Rhys does not trust easily and he suspects you are here to join with Ulf. Please tell me I am not too late!' She looked around at her family, who looked at their feet guiltily. 'Please. You have come this far for me. I only ask that you now raise your swords to fight against Ulf—a man who does not deserve to win this fight or rule this land.'

Brynhild glanced at Erik and a silent agreement passed between them. 'You have our blades, Sister, but I will be having words with your *husband* once this is all over.'

Porunn smiled. 'Helga, I will always guard your back—if you insist on us joining with Rhys, then I will do it. What say you, Sihtric?'

He nodded. 'I never liked Ulf anyway.'

Tostig slapped his palms together cheerfully. 'Wonderful!'

Chapter Twenty-Six

Rhys stood at the gates and watched as three hundred warriors climbed up one side of the mountain and Ulf's horde climbed up the other. He wished he could swoop down, gather up Helga's force and fly them back to the safety of Cadair y Ddraig walls.

But he could not, helpless to wait and watch as the two armies raced to reach the mountain peak.

'They have joined forces against us!' cried Madoc in horror as he squinted down at the approaching warriors.

'No,' said Rhys. 'See how they are split?'

'It could be a first wave followed by a larger second?' suggested Madoc and he glanced with worry down at the saddled riders behind the gate. 'This could be a terrible mistake, my lord.'

'No, it's not.' Shouting down to the riders, he said, 'Prepare yourselves!' But when he turned back, the blood drained from his face and he felt light-headed. 'Is Ulf's force turning?'

Madoc leaned forward. 'I… Yes, my lord, I believe it is… They must be joining forces now.' Madoc was convinced Helga could not sway her family, but he had made the mistake to think of her as only a young woman, not a shieldmaiden of influence and strength. Rhys had also made that mistake, but he refused to do it again.

Rhys strode to the palisade ladder and rushed down it, leaping before he reached the bottom to mount his horse. 'Make ready!' he ordered.

Harald and his brothers moved forward. 'We will come with you.'

Rhys wondered for a moment if he should trust them, then with a curse he decided that he was done fearing the worst. 'If Helga trusts you, then so shall I.'

Porunn looked grimly down at Ulf's advancing army behind them. They'd made it to a small ledge, not far below the larger plateau Rhys's fortress was built on. But many of Sihtric's warriors were behind them, still making the climb.

Helga and Brynhild stood either side of their mother. They were on horseback, but most of the warriors were not, and although they had made impressive progress up the mountainside, they were beginning to tire. Even Helga, who knew little of strategy, knew things were not going well.

Ulf must have had men watching them and had guessed their decision to join with Rhys. He trusted no one and therefore was unsurprised by such treachery.

Would Rhys think the same? Until it was too late and he watched their defeat?

Ulf's army was far greater than Sihtric's and so the only chance they had was if they made it to the fortress before Ulf could catch up with them. Unfortunately, the thunder of boots and the clamour of weapons that chased them was growing louder with every step.

Helga looked up at the cresting ridge above them. It

was a steep climb from here, but at least Rhys's fortress lay just beyond it.

But how would they be received? A warm welcome? Or a closed gate and a volley of arrows?

Sihtric pulled his horse up beside them.

'The first wave will be upon us before your men will be able to reach the ridge,' said Porunn.

Sihtric nodded, his eyes narrowing at the dust rising up from the forest beneath. 'Then we shall have a line of bowmen here, as well as at the top of the ridge, and another line of fighters at the tree line below. That will stop them from using archers at our back as we climb.' He cantered down the rocky hillside, shouting orders as he went.

Brynhild moved forward, unstrapping her battle axe. 'Erik and I will join the shield wall.'

Porunn reached over and stopped Brynhild with a hand to her arm. When she had Brynhild's attention, she turned, and took Helga's hand in her other. 'Fight well, my daughters. May Odin keep you safe, or grant you glory.'

Brynhild nodded with a reassuring grin. She was happiest with a plan of action. 'I will see you soon.'

Usually, when Helga said goodbye to them, she was certain of seeing them again. But not this time and her throat closed up with fear. Not wanting to place any shadows of doubt in Brynhild's mind, she did what she always did—she smiled brightly and replied, 'You shall!'

Brynhild jogged down to the first line, Erik walking in step beside her. They looked like two gods walking calmly into battle, while mortal men hurried past them in the opposite direction, climbing on all fours up the slope and scrabbling to find purchase on the rocky ground.

Those that were quicker stood their ground upon the

ridge above, or stopped beside Porunn and prepared to stand as archers to protect their friends' backs.

Porunn squeezed Helga's hand, forcing her attention away from her impressive sister. As if sensing the unease behind Helga's earlier bright smile, she said, 'You should go up to the fort, tell them to make ready for us.'

Helga shook her head. 'I will not leave you. I brought you into this fight and I will see it through to the end. Besides, Rhys will have seen us approaching and he will open his gates to us…if it is not too late.'

'Pah!' Tostig laughed as he handed Helga a bow and a quiver of arrows. 'I have been in worse scrapes than this. This will be a minor scuffle, nothing more.'

Helga and Porunn smiled at his unusual optimism. Then Porunn looked at her deeply, as if she longed to say something, but struggled to find the words. In the end she said briskly, 'I have had the honour to fight with Valda and Brynhild on the battlefield, but never with you. I am grateful for this opportunity.'

'Mother…' Helga said quietly. She was unsure of how to say it, but she felt compelled to speak her truth before it was too late. If anything, her time with Rhys had taught her that it was always best to speak about the past and not let it fester. 'I know that I have been a disappointment to you in many ways. I am not as strong or as skilled as my sisters, and as you know, I prefer…a gentler way of life. But…I am so grateful that you are here by my side. I will try my best to prove myself worthy of you in the battle ahead.'

Her mother said nothing and Helga was a little surprised to see Tostig thump Porunn's arm and truly shocked when she saw the subtle nod of acquiescence she gave in response.

Porunn cleared her throat gruffly and pointed at Helga's

bow. 'Let your arrows fly, Daughter. Show everyone the mistake they have made in misjudging you…including me.'

Helga smiled and nodded, understanding this was her mother's apology.

'There goes the last of my men,' said Sihtric, returning to their side, his horse snorting loudly. He pointed down at about fifty men who were making their way out of the forest and up towards them.

'Here come Ulf's mounted warriors,' said Tostig.

The horses crashed from the forest and headed straight towards the shield wall. There weren't many, which suggested most of Ulf's horses had been exhausted, or possibly eaten on the journey from Jorvik to Wales.

The Norse preferred to fight on foot anyway and used horses primarily for transport or food, a fact made very clear when Brynhild and her men began thumping their spears and shouting at the top of their voices at the oncoming horses. Spooked, the horses bucked, shying away from their charge, and the warriors were forced to dismount and release the animals. Ulf screamed orders at his men to form a wall of their own and advance upon Brynhild's.

As they struggled to organise themselves, Helga's line of archers let loose their arrows upon Ulf's first wave of warriors and many struck home. Helga was disappointed when her arrow thudded into Ulf's shield—it would have gone in his chest if he'd not raised it in time.

With his men organised, they began to advance on Brynhild's line while Brynhild's men began to calmly and with firm discipline walk backwards up the slope, in a horseshoe formation. Helga and the rest of the archers' rained arrows down upon Ulf's raised shields, occasionally striking true through a crack in his defence.

The bang of steel against shields thundered up the

mountain as the two walls collided, meeting blow for blow. Spears pierced through gaps in the wall and warriors screamed on both sides, but Brynhild's line held firm, shifting to cover the gaps left by fallen fighters.

As more men emerged from the trees to help reinforce Ulf's fallen warriors, Helga's archers loosed as many arrows as they could to keep Ulf's reinforcements back from curving around her sister's shield wall.

If the enemy engulfed the sides of Brynhild's wall, her defence would collapse and they would be surrounded on all sides. With resolute courage they beat forward with their weapons and stepped back with their feet. They had the advantage of higher ground, but the slope was steep and it made their retreat unbearably slow.

Two men flanked Ulf with raised shields as he brought a two-handed battle axe down heavily upon Erik's shield. Helga's breath caught in her throat as she realised the wall's fate was held in the balance. Erik fell to one knee, but manged to keep his shield raised, despite the wooden shards flying from it. She heard Brynhild's battle cry as her sister punched forward with her shield, knocking down one of the men guarding Ulf's side, then felling him with a swift blow of her axe. Ulf snarled and struck down again, but Erik had righted himself by then and tilted his shield to deflect its force.

Ulf's guard was down on one side, but another man moved in quickly to fill it, and Brynhild barely had time to recover her position before Ulf hammered her, this time with a vicious blow.

More men swelled from the trees, adding to the carnage. Helga continued to let loose her arrows, not caring how many she killed as long as it kept her family safe for one more step.

One side of Brynhild's shield wall crumbled as two

men were felled and others had no time to take their place. Ulf's men poured through the opening, cutting down men as they struggled to regain footing. Helga concentrated her arrows on the break, but knew it was already too late as Brynhild and Erik sprang back, trying to gain distance between Ulf and his pack of wolves.

'Retreat!' bellowed Sihtric and the line broke fully as men turned and ran for their lives.

Helga kept watch for her sister and Erik, desperate to see them safe. Two men attacked Brynhild at once. Erik cut down one, while Tostig's arrow took the other, and then they, too, were running up the hillside with the rest of their men. Those not fast enough were cut down by Ulf's charge.

Helga's fingers bled, the string of her bow crimson. But she did not care, as long as she could still let loose her vengeance on the men who chased her warriors.

Porunn, Sihtric and Tostig stayed with her, not caring that Ulf's army were closing in, or that by remaining they hindered their own retreat. They didn't have enough horses anyway.

A thunder of hooves and dust from behind distracted Helga from her grim task. Turning instinctively, her bow raised, she gasped when she saw who was approaching.

It was Rhys on horseback, followed by his entire *teulu*—she even recognised Harald and his brothers' faces among them.

Rhys raised his sword and in response every man behind lifted his spear and shield. 'For Helga, Lady of Gwynedd!' he shouted and the men echoed the battle cry.

They swept down in an arc, cutting between Ulf's men and Brynhild's retreating warriors. Their horses had been trained well and did not flinch at the smell of blood, or the sounds of chaos. They crashed through the men, scattering them like twigs, barely slowing as they ran them through, their spears darting out to pierce flesh and bone.

Their intention was clearly to surprise and disrupt Ulf's warriors long enough to allow a safe retreat. The strong mountain horses galloped onwards, curving back up the mountainside, having successfully carved a trench in the enemy's side. Rhys was still at its head and, as he galloped towards Helga, tears of relief streamed down her cheeks.

He had come for her—despite the risk it posed for his people and for his land. Finally, he had realised that she would never betray him.

Pulling up his horse beside her, he offered her his hand. 'Come, we cannot stay. As I told you, it would be madness to meet Ulf in the open.' But he said it with a smile, and she gladly reached up to take his hand.

Rhys pulled her up swiftly, seating her in front of him. It was a familiar position after their journey together and she pressed her mouth against his in a quick kiss of greeting.

'Thank you,' she said.

'Do not thank me. I failed you earlier, but I swear I will never do it again.' Rhys's gaze flowed coldly over the approaching army. 'Let us hope we survive this, so that I can beg your forgiveness once more.'

'On your knees?' she asked innocently.

A smile cracked upon his face and he looked down at her with warm eyes. 'If you wish.'

'Brynhild!' Her mother's desperate cry drew Helga's attention back to the hillside.

Nearly all of Sihtric's warriors were at the top of the plateau now or were climbing on to the *teulu*'s mounts. All except for Brynhild and Erik.

Erik was limping, an arrow in his thigh, and Brynhild was covering him with her shield as they made slow progress up the mountainside. A volley of arrows flew at them, but thankfully most were not in range—except one, which struck dangerously close to Brynhild's exposed feet.

Ulf was the man who had sent it. He screamed with furious rage, striding forward with a bow in his hands, grabbing arrows from the bodies of fallen men and launching them at Erik and Brynhild with insane fury.

Sihtric let loose an arrow, but Ulf rolled out of its way, and sprang up with his bow notched. For all of his wickedness, Ulf was still a jarl and a master in warfare. As more of Ulf's men recovered from Rhys's charge, several arrows sank in the earth close to Brynhild and Erik's feet and the enemy line began to rush up the hillside with bloody swords raised.

Tostig pushed the man whose mount he was sharing off his horse. 'Sorry!' he called down as he grabbed the reins and galloped his horse towards Erik and Brynhild. Porunn did the same—although Harald had already seen the way of it, jumping out of his saddle to then climb on to one of his brothers' mounts.

'Hold me steady and ride towards Ulf!' Helga ordered, raising up to stand on Rhys's saddle as she aimed her bow and arrow. His arms wrapped around her legs holding her tight, but without question he did as she said, kicking with his heels and using his shield to protect her body as best as he could.

They cantered forward down the slope, the wind whipping back her hair, her feet carefully placed and her knees bent to take the movement of the horse beneath.

Brynhild was helping Erik on to Tostig's horse, Porunn not far behind.

Ulf was closer to them now and he aimed his arrow at Erik's exposed side with a cruel smile.

Helga did not hesitate.

Ulf's hand went slack, the arrow falling uselessly from his fingers to the ground at his feet. Lifeless, his body fell backwards, an arrow in his eye.

Helga dropped down into the saddle and, with a yank of his reins, Rhys turned them back. Glancing over her shoulder, Helga sagged with relief when she saw her whole family riding safely after them.

Chapter Twenty-Seven

Rhys's *teulu* had given Sihtric's warriors the extra time they had needed. Safely behind the gates, they waited for Ulf's now disorganised and leaderless army to crest the ridge.

Sihtric, Porunn and a man Rhys recognised as one of Halfdan's kinsmen came to join him on the battlements. Helga was currently busy examining Erik's arrow wound.

'I am Jarl Sihtric, Helga's father. This is Tostig,' he said, gesturing to Halfdan's kinsman, and then he turned to the fierce shieldmaiden who was glaring at him as if she wished to cut out his heart and feed it to him. 'And this is Porunn, Helga's honoured mother.'

Rhys swallowed the ball of nerves in the back of his throat. He pulled his gaze from his father-in-law to the true power behind Helga's clan.

Why would anyone fear meeting a woman's father when a mother like this existed?

Porunn's hand rested on the hilt of her sword as she continued to stare at him without saying a word.

'Honoured Mother,' he said, inclining his head with respect.

'Am I?' The question was clipped and full of discontent. 'I do not feel *honoured* by your actions. Not only have you stolen a beloved daughter from me, but you have also put my other daughter's life at risk. I gave no permission for you to marry my daughter. How dare you call me *Mother*? Where is the proof of your marriage? Where is Helga's bride price?'

Tostig smirked at Porunn's words and raised a snowy eyebrow at Rhys in question. Sihtric, on the other hand, seemed more reasonable, if only marginally.

'Porunn is right. We require a bride price and reassurance that my daughter is safe behind your walls before we leave. You may have one hundred of my warriors as part of her dowry. It appears you need them.'

'A bride price?' Rhys asked, confused by the unfamiliar term.

'Gold and silver,' Tostig explained cheerfully. 'Enough to give her independence if she later wishes for a divorce, or you die in battle. It will be hers to keep forever.'

'I am sure we can come to an arrangement.' Rhys looked helplessly at the ridge in the distance. None of Ulf's men had crested it yet. How long would it take for them to regroup?

As if understanding his fears, Sihtric said with a shrug, 'Ulf is dead. They will be electing a new leader as we speak and deciding on how much silver to demand.'

'They will get nothing,' snapped Rhys. 'I do not pay tributes to raiders. If they wish to steal from me, they must be prepared to die for it.'

'Oh, they are prepared for battle. But they will likely have more sense than Ulf, especially now that my forces are behind your gates. I would imagine that they will make camp out of range of your arrows and will block anyone from entering or leaving your fortress. They will hope to starve you out, or at least cripple you slowly by raiding the surrounding land. Now, where can we discuss my daughter's future in privacy?'

Rhys turned to Madoc. 'If they demand *anything*, come get me from the hall. I will take great pleasure in informing them of our King's imminent arrival. They will soon find themselves pushed between my gates and the cliff.' He turned back to Helga's family. 'Jarl Sihtric, Porunn and…' Tostig smiled gleefully at him '…*Kin*… Please, follow me.'

As they made their way to the Hall, Porunn fell in step beside him. 'Do you love her?' she asked stiffly.

'I do.'

'She deserves better,' Porunn replied bitterly.

Rhys caught her eye. 'I know. She deserves better from both of us.'

She stopped sharply and blustered. 'How dare—'

Rhys interrupted her, 'She thinks she is a disappointment to you. Did you know that? She believes you never thought her good enough.'

Porunn's eyes widened, then she continued walking, a pained expression on her face. 'It seems we both owe her an apology…'

Helga sank against the bench with a deep sigh of relief. She'd placed Erik in a side chamber of the hall, one of the few private spaces left. Benches had been pushed aside or used for the wounded to sit or lie upon—not many, thankfully, but enough to remind them of the severity of what might have been. It was also worth remembering those who had fallen on the battlefield. A score of Sihtric's men had sadly not made it over the ridge and into the fortress.

Thankfully, all of the wounded would most likely survive, including Erik, who now lay resting on a pallet.

Brynhild sat on a stool beside him, her hands clasped around one of his, her big back arching over him.

Helga's heart swelled when she saw the tender way Erik reached up to cup Brynhild's cheek. 'I will be fine, my *sweetling*, do not worry.'

Brynhild was a fierce woman, but she had a heart as soft as butter. Seeing her lover wounded was a blow that had shaken her to the core.

'He could have taken you from me,' Brynhild whispered and Helga looked away, not wanting to intrude on the intimacy of the moment.

'Never!' scoffed Erik. 'No tiny arrow could take me from your side. Besides, Ulf is dead now. We have your sister to thank for that.'

Helga flinched. There was no bitterness in Erik's tone, but she still feared what her actions had cost him. Not because she regretted what she had done, but still—Ulf had still been his father.

She stepped towards them. 'I am sorry. I wish there could have been another way.'

Erik's brown eyes softened with sympathy. 'Ulf made his choice many years ago.'

'I hope Halfdan feels the same.'

Erik eased his head back against the wall and closed his eyes untroubled. 'He will.'

Brynhild smiled. 'Thank you, Helga.' Then she turned back to Erik and kissed his hand.

Despite their words, guilt still churned like a poisonous serpent in her belly. She had never killed before, but today she had taken many lives with her bow. The fact that she could not even say how many hurt deeply, like a cracked bone.

She walked over to Efa, who was fussing over a cut on Harald's calf.

'I did not realise you were wounded,' said Helga suspiciously, not missing the satisfied smirk on his face, or the freshness of the wound.

'I barely noticed it myself, until I returned. A spear must have caught me as I rode through the enemy lines,' replied Harald smoothly.

Efa seemed relieved when she saw her. 'Oh, Helga, could you advise me? I have cleaned it, but do you think it needs stitching? He was still bleeding when he walked in.'

Helga frowned down at Harald. Efa had dealt with far worse wounds today than this tiny scratch and all without her guidance. 'It is not deep. Apply some honey, that should be sufficient.'

'Of course!' gasped Efa with a blush. 'Why did I not think of that?' Leaping from her stool, she hurried towards the pantry.

Helga sat down to examine Harald a little more closely, although she focused on his face and not his leg. 'Let us hope you can still fight if needed.'

Harald shrugged, looking far too pleased with himself. 'It is only a scratch.'

'Even a scratch could lead to a fever... You should be more careful.'

'Now that you mention it,' Harald said, looking over at Efa as she hurried back, 'I do feel a little feverish.'

Helga slapped his wound with a sharp flick of her wrist. He hissed at the unexpected pain, but Helga ignored him and spoke loudly for Efa's benefit, as she stood. 'Ahh, good, no more bleeding. You should heal well, with or without treatment.'

'I should probably put a little on...just to be sure,' said Efa, sitting back down on the stool.

Rolling her eyes, Helga turned away from them with

a smile. They were hopelessly falling for one another and would probably make greater fools of themselves in the weeks to come.

That's when she noticed Rhys, Tostig and her parents entering the hall and her heart stumbled on its next beat.

'Come, Daughter,' said Porunn, gesturing for her to join them at one of the tables.

Helga joined her family and Rhys as serfs hurried around them to pour ale and place a platter of bread and cheeses in front of them.

'I want reassurances that my daughter will be well cared for,' said Sihtric. 'Her bride price should be of fitting value.'

Rhys took off his mother's rings. 'Are these enough?' Reaching for Helga's hand, he placed them gently in her palm, then closed her fingers around them with a smile. Helga melted into a puddle at the sweet gesture. Turning back to Sihtric, he added, 'I can also offer silver and gold. What do you suggest?'

Sihtric said an amount that smacked the air from her lungs. 'Father! That is too much!'

Rhys sighed. 'You think me much wealthier than I actually am.'

Sihtric's eyes swept around the grand hall. 'Do I?'

'My gold mines dried up many years ago. But we do have other precious metals such as copper—'

'Land would be better,' interrupted Porunn. 'A nearby settlement, perhaps? Something that can be managed in her name.'

Helga felt a prickle of awareness run down her spine. She suspected her mother had planned this all along. 'And who would manage it?' she asked lightly.

'How about Brynhild and Erik? That way they could stay close enough to ensure your well-being.'

More than happy to support her mother in this, she smiled at Rhys. 'Yes, that is what I would like. A farm-stead for Brynhild and Erik. Something nearby, like the one down at the bottom of the mountain? They can help defend and train your men as well.'

Rhys nodded. 'If that is what you wish.'

Helga's joy was incandescent. 'Very much so. What of you, Mother? Will you stay with us?'

'No… Tostig has asked me to join with him.' An un-expected and completely uncharacteristic blush stained Porunn's cheeks and she reached across to take Tostig's hand. 'Valda and Halfdan will continue to trade along the silk route and beyond, but they will need help now that they are to become a family…'

Tostig nodded and Helga gave them both a wide smile. 'I will miss you. But I am overjoyed to know that you are beginning a new adventure together.'

Helga glanced at her father, but he did not seem dis-turbed by the news. Respect had lasted far longer than lust and his admiration of her mother had always been clear.

'Then, my daughter's future is settled,' said Sihtric and he raised a cup of ale. 'Skol!'

'Skol!' cheered everyone, even Rhys.

'Now, let us speak of the army at your gate. Why has your King not come to your aid before now?' asked Sihtric.

Rhys set down his cup. 'He feared my position has grown too strong. I am sure he only hoped to humble me, but then it was too late. He saw you sailing past and grew fearful. When he hears you have joined with me and are not another threat, he will send reinforcements. I suspect they will be here before the end of the week.'

'Good. When the new leader of Ulf's army emerges, we can tell him of that fact. They may even learn of it from their own scouts and scatter. But I do not like the sound of this King who fears you. How can you guarantee my daughter's safety from him?'

'Helga has ensured it by marrying me. By aligning myself with no other kingdom or powerful house, he has nothing to fear from me.'

Porunn bristled with offence. 'Helga is not without power. She is the daughter of a Jarl!'

'But she is not due to inherit anything, correct? No land or titles?' asked Rhys.

Sihtric nodded. 'None. I have four sons already. As I have said, one hundred of my warriors—men who wish to settle—will be yours as part of Helga's dowry, but that is all. We could trade if you wish…'

Rhys and Sihtric began to discuss the finer details of their alliance and Porunn reached across and took her hand in hers.

'Helga…' she said and then stopped as if struggling to find the words. 'Rhys said something… Well, it was more of a reminder really… I have realised in your absence…' She stumbled and frowned with irritation.

Hating to see her mother so uncertain, Helga squeezed her hand reassuringly. 'What is it?'

Sucking in a deep breath, as if she were about to dive into an ocean, Porunn said, 'I am so sorry, Helga…' When Helga opened her mouth to speak, her mother shook her head. 'For years, I have pushed you into learning to fight. I did so because I believed it was the only path a woman could take to give herself independence and security. But I was wrong to try to force you into a life that did not suit you.

'You have more wisdom and courage than I could ever hope to possess. Out of all of us, *you* are the fiercest shieldmaiden. *You* have held firm, no matter what struggle or defeat came our way. When we are down, you are the hand that lifts us up. You wield your faith in us like a fiery sword, casting away all shadows of doubt. No matter how large the foe, or bitter the disappointment, *you* always had faith in us. When we are broken, you have given us courage. When we are wounded you have healed us and made us whole again. You are our shield and strength. I am sorry that it took you leaving for us to realise it. To realise how *truly* special you are. You are the greatest shieldmaiden and I am proud to call you my daughter.'

Helga's throat tightened painfully, sharp tears pricked at the back of her eyes and then she fell into her mother's arms. Embracing her mother's words with a relieved sob, and a grateful heart.

'Helga, may I speak with you in our chamber?' asked Rhys hesitantly a moment later.

She nodded and stood, pressing a hand to each of her kin's shoulders as she passed.

In their chamber, she was surprised to see the covers had been removed from the stored furniture and they were now placed carefully around the room.

'Why did you cover them?' she asked, running her hand along a beautifully carved crib.

'They were made for a family. And I had none.'

'And now you do,' she answered and he smiled tenderly in response.

'Hopefully… If you can ever forgive me for being so stubborn and blind.'

She didn't answer immediately, then she noticed something still covered at the side of the room. It was tall and narrow and she suspected what it might be, but needed to know for certain. 'What is that?'

'My mother's chair.'

'The one that matches the throne?'

He chuckled. 'It is not a throne and you will get me hanged if you say that in front of the King.'

'Will I have to meet your King?'

Rhys shook his head. 'I doubt he will have much interest in us, especially once he realises he has nothing to fear from me, and I do not plan to journey to court unless necessary… Anglesey brings back bad memories for me.'

The confession was brief, but heartfelt, and Helga felt the knots ease just a little. 'Did you only marry me to appease your King?'

Rhys's spine straightened and he strode towards her, cupping her face in his hand to force her to meet his jewelled gaze. 'No. I married you because I love you. I know I doubted you and you have no reason to show me the same trust, but please believe it. I love you with all of my heart. You once said that you only found peace in nature… Well, I have only found peace with *you*.'

Helga felt as if a great weight had lifted from her chest and she wrapped her arms around his waist and hugged him. 'I love you so much!' Then she saw the covered chair and sighed. 'Although…I cannot imagine myself on a dragon throne.'

To her surprise, Rhys laughed. 'My mother was not a dragon.' Untangling himself enough so that he could reach the cloth, he pulled it away with a flourish.

Beneath was a beautifully carved chair, so like his own and yet so different. There were no lethal beasts coiling around the arms, instead there were flowers and vines. Rhys kissed the top of her head. 'She was a rose, like you, beautiful and sweet—but not without thorns.'

Helga reached forward with a smile, stroking her fingers over the intricate carvings including the blunt thorns. 'I can see myself sitting in this…by your side.'

'Good,' he said, tilting her face back to him, and dipping his head to taste her lips. 'Do you forgive me?'

'First you have to beg.'

His eyes widened, but then closed leisurely as a deep chuckle tingled against her lips.

'Of course, shieldmaiden, I am yours to command.'

Epilogue

Cadair y Ddraig—spring AD 914

'How is she?' asked Tostig, leaping from his seat beside the campfire. The rest of Halfdan's crew looked as fretful as he did, all of them anxiously awaiting news of Valda's labour.

'The babe will be here very soon,' replied Helga, only giving him a cursory glance as she checked the pot. The water was boiling and she reached for a cloth to help her lift it without burning her hand.

'Let me help you.' Rhys was already there before she could take it, lifting the boiling pot off the flames with ease. She smiled gratefully at him, then grabbed another pile of linens from the wagon of supplies.

'Is there anything we can do? Anything at all? Do you need more linens? More water boiled?' asked Tostig, wringing his cap.

Helga looked at Halfdan's crew and smiled. Birth was a worrying time for everyone, especially the mother, but Helga had a feeling these men would move mountains if it meant helping their friend. 'All is well... But maybe you should prepare a meal for her to eat afterwards?

Something simple and not too rich. Oh, and, yes, more hot water. She will need to bathe after delivering the baby—to ward off a fever.'

The men's eyes all lit up as if she had offered them the greatest treasure in the world. Tostig began shouting orders and they all hurried to do his bidding, grateful for a task.

'That should keep them out of mischief for a while at least,' Rhys muttered with a dry laugh. 'Although, if we were at home there would be no need to run around for supplies...' He frowned meaningfully at the small encampment, which stood beside the lake.

'Valda's babe must be born in her household. That is our way,' Helga answered patiently. She'd already argued this many times already.

'*That* is not a household,' Rhys said, jerking his head disapprovingly at Halfdan's longship. The magnificent red and black dragon glared back at him proudly.

'It is home to them.'

They made their way along the wooden jetty towards it. Rhys had had it built to allow Norse ships to anchor more easily. It must have gone against his instincts to do such a thing, but it made sense as they now had trading links with Sihtric in Ireland, as well as Halfdan. Connections that Helga hoped would only lead to greater prosperity for Rhys and his people. *Her* people, too, she reminded herself with a smile.

They no longer feared the old Welsh King's disapproval as he was ailing and his son Idwal had taken over. This had worked in their favour, as Idwal seemed a far more reasonable man to deal with and did not fear Rhys as his father had.

'You are going to miss them when they are gone,' Rhys said with a frown, as he helped her aboard with his free hand. He had seen how happy they were—sisters and mother all back together—and he was evidently worried how much the parting would hurt her.

'Yes, but at least Brynhild and Erik will be close.'

'That was a *pleasant* surprise.' Rhys scowled and Helga laughed. They butted heads like goats on occasion, but they *all* wanted the best for their homeland and she knew he was secretly pleased to have their help.

Brynhild and Erik came as a pair, but with the loyalty and soul of one person. A long and fulfilling life awaited them, working side by side at Cadair y Ddraig, nurturing and strengthening everything around them with their presence.

Halfdan and Valda's tent had been stripped of all unnecessary items, crowded as it was with the birth. Erik sat on a table outside surrounded by other odd pieces of furniture, he waved at them as they passed. He'd said he was carving a toy for the baby and, after so long waiting, it was actually starting to look like the ship he'd intended.

A low moan that sounded like a cow mooing came from inside the tent and Helga picked up her pace as Brynhild's head poked outside. 'Hurry, I think she's almost ready!'

Helga rushed inside, putting the fresh linens down on the straw mattress. Valda was on her knees, her upper body draped over Halfdan's as the labour pain swept through her. Her mother knelt behind her, rubbing the small of her back.

Her sister began to grunt with increasing pain, and Helga knew the baby's head was about to crown. 'I will wait outside,' Rhys said, quickly handing the pot to Brynhild and ducking back out. Helga exchanged an amused look with her as they watched Rhys practically run from the tent. But then Valda cried out in pain and they both hurried to her side.

'The baby's head is out. Well done, Valda, well done!' said Porunn, stroking her daughter's back with pride.

Helga reached down to help turn the baby. 'Now for the shoulders. When the next pain comes, push down hard.'

'I am trying!' growled Valda and Halfdan kissed his wife's head.

'I know, my love. You are a natural at this!'

Valda hissed a curse and all of the women chuckled. But then the pain began again and everyone in the tent urged Valda on.

Her niece slipped into Helga's waiting hands like a fish and she carefully cleaned the baby's mouth, nose and eyes with some damp linen, rewarded with a hearty cry.

Valda sobbed with relief, clinging to Halfdan's neck as if he were her raft in a storm.

Helga beamed. 'She's perfect! A baby girl, just as I predicted.'

Valda groaned at her sister's smug declaration. 'When will you ever be wrong?'

Soon after, mother and baby were settled in bed and Valda looked exhausted but happy as she nursed the newest member of their family. Then the crew arrived one at a time to reassure themselves that child and mother were both well. They bought little gifts of clothes and toys, as well as a feast of food that Valda looked a little horrified by.

'I am not even hungry,' she whispered to Helga.

'It doesn't matter, they wanted to help.'

Valda's eyes softened and she eased her head back against the headboard and closed them with a sigh.

'Time to rest,' said Helga and, after a meaningful look

to her mother, everyone was ushered out of the tent and told to celebrate the birth at the campfire on the shore.

As Rhys and Helga walked down the jetty to join them, he asked, 'Have they chosen a name?'

'The father names the child in nine days' time. The number nine is very important to us,' she replied with a wink, but at his sober expression, she added, 'Is something wrong?'

'Would you like to have a Norse wedding ceremony?'

Helga's heart skipped a beat and then overflowed with love. 'You would have a pagan ceremony...for me?'

'What better time? All of your family are here and if it would please you—'

She leapt into his arms, his words cut off by the crush of her lips against his mouth—a searing brand of her love. He blinked, his eyes darkening as his arms swept around her and tightened.

'Yes,' she gasped, pulling only far enough away so that she could speak. 'More than anything.'

Nine days later, on Halfdan's boat, baby Ula was officially named by her father. It meant 'gem of the sea', appropriate for a girl treasured by her seafaring parents.

Helga and Rhys's handfasting would take place in the afternoon, up at the fortress.

'Will you stay a little while? Surely you will need to recover from the birth before you sail again?' asked Helga hopefully. Her mother and sisters were all gathered around her, as she bathed in a barrel in Halfdan's tent. The water was warm, scented with soaps and oils from exotic lands.

Valda brushed her hair while Porunn rocked the sleeping Ula in her arms.

Brynhild sat on the bed, trying hopelessly to weave

spring flowers around a silver *kransen*—a bridal crown fit for a princess. She set them aside gladly and focused on the conversation instead. 'You should stay at least a year. A baby should not be out on the open sea.'

'Ula will probably be happier at sea than on land. Look how much Mother has to rock her!' argued Valda.

'That means nothing, *all* babies like being rocked,' grumbled Brynhild, and Helga smiled at her sister's bad temper.

'I think Brynhild is trying to tell you she's going to miss you.'

Brynhild scowled, but did not argue with Helga's point.

'I will miss you both, too. At least with the new trade routes we will have an excuse to visit more often,' Valda said, offering her a length of linen. Helga stepped out of the barrel and, after wrapping herself up, joined Brynhild on the bed.

'There is that, I suppose.' Brynhild sighed, standing up so that she could help Helga into her blue gown. Valda had offered her Byzantine silks to wear, but Helga had refused. She wanted to dress as a Welsh lady, showing her love for both Rhys and their people. 'Although, why Mother and Tostig wish to leave with you, I still do not understand.'

'Because you are all settled, Brynhild,' said Porunn. 'You do not need me any more. You have Erik, and Helga has Rhys. Although, I confess, I am glad you will be so close to one another.'

'And you are about to begin a new adventure, too… with Tostig,' Valda said with a wiggle of her eyebrows.

Porunn rolled her eyes at her daughter's unsubtle remark. 'Yes, Tostig is too much of a traveller to settle down and it's a life that suits me well.'

'I think we will need to add more,' Valda warned, putting the half-finished *kransen* on Helga's head and weaving her hair through it. They each wore a wreath themselves, even Brynhild, although it was a simple circlet of ivy and less elaborate than the others.

All three sisters began to add more flowers. When they were done, Porunn cupped Helga's face and tilted it up to the dappled light of the tent. 'So beautiful.'

'So, are you, Mother. You all are…' Helga gazed happily at the extraordinary women in her family. 'I am glad we have all found someone to love—it has made us stronger.'

Ula began to grumble at the lack of rocking and Porunn looked down at her with a tender smile as she began to sway once more. 'You are right. My girls are the greatest loves of my life. Even so, Tostig has given me a new adventure to look forward to and he is the best of men. For once I am not fearful of the future; I welcome it.

'For a long time, I was living only to ensure all of you were happy and safe, but Tostig has made me realise that I am still capable of so much more, that life and opportunities are not yet over for us and…I think…I have done the same for him, too.'

Their mother's open admission surprised them all into silence, but as usual Brynhild was the first to break it 'Who would have thought such a thing possible when we were all living in that mud hut last year?'

'Do you remember that game of runes we played as children?' asked Helga and each of her sisters nodded.

'Of course, how could we forget! I had the Laguz—a water rune. Brynhild had the warrior rune of Tyr and you picked the black dragon—which isn't even an actual rune—you cheated! So, yes, we are all very impressed with your prophecies, Helga,' Valda remarked dryly, although Helga could see the flicker of admiration in her sister's eyes.

'And your dream that we would all be married with flowers in our hair,' said Brynhild with a roll of her eyes.

Helga chuckled. 'Sometimes, I can be wrong. Brynhild and Erik have yet to marry and I would have sworn they would have done so before me. Maybe we should not place such great value on my visions and accept life as it comes.'

A sly smile passed across Brynhild's face. 'Well, Erik and I did have a ceremony…of sorts…and it did involve an accidental flower being in my hair.'

'You did?' Helga laughed.

'We did.' She gave a firm nod and slung her arm around her little sister's shoulders. 'So, I, at least, believe in your visions, even if you do not.' Valda and Porunn nodded in agreement and Helga grinned.

Rhys stood with the men at the waterfall's pool.

'Do you think I chose the right place?' Rhys asked, feeling oddly nervous.

Erik looked around the tranquil setting and smiled. 'It is perfect.'

Despite it being a pagan ceremony, everyone from his settlement had gathered to watch. The Norse crews from Sihtric and Halfdan's ships were also there and the clearing was crammed with well-wishers.

Rhys shifted the hilt of his sword from hand to hand, its point balanced on the rock between his feet. Sihtric had said that a family weapon needed to be given from both sides, preferably one that had been passed down through the generations or had seen battle.

Rhys's sword fulfilled both requirements.

The talk from the crowd died down, signalling the bridal party's arrival, and Rhys looked over to the narrow path. Porunn, Valda—who was cradling baby Ula—and

Brynhild walked towards him, each wearing costly Byzantine silks in sky blue embroidered with silver thread.

Porunn wore wild flowers of all colours wrapped in a
crown of twisted hazel. Valda wore roses, the thorns still
visible through the white linen wrapped around the crown
to protect her head. Brynhild wore flowering ivy, its yellow-
green blooms barely visible in her circlet. She was also the
only one not wearing a gown, choosing instead to wear a
long tunic and matching wide-legged trousers.

Rhys glanced at the men around him. Tostig, Erik
and Halfdan all beamed with pride as the women walked
single file towards the rocky ledge for the ceremony. He
searched the path for Helga and was rewarded when she
stepped into the dappled light.

She didn't wear the exotic Byzantine silks of her family. Instead she wore the sapphire wool from their wedding day, except she had edged it with the matching blue
and silver from her family's silks. The fact that she would
choose to wear it twice made his heart leap with pride.

Murmurs of approval whispered through the crowd, as
she walked up the path to join him, Sihtric's sword laid
in her open palms, pausing only to accept a tearful kiss
from Efa, who was then comforted by a more than willing Harald. Normally, Rhys would have glared at him,
but today he didn't have the heart. He wouldn't be surprised if Harald joined his family in the not-too-distant
future—when his aunt felt ready.

Helga's crown was a circlet of silver wrapped with
flowers from his land. So many blooms were on her head
that they cascaded around her shoulders and showered
her with petals. Flowers of oak, primrose, broom and
meadowsweet. Blooms of Cymru in yellow and white that
illuminated her pale blonde hair with vivid brilliance and
a single red rose tucked at her ear in honour of his mother.

His eyes stung with emotion as she joined his side.

'Thank you for doing this,' she whispered, her face bright with happiness, 'It means so much to me.' She balanced Sihtric's sword on its point like he had done.

The grip around his throat tightened, but he was able to clear his throat enough to say, 'I am glad…' It wasn't about their differing faiths, or traditions, any longer, it was about making a true promise. 'Because this feels right and better than before. This is what you deserve.'

Her eyes widened and became misty. Taking his hand in one of her own, she pressed it against her lips gently. 'You deserve it, too…to be happy.'

No one on earth could cut him down like Helga could. Fighting back against the rising tide, he looked to Sihtric and gave him a brisk nod to continue.

The ceremony was in Norse and translated to the crowd by Old Aneurin.

They placed their wedding rings on the tips of their swords, then raised the blades to cross one another, high up in the air.

Sihtric held up a bunch of the sacred nine herbs of Odin. The bundle represented the nine realms of the world tree, a charm to bless their marriage. Dipping it in an oil Helga had made especially, he sprayed the weapons with its fragrant scent.

Then it was time to carefully lower the blades and offer the rings. They each took one and then the swords were handed to Erik and Halfdan for safe keeping.

After Sihtric's blessing, Porunn stepped forward. In her hands was a length of braided silk, in blue, silver and gold. 'Take her hand,' she said to Rhys. 'Odin's wife, the goddess Frigg, binds you,' she said as she took their joined hands and began to wrap the braided silk around them.

Helga caught Rhys's eye, and with a nod they began

to recite the words she'd asked him to remember. 'There shall be one end for us. One life and one death. No other shall part us. We are bound together from this day forth. I am your heart, and you are mine.' As the braid was pulled away, Porunn said, 'The bonds that tie you are invisible, but they are unbreakable. Go forth, love and be happy.'

Rhys stared at their clasped hands and then at Helga's beautiful face. Overwhelmed, he reached for her, cupped her cheek and kissed her thoroughly.

She sighed against him, her body bending like a flower to bask in the light of his love as her fingers reached up and threaded through his dark hair, gripping him tightly. She was strong and passionate, as well as soft and gentle. Cheers filled the sky as the couple kissed, intoxicated with one another.

Helga might have awoken the dragon, but they had set each other free.

* * * * *

*If you enjoyed this story,
make sure to read the other books in
Lucy Morris's
Shieldmaiden Sisters trilogy*

**The Viking She Would Have Married
Tempted by Her Outcast Viking**

*And why not check out
some of her other exciting stories?*

**The Viking Chief's Marriage Alliance
A Nun for the Viking Warrior**

HARLEQUIN
HISTORICAL

Your romantic escape to the past.

Be seduced by the grandeur, drama and sumptuous detail of romances set in long-ago eras!

Six new books available every month!

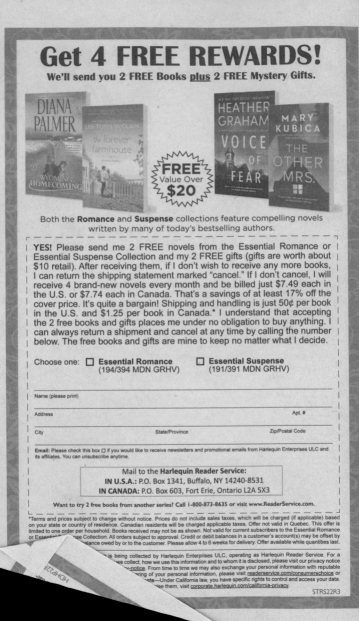